"That's it? You're agreeing to the plan? To going to the safe house?"

"Of course I am," Jenny answered. "I'm grateful for the offer."

Ben's brows rose with what looked like genuine surprise.

"How could you think I'd do any differently?"

"All I ever had to do was suggest a safety measure to you and you'd balk. An argument would be tripping off your tongue before I even had a chance to state my full case..."

His words hit her between the eyes.

Jenny saw something she'd never seen before.

The way her fight to maintain her sense of optimism, to be able to live without fear and the constant anxiety that had threatened to overcome her, must have appeared to him.

As though she was willing to put herself in danger just to not give in to him. To have her way. To win.

"It wasn't about winning. I wasn't fighting you, Ben."

He shook his head. "We must have been living in two different houses. Living two different lives."

"I was fighting. But not you."

"What, then?"

"I was fighting for my ability

T0197863

Dear Reader,

I'm a firm believer in reaching for what you most want or need. In never giving up hope in happiness. Every day brings new opportunities for bright moments if we try to find them. If we do all we can do to bring them to us.

And I'm also one who suffered tragic loss young and whose life was shaped by the knowledge that sometimes things happen that change our lives forever and there's nothing we can do to stop them. We can only try to prevent them from ever happening again. To be aware, every second of every day, and make safe choices.

Meet Jenny and Ben. The dichotomy that is me. This book started as a story about a divorced couple in their forties who still love each other getting a second chance. And somehow it became the two parts of myself vying for...I don't know what. But what I found, through Jenny and Ben and an abandoned baby, was my own inner peace. An acceptance of what I can't change and the ability to reach for happiness every day because of it. Not in spite of it.

I hope that you hold on to this book. Read it. That the story captures you, keeps you on the edge of your seat a time or two, makes you smile and swoon, and calls you back. Even more, I hope, when you reach The End, you come away with a sense of peace in your heart, too.

Tara Taylor Quinn

BABY IN JEOPARDY

TARA TAYLOR QUINN

ROMANTIC SUSPENSE

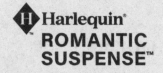

Harlequin®
ROMANTIC SUSPENSE™

ISBN-13: 978-1-335-50247-6

Recycling programs
for this product may
not exist in your area.

Baby in Jeopardy

Harlequin Enterprises ULC
22 Adelaide St. West, 41st Floor
Toronto, Ontario M5H 4E3, Canada
www.Harlequin.com

Printed in U.S.A.

A *USA TODAY* bestselling author of over one hundred novels in twenty languages, **Tara Taylor Quinn** has sold more than seven million copies. Known for her intense emotional fiction, Ms. Quinn's novels have received critical acclaim in the UK and most recently from Harvard. She is the recipient of the Readers' Choice Award and has appeared often on local and national TV, including *CBS Sunday Morning*.

For TTQ offers, news and contests, visit www.tarataylorquinn.com!

Books by Tara Taylor Quinn

Harlequin Romantic Suspense

Sierra's Web

The Bounty Hunter's Baby Search
On the Run with His Bodyguard
Not Without Her Child
A Firefighter's Hidden Truth
Last Chance Investigation
Danger on the River
Deadly Mountain Rescue
A High-Stakes Reunion
Baby in Jeopardy

The Coltons of New York

Protecting Colton's Baby

The Coltons of Owl Creek

Colton Threat Unleashed

Visit the Author Profile page
at Harlequin.com for more titles.

For Rachel: Whenever you are ready,
I am here. Always. Forever.

Chapter 1

Was that a baby crying?

Looking away from the columns of numbers on her computer screen, forty-one-year-old Jenny Sanders muted the soft pop station she'd been streaming and listened. As a child life specialist and long-time director of the secular preschool she'd helped establish on the sprawling church campus, she lived with sounds of children all day every day.

But not babies.

A full minute later, silence and the sound of her own breathing were her only two aural companions.

Shaking her head, she turned the music on and went back to work, switching screens from financial reports to the classroom charting. She required her four teachers to complete charts for every one of the preschool's one hundred and two students every week. Since her first week on the job ten years before, Tuesday evenings had been her time alone on campus to go over those charts. The only quiet time, and guaranteed uninterrupted time, she ever had at work. The only night the church was free of functions.

Seven of their nine three-year-olds had had some minuses in their behavioral reports over the past week. Minuses weren't lightly given, meaning their actions had to have been severe enough to disrupt the class. She frowned.

Seven out of nine told her something wasn't right in that classroom. She'd have a talk with the teacher first thing in the morning, and she decided she'd spend more time in that classroom in the coming days. And she'd be talking to parents within the next day or so, too. Adding all three items to her already full schedule, she read each of the nine charts again, going back a month this time.

Her general philosophy was to let youngsters find their own way, within boundaries that allowed others to do the same. Something she and Ben had clashed on since the first time they'd babysat his young half brother, Simon, together. They'd been teenagers at the time, the summer between their sophomore and junior years of college. Even back then her detective ex-husband had believed in living cautiously. Protecting rather than enjoying. Not allowing Simon to roll on the floor, for fear of what could possibly hurt him, rather than allowing the baby to explore his world. She'd struggled to help him see that children needed boundaries that set them free.

She encouraged individualism in thought, discovery and expression, and also fully believed that toddlers who learned to understand and respect the boundaries that protected their freedoms grew up to be happier and more productive adults. Her idea of boundaries was rooted in physical safety and being respectful of others. Ben had thought her far too lenient. She'd found his protectiveness— mostly where Simon was concerned, but sometimes her, too—almost suffocating. He'd encouraged them in their endeavors. He'd just always had danger warnings—and had worried about them. Had checked in just to make sure they were okay. Far more than Simon had liked.

It was tough being raised by a serious-minded cop.

She and Ben had loved each other. And they'd both loved

Simon, who they'd ended up raising, to distraction. They'd been a close family and had always taken time for date nights and special moments, too.

And yet, it had all fallen apart. She'd blamed Ben. He'd blamed her. They'd both tried incessantly, each beseeching the other to understand.

Simon grew up in the clash and decided, in his junior year of high school, to emancipate from them.

Wait. The speakers on her desk silenced again at the touch of her finger. She'd definitely heard something. A squeal? A cry?

Getting up from her desk, she proceeded quickly, but quietly, out to the hallway that was dimly lit by the security lighting that shone all night. A quick glance showed all four classroom doors closed, as they were every night. They'd be locked, too. Jasper Gulley wasn't a huge city, by any means, but it was big for Northern Arizona and had its share of crime.

The church being a haven for people experiencing homelessness and hardships—people who were sometimes desperate enough to break the law—put her at a slightly higher risk. Most knew to come during the morning hours when the store and kitchen were open for sustenance. But there'd been one or two people over the years who'd sought more than the church had to give...

She pulled out her cell phone. Her finger on the speed dial for 911.

Ben had never quit nagging her to carry the little pistol he'd taught her to shoot before they'd even married. Another bone of contention between them.

But if there was a rabid animal between her and her car...

A thought flashed through her mind, how it might be

good to keep the pistol locked in the safe in her office, just in case. But she was interrupted by a definite cry.

Human. Not animal. Young. Newborn young. And in distress.

The sound suddenly unmistakable, Jenny ran toward the wails coming from outside the preschool door, phone to her ear. If the baby was bleeding...

"911, what's your emergency? Jenny Sanders, is that you?"

Her name would come up, of course. Ben, Jasper Gulley's lead detective, would have seen to it that dispatch would always be aware of her name and address.

Divorced or not...

Oh, Dearest God in Heaven, who'd leave a helpless little...?

"Yesss," she said slowly, as she saw the bundle of blanket lying in an opened suitcase in the courtyard just outside the front door of the preschool. The brighter, outdoor security lights illuminated a small, scrunched up, reddened face. "I have a baby..." she said. "I'm at the Community Church and this baby is outside the door..."

Without waiting to hear a response, she dropped the phone on the ground as she knelt by the squalling infant.

Unwrapping the lightweight summer blanket to reveal a thin pink cotton long-sleeved sleeper, she glanced quickly around the deserted area and then watched as both legs and arms directly in front of her squirmed, seemingly healthy. She couldn't see any blood. And, slowly sliding her arms under the small body, she lifted the baby to her shoulder, carefully holding a neck and head that clearly wasn't mature enough to support itself.

The baby could only be days old. And judging by the weight against her, was a mere six or seven pounds.

Facts registered, including the sound of sirens coming

her way and footsteps sounding off to the left of her, in the shadows. She shielded the squirming bundle in her arms, holding the baby close.

The crying stopped almost immediately, as though the infant recognized that she was in caring arms—and as Jenny's heart pounded in fear, it also burst wide open.

It seemed as though, in the space of seconds, she'd fallen in love.

Detective Ben Sanders was at home in the little two-bedroom cottage he'd purchased after his divorce, listening to his scanner while he grilled up a cheese sandwich for dinner, when he heard the call come through.

A woman reporting a possibly abandoned baby at Jasper Gulley Community Church. He already had the stove off, pan with a half-baked sandwich on the back burner, and keys in hand when his cell rang, telling him that Jenny, Jen to him, had found the baby—and asking him if he wanted the case.

He knew his ex-wife's routine—had known she'd made the call the second he'd heard the dispatch come through—and was out the door and in his sedan before he'd hung up the phone.

Of course he wanted the case. The question had been rhetorical.

Still in the light-colored pants he'd worn to work with a short-sleeved brown shirt and brown and beige tie, with its half-neat knot, he put out his bubble light and sped the five miles to church. He arrived just behind an ambulance and a cruiser that had already been on the road and close to the church when the call came in.

From the time Jen had taken the job at the church—and had insisted on her time there alone each week to focus on paperwork aspects of her job—he'd been concerned about her being there alone at night, the same night, at the same time, every week.

He'd worried for ten years about having a Tuesday night call to the church. Had known it would come someday.

Never once had he imagined it would involve a baby.

He recognized Jen's butt immediately as he pulled onto the lot and saw her climbing into the back of the ambulance. She wore jeans to work on Tuesdays, because her times alone at the preschool often involved rearranging as well as paperwork, and she'd left her long curly dark hair down. He'd always liked it best that way.

By the time he was stopped and out of his car, the doors had shut and the ambulance was pulling away. Leaving instructions for the officers on scene to do a canvass and keep him posted, he was back in his car within five minutes and heading to Jasper Gulley Hospital—a four-story facility that served most of the small towns in Northern Arizona.

Jen had discovered the baby. She was his key witness. In addition to the child, of course. Any identifiers the doctors could give him would help him possibly locate the person who'd abandoned the infant. Experience told him that if he didn't get out there looking quickly, the chances of him bringing the case to a rapid and successful close lessened.

With Arizona safe haven laws, leaving a baby less than thirty days old at a church wasn't a crime. Leaving any child without handing it to a person or placing it in a safe haven drawer at the hospital—that was most definitely a criminal act.

The bubble on top of his car spun as he broke the speed limit by twenty. He was rounding the curve at the base of a mountain, just before the hospital, his mind on his big-hearted ex-wife who failed to take danger seriously enough, when a loud bang sounded and the car lurched. Hands tightening on the wheel, his entire body stiffening, Ben tried to maintain control of his vehicle. He spun out, around, threw the steering wheel into a counter turn, but the car wasn't responding to his efforts at all. He saw the base of the mountain in his headlights. Slammed both feet on the brake.

And then, as four thousand pounds of metal slid into solid rock, he just held on.

Wiping blood from a small cut beneath his chin, from where he'd gouged it with his thumbnail as the impact shot his head forward, Ben was out of his car while the air was still filled with dust from the crash. He called for a car to come get him as he took his first glance at the scene.

He'd managed to slow his vehicle enough that the airbag hadn't deployed, but the front end was mangled around a wall of rock at the side of the mountain. No way he was going to be able to back out of there and get to Jen and the baby.

After his call, it took him about thirty seconds, with the help of the flashlight on his phone, to see that his back two tires had been cut, clean, as if with the blade of a knife. A small knife that hadn't penetrated all the way through the radial tire, allowing him to drive away from the church, but still causing one of the tires to blow as he drove. Any bump could have done it.

And both back tires, not one back and one front. As though whoever had slashed them had known that when a back tire blew, the driver lost all control of the car.

He'd been at the church no more than five minutes. With police swarming around. And someone had managed to slash his tires?

Someone who hadn't wanted him to be able to go...where?

And why?

Too much of a coincidence for him to think that the slashing had been random. And yet…what on earth did an abandoned baby have to do with someone wanting him out of commission? Maybe permanently?

Depending on where that tire had blown—and on his ability to hit the brake in time—he could have been killed. Instead of just shaken from impact.

He could be dead instead of just pissed.

Jen.

What if whoever had slashed his tires had continued to the hospital…to lie in wait?

What if the perp was already in the emergency room? Grabbing his phone, he made a terse call to hospital security, alerting them to keep an eye on Jen and the baby. And then, ignoring the throbbing in his ribs, he dialed dispatch, checking on the ETA of the car he'd called. Stayed with them until the cruiser pulled up, calling for another crew to deal with his car, as he jumped inside the police vehicle and barked an order for the uniformed officer to get him to the hospital immediately.

"You okay, sir?" the young man asked as Ben told him to go even before his door was fully closed.

"Fine. Just go," he said, thinking only of Jen. Of the baby. His shaken nerves could just get over themselves.

Striding through the emergency room door, Ben sought out someone with enough clout to get him to where he needed to be.

He wasn't even fully in the back area before he saw a silhouette of Jen's form standing behind a pulled curtain. He'd been head over heels in love with the woman since he was fifteen. He'd know that shape anywhere.

"Can I help you?" A nurse, in his thirties or so, approached him, and Ben flashed his badge. Told the man why he was there and was immediately led to the curtain he'd already homed in on.

Taking a deep breath, he slipped behind the curtain the nurse held for him.

The first glance he saw of his ex-wife's face in more than three months was breathtaking. The glow of her expression as she gazed at the baby she held…

It sent him back twenty-three years, almost to the day. Simon had been born in the same hospital. Also in July. And the first time Jen had held him, that look on her face… that's when he'd first seen her as a mother. And had known he'd wanted no one but her to mother his children.

When she'd told him that was what she wanted, too, Ben had thought every hope he'd ever had had just come true. Thought he'd be spending the rest of his life living his dreams.

They'd been eighteen and nineteen at the time.

By the time Jen glanced up and saw who'd entered the cubicle, he'd come back to reality enough to school his face.

His only dream these days was to keep a distant watch on his half-brother as Simon threw away his life. No matter what he learned, Ben kept tabs, with the idea that he'd be able to come to Simon's rescue if he was ever in trouble with the law.

It was all he *could* do, since Simon had threatened Ben with a restraining order. He wasn't going to risk being legally prohibited from watching out for him.

And as for Jen… "Ben? What happened? Your chin's bleeding…"

A surface cut. He swiped at it with his sleeve. "I scratched it with my thumb." He gave her the one fact—and nothing more.

She didn't ask questions. Turned to the baby, instead.

"The doctor met us at the door and has already said her vitals are good and, overall, she looks well cared for. We're waiting on someone to come in to draw blood. She's only six pounds and seems a little underfed, though not malnourished, and she's still got her umbilical cord. Based on its state of dryness he figures she's at most a week old. He also says the cord cut looks professional, so she was likely delivered with medical supervision."

She'd glanced at him a couple of times, but only briefly, her focus fully on the baby she held. As he'd expect. As his had to be.

On finding the baby's family, in case the child had been abducted. Or had biological family members who wanted it. Finding who'd illegally abandoned the baby. And why someone had tried to hurt him within minutes of the baby having been left.

He couldn't help feeling a pang in his gut that he'd thought he was past as he watched Jen nurturing the child. She'd been born to have a houseful of children. Yet when the time had come, after they'd spent a year adjusting to having custody of Simon as soon as they'd graduated college, she'd demurred.

"Is she wearing what she came in with? I'll need to take it to the lab," he said. "And was there anything else with her? Blankets? I'll need it all. Maybe we'll get lucky and find some fingerprints…"

Lucky was such a transient word. Yeah, how lucky to be able to easily identify the abandoned child. And yet, if fingerprints came up that easily, it would most likely mean whoever had had the child also had a criminal record.

Lucky that Jen had fallen as hard in love with Ben as he had with her. Yeah, and yet…their marriage had brought far too much heartache to both of them.

And to Simon, too, he was sure.

Kids didn't just emancipate for no reason. Most often, as he knew full well from more than twenty years of police work, their home environments played a factor.

A pang hit his chest. He put it down to his recent visit with the side of the mountain.

"The outfit she was in is in that bag," Jenny said, pointing to a plastic zip-sealed bag on the back counter of the room. "The nurse who removed it wore gloves, but I held her, so my prints will be there."

He nodded. Moved to take possession of the bag. Taking responsibility for chain of evidence. No matter who'd left that child, doing so without placing her in the hands of a person was a crime. She could have lain there all night. Been attacked by coyotes…

"And she was lying in, like, a small carry-on suitcase, black, with a blanket tucked around her. I picked her up and didn't look at the suitcase again. I have no idea if there was anything inside except the blanket. I'm assuming an officer on the scene has it."

She'd been a cop's wife for two decades. Knew what he'd be looking to know.

There were other questions he could ask. Would ask. And yet, he just kept watching her with that baby. Jen was safe. The baby was safe. Emotions swamped him. He pushed them back. Walled them off as best he could.

Something he'd perfected over the years.

Coughing, he ran a hand through hair that was still as thick as always but starting to show a bit of grey at the temples, too. Wondering if he'd ever feel whole again.

"Did you… Can you tell me what you heard? What alerted you to the fact that she was there? Or did you find her when you were leaving?" He had to find out who'd dropped the child.

Then they'd figure out where she was going to spend

the night. Social services would have been alerted, but this late…

Of course, the doctor might admit the child overnight.

Jenny told him she'd been listening to music and thought she heard a baby cry.

"What time was that?"

"A little after seven. I know because I logged in to charting right after that and it always gives a time stamp."

"And how long were you there before that?" His mind was working again.

"About an hour."

Yep, she'd always gone in at six. For years, Tuesdays had been his and Simon's guy night. Until Simon had decided to hang with friends, instead. Because Ben had angered him too much.

"As far as you know, were you alone on campus the entire time leading up to that?"

She nodded. Glanced at him, then away, as the sore subject reared right there between them in a room far too small to contain it.

He'd hated her on campus alone after dark. Saw the inherent danger. She insisted that she was locked in. That her car was right outside the side door. And that she was at a church. If it was her time, it was time. Otherwise, she'd be safe.

It was a testament to the state of his mind and emotions that he managed to keep his mouth shut on the issue. There was too much else taking up his immediate focus.

Like the fact that the love of his life was holding a baby and the sight was doing things to him that he'd thought had been killed right along with their marriage. Fate definitely had a sense of humor.

"I thought I heard footsteps, after I picked her up, but…" She shook her head. "I thought they were running toward me, but the sirens got louder, drowning out the sound and no one appeared…"

The baby was sleeping. "I wonder if she's been given a name." Jen's soft voice—the tone—he hadn't heard it in so long. Far too long.

Another lifetime.

One that had to stay out of his present.

"For now, we're calling her Ella. Ella Doe," Jen continued, as though footsteps didn't matter at all.

Ella. The name she'd talked about when they'd first talked about having kids someday. Before Simon's shocking advent into their lives.

The name choice couldn't be a coincidence. And didn't bode well for Jen getting out of the situation unscathed.

Why on earth did she have to be the one who found the baby?

"If you want me to wait until social services gets here, I'll take her," he said then, moving farther into the room. He had to take control. To do what he could to make the situation better. That was what was mucking him up. He'd never been good on the sidelines.

He was the doer. The fixer. The one who'd run into a burning building to save a life without a second's thought.

The one who'd faced bullets to protect people he didn't know.

And who'd failed to hold his own family together.

"I've already talked to them," Jen said. "A woman was here at the hospital when I came in. Since I'm a licensed child caregiver, they're letting me keep her tonight."

"That's not a good idea, Jen. My tires were slashed at the church. I was in an accident on my way here…"

Eyes wide with concern, she gave him a once-over. "You're okay?" she asked, meeting his gaze, but only for a moment before she looked away again.

"Obviously."

"So…surely you don't think slashing the tires of a car with a bubble on top at a scene has anything to do with this baby," she said. "Cop cars are vandalized sometimes. Even I know that."

And he knew that though there had to be a connection, Jen was conditioned, by his own overprotectiveness, to blow him off anytime he tried to impress danger on her. He'd cried wolf too many times.

Ben had to get out of there.

To do his job.

Daylight would come again before he knew it.

And if he was going to keep Jen safe, keep that baby safe, he had to get busy.

And maybe, just maybe he could get his ex-wife to smile at him again.

Or at least be able to look him in the eye for more than a second.

Chapter 2

Making a call to the church minister while she sat in the emergency department waiting room after Ben left, Jenny not only procured permission to borrow a pack-and-play portable crib from the church nursery for the night, but Bonita, the preacher's wife, said she and her two daughters would head to the local box store and purchase newborn diapers, bottles and other necessities, as well. Enough to get her through a couple of days.

While Jenny wasn't a member of the church that housed the preschool, she'd been a full-time employee for so long, they treated her as one of their own.

And knew of her heartaches, too.

Hanging up the phone, Jenny held the newborn baby girl to her chest. Other than when the hospital personnel had laid the infant on the table to examine her, Jenny had had her in her arms since they'd left the ambulance. The phlebotomist had even let her hold the infant when they came in to take blood. The baby would need a normal procession of shots. But first they had to determine if she'd had any yet.

And they needed to make certain she wasn't suffering from any unforeseen immediate complications.

Like being born with a drug addiction. It happened more

often than a lot of people wanted to believe. And low birth weight was a symptom.

They'd given the baby some IV fluids when they'd pricked her to take blood, and she'd already had a wet diaper, which was good. Either way, Jenny would be spending the night with the newborn. At home, or at the hospital. She'd been temporarily charged with her care. She'd qualified due to her foster parent status. The fact that she was a nationally certified child life specialist, having done her internship at a children's hospital in Phoenix, had pretty much guaranteed her the privilege. No one else in Jasper Gulley was as qualified as she was to handle the situation. Advocating for children was her forte. She'd just never, ever expected to be doing so for a baby she'd found.

Life certainly twisted and turned in weird ways. She knew it was way too soon to see the night's astounding events as a second chance. But…could it be? Ben didn't know about her recently completed foster parent certification. She hadn't been eager for him to know. They hadn't fought Simon's right, and choice, to emancipate, but it had hit them both hard.

Since the divorce, she'd been starved for family. And yet, upon certification, she hadn't put in for any children. How could she? After failing so miserably with Simon?

She'd been waiting for some kind of clearance from herself. Some sense that she was good enough.

So…was this it? This baby?

Dropped at the church, right outside her work door… Was this precious little girl a sign to her?

Could it get any clearer?

The doctor came back in with the news that the little one's NAS, neonatal abstinence syndrome, numbers were a little high, indicating that the mother had ingested some opiate drugs during her pregnancy. But they weren't high enough to even require medication. He'd told her his educated guess was that the mother's drug use had been minimal, at least during the last trimester. And, based on all reports, there was no reason to keep the baby overnight. She was, in his estimation, a healthy baby.

She'd been given a supply of higher calorie baby formula and a car seat donated by a special program through the hospital. Ben had made sure her car was delivered to her. So, just before midnight on a night that had started out like any other Tuesday, Jenny was driving home with a brand-new baby in her care.

She'd told the uniformed officer who'd been assigned by Ben to see her home that she didn't need or want his time. And was fully prepared to stand up to her ex-husband when he found out she'd refused escort and overnight watch outside her home. Ben would call her to tell her how foolish she was being. That much was guaranteed.

The streets were dark, but she wasn't afraid. She knew the roads, the trees and the people who lived in the houses she passed. Jasper Gulley had been her home for her entire life.

And it would be a wonderful, welcoming place for the precious new life in the car seat behind her. She had flashes of the day care, for the baby's first social interactions, and then jumped ahead to kindergarten and school programs... piano lessons from Mrs. Larson and ballet class at the studio by the grocery store...

She stopped herself long enough to qualify the visions with the fact that they could happen whether she was the one raising the child or not.

She was smiling, her heart filling with an anticipation, and purpose, she hadn't felt in a long while. She glanced in the rearview mirror to get a glimpse of the car seat, as though to reassure herself that it was really there, and noticed instead the headlights shining in the distance behind her. A like soul, someone out late in a town that closed early. Someone she knew?

Hopefully not someone coming from one of the bars in town and driving when they shouldn't be. She glanced back again. The car wasn't speeding. Jenny was just below the limit, and it wasn't gaining on her. And didn't seem to be swerving at all, either.

Thankful that all seemed well, that the baby in her care wasn't in immediate danger of an alcohol-induced car accident, she made the turn that would take her across Main Street and into her neighborhood. Once again she allowed her mind to travel over and around the stupendous events that had led to a baby girl in her back seat.

The newborn hadn't made a peep since Jenny had put her in the seat. Not being able to actually see the little one due to the law-required rear-facing safety carrier made her nervous. Glancing in the rearview mirror again anyway, somehow taking reassurance from the back of the seat visible to her, she noticed headlights again. The same headlights. The left one dimmer than the right. Still behind her even though she'd turned twice.

Was she being followed? Her first instinct was to push the hands-free dialing button on her steering wheel, to call her ex-husband, the cop. But she wrenched the wheel instead, turning a couple of roads before her own—onto a road that led right out to Main Street and toward the police station.

If she was overreacting due to the drama the night had brought, there was no way she wanted to alert Ben. But if there was any way that baby was in immediate danger...

The car that had been behind her went by the turn. She caught a glimpse of it heading at the same steady pace as it went past.

If she was being followed, she'd lost the tail.

And was not going to allow Ben's constant focus on the bad that could happen insinuate itself into this new venture in her life. Whether she was allowed to keep this baby or not, she was going to be a foster parent.

One who didn't suffocate the children in her care with the fear of what could happen out in the big bad world.

She reiterated the promise to herself a second time half an hour later as she laid a fully fed baby girl down to sleep in the portable crib set up in her living room. Jenny refrained from peeking out the front curtain just to make sure there were no unknown cars parked out in the dark. Ben's paranoia was not going to invade her home again.

In a pair of lightweight pajama pants and a T-shirt, she planned to lie right there on the couch, next to the portable crib, to get the couple hours of sleep she expected to be allowed before the baby woke up needing to eat again. Had just lain down when her phone beeped a text.

It's me. I need to talk to you. I'm here.

The blinds were drawn, but he'd still be able to see a glow of light from the living room. He knew she was up. Probably knew she'd only been home a short time, too, and maybe even that, for a second there, she'd been scared. Ben Sanders seemed to have a way of knowing everything.

There'd been times over the years that had been a comfort.

But not always.

Heading to the foyer, because she'd be answering the

man's call for the rest of her life, she took a quick glance outside. She recognized his dark SUV—and him standing on the front porch—and pulled open the door.

He was still in the beige pants and brown shirt, that endearingly sloppy knot in his tie, and, as always, she had to tamp down her heart's immediate reaction to the sight of him.

"I'm sorry it's so late," he said. "But if we're going to find the little one's family, we have to move quickly. The trail grows colder with every passing hour."

Nodding, she didn't bother to shut the door behind him. He'd get it. And lock it, too. Just as he'd follow her into the living room they'd furnished together.

Shared seventeen Christmases in.

Loved in.

Fought in.

She'd thought about moving, many times. But her heart was in that home. Even if the people she loved were not.

Shame hit her as she realized a big part of her didn't want him to find her little girl's family. They'd abandoned her. Left her all alone and crying in the dark. Who knew what else they might do to get rid of her if they got her back?

Someone had abandoned the child. And with Ben on the case, that person would pay. But the baby likely had other biological family who would love her to distraction. Even as she yearned for the child to stay, Jenny knew she most wanted what was best for the baby.

And trusted Ben to find any loved ones who might be out there, grieving for her.

Taking a quick look in the crib as he passed, Ben sat on the edge of his half of what had been their couch—two recliners with a console between them. She settled on the matching full-length couch, also brown, that already held her pillow and a blanket.

When he pulled out his pocket-size spiral notebook and a pen, she glanced fully at his face. She'd never been on the receiving end of one of his investigative interrogations.

No, the ones she'd endured in the past had been far more personal.

Thankful that he was treating her professionally, rather than like a woman who worried and displeased him, she found it easier having him there.

And thought again about the fact that there could be a family out there who'd had their baby stolen away from them. A mother whose newborn had been kidnapped. People who were facing an unbearable heartbreak, made stronger by the fact that they didn't know their little one was safe.

There'd been evidence of drugs in the mother's system. But only trace. And no other sign of poor care.

That said something.

"Nothing showed up on the church security cameras, but they wouldn't have caught the area from which you heard footsteps. The suitcase was left just out of sight of the camera focused on the front door. I need you to think about earlier this evening when you found the baby," Ben started, his voice holding that serious tone with kindness mixed in. She didn't just hear that voice, she felt it. Deep inside her. The one that had been speaking to her since the first day she'd met him.

He was a good man. A caring man.

Which was why she'd loved him since she was old enough to know what love was, and why she knew she was going to love him for the rest of her life.

Even though they were so diametrically opposed on important matters. Philosophies. Views of the world and how to live in it.

They'd grown up so differently. Her within the arms of a loving secure family where optimism abounded, and all ideas were considered.

He'd been the man of his house since his daredevil father's accident had left Ben's mother a widow. Ben had been six.

From the very beginning of their relationship, he'd tried to influence some of her choices. Warning her of possible pitfalls. He'd been protective. But only because he'd needed to know she was safe. Same with Simon.

It had never been about him having control of them. Or wanting to make them into who he wanted them to be. It had been about keeping them safe.

And he'd lost them both.

Sadness engulfed her, for him, as she watched him glance toward the portable crib on the floor a foot away from her.

"Try to remember the campus," he said. "You must have looked around, at least superficially. You always check out your surroundings."

Because he'd drummed the need in her. But he was right. She did. It was the smart thing for a woman alone to do. Be aware of her surroundings.

Thinking back to the first moment she thought she heard a baby crying, she replayed the minutes for him, with every detail she could remember. Switching from financials to the charting app, the station she was streaming, the song that was playing…

"So you're outside… Was it chilly?"

July in Jasper Gulley could have a cool breeze or two at night.

She shook her head. "The air was still. The campus

was quiet. I glanced around but didn't see anyone. Or any movement."

"Think carefully," he said softly, reminding her of the time he was trying to help her find her engagement ring when she'd feared she'd lost it forever. He'd been so kind, so gentle, helping her retrace her steps. "There was some-one out there. Someone in the shadows…"

Someone who loved the baby?

"Someone who ran at the sound of sirens."

Closing her eyes, she pictured her memory of the night, the moments she'd seen that suitcase, the glance she'd taken of the open space and columns of breezeways around her as she'd knelt to the crying baby.

And shook her head. "All I see is emptiness…" she said.

Just because she'd been looking for answers to her future and a baby had shown up didn't mean that fate had given the newborn to her. And even if it had, she might only have the child for a minute. For some unknown purpose yet to be revealed. Her job was to love the baby while she was in her care, and to want what was best for the child. Not what Jenny thought was best for Jenny.

But she had a full heart brimming with the need to give. And if this sweet new soul needed love…

"We found a note, Jen." Ben's tone hadn't changed much, but she noticed a difference. Almost a warning. Or prepa-ration for the news he had to deliver?

She glanced at him, and away. Looking him in the eye… that was a thing of the past. An intimacy she could no lon-ger afford. She wasn't one with him anymore. And couldn't share her deepest soul. Or look into his.

"I believe, as does Drake, that whoever left that baby there tonight did so knowing that you would find it."

Drake Johnson. An unmarried thirty-five-year-old detective who'd shown up in Jasper Gulley five years before, already hired on before his arrival in town, for reasons no one really knew. He and Ben had been friendly from the beginning, but they'd seemed to spend more time together since the divorce—golfing, fishing. Ben had told her it was because Drake didn't know anyone in the area and didn't like hanging out in the bars every night any more than Ben did.

"My car was parked by the door of the preschool," she said, gathering her thoughts. "And there were lights on inside the building." Watching the baby sleep, she couldn't imagine anyone willingly giving her away. Putting her down and walking away. "If someone wanted me to have the baby, they'd just have brought it in to me."

"Not necessarily," he told her, and she had to know what he wasn't telling her.

"What did the note say?"

Glancing just over her shoulder, Ben replied, "I belong here. Please love me and keep me safe."

Chills ran over her as he said the words. *Keep me safe.* Ben's specialty. She glanced at her ex-husband, wondering if he got the inference. Was helping this baby find her rightful place in the world something they could do to atone for the mistakes they'd made with Simon?

A way for them to find peace of mind? And comfort for their aching souls? By working together rather than at odds?

Or was she losing it, floating hopelessly along in her well of optimism-lined loneliness?

Keep me safe. As though the baby's life was in jeopardy. Which meant they could both be in danger. A flash of headlights, one dimmer than the other, crossed her mind.

Giving herself a mental shake, Jenny sat up straighter.

She was a strong, capable woman, not some helpless damsel needing a man's protection. Ben's protection.

"You've been at that church alone, every Tuesday evening, for more than a decade. Hundreds of people would know you'd be there. I need you to think, Jen. Who do you know who could have given birth in the past week?"

A quick mental rundown of the people in her life, sorting by known pregnancies, brought up...nothing. Shrugging her shoulders, she shook her head.

"It could just be someone you know who knows someone," he told her. "Anyone in the past seven to nine months who's talked about a sister or friend in a hard situation? One that the pregnancy might have complicated?"

Giving more time to her internal search, she still came up blank.

Glancing his way, she was bothered by the frown on his face, more so when he prompted, "Could be a grandparent whose underage daughter gave birth...or a boyfriend who stole her from his girlfriend, so he won't be held responsible..."

Could be anything.

But whoever had abandoned that suitcase had committed a crime.

And that baby girl deserved to know who she was. How and why she'd come to be left in a suitcase on the ground.

"How about in the church congregation? Have you heard of anyone who's pregnant?"

"A woman named Maria. I saw notice of a shower for her. But she had her baby three weeks ago. A little boy. He's adorable and already sleeping at four-hour stretches." Which meant nothing in the current situation.

"This person knew you were there, Jen. And they knew

enough about you to trust that you could and would take care of the baby. The note says 'I belong here.'"

"Does that mean at the church?"

"Or Jasper Gullcy. Or…"

She glanced at him as his words dropped off, and then, as she glanced quickly away, heard him say, "…with you. There's that plea to 'please love me.' It's as though the person knows you personally. Knows how nurturing you are…"

She could hardly breathe. Hearing him speak of her in such warm tones…about the very things that had driven them apart…

"How about this," he said, inching forward on his seat. "Can you think of anyone who's been gone for the past several months? Say a teenager…or some other person who could possibly need to hide her pregnancy for whatever reason…"

"You think she'd leave the baby with me in the hopes that she'd still get to see it?" The idea both horrified and gratified her. If she could give a mother a chance to have contact with her baby girl…

If she could ease another mother's broken heart. Surely, if they could prove extenuating circumstances, the girl could get a slap on the wrist for abandoning the baby. If they could prove that she'd knowingly left her for Jenny to find—and maybe even waited around to see that Jenny had custody of her?

And then she had another thought. "I can't think of anyone who's been missing," she told him. "But I've recently completed a months' long certification process for foster parenting…"

"Through the Family Alliance," he said, nodding.

"You know?"

"Your background check was run through the Jasper Gulley Police Department."

With a quick look, she tried to determine his feelings on the matter and saw only a face masked with professionalism.

Which could be hiding a lot. Or nothing.

Did it bother him that she could be starting her own family without him? Did he think her capable of doing so? Wish her luck?

Or didn't he care at all?

"I was just wondering if maybe someone in the alliance knew of a child who needed a safe haven," she said when her personal issues came up without answers. Again. "They'd know I'm recently certified. And that I don't currently have any kids in my care. And some of them know that I work late on Tuesday nights because we conducted an interview at the preschool."

If that was true, did that mean that the sweet baby girl sleeping just inches away from her was going to be hers to keep? At least as a foster?

For long enough to allow her to start adoption proceedings?

Could life really give such incredible second chances? Not that any baby would ever replace Simon in her heart or ease the pain of never having had a child of her own because of her marital issues. But loving another child would open up new places in her heart.

If it was someone from the alliance, they wouldn't have abandoned the child. They'd have brought it to her, following protocol.

Unless…there was some reason not to have done so.

Was she crazy to see someone's abandoning of a newborn baby as a sign that she was supposed to mother that child? Even for a short time?

Was she that lonely? Her life that empty?

Ben stood, sliding his notebook into his front shirt pocket, adjusting the gun on his hip. "You might be on to something," he told her. "I'm going to head back to the station. Get someone from the alliance on the phone."

"It's after midnight," she said, following him across the room toward the front door.

"And every minute counts," he told her.

Glancing at the infant, she tried to still her thoughts. To let her heart flow with whatever truth it had to give her. And knew only a huge swelling of love.

Because of how badly she needed a child to love?

Loving wasn't a selfish act. It meant that she had to do what was best for the baby. Whether that was a blessing in her own life or not.

"You can count on me to help in any way I can," she said aloud as they reached the door. "I want what's best for her."

He glanced at her, lifted a hand as though he might touch her face, but then dropped it back to his side as he nodded. "Just be careful, Jen. I don't want you to get hurt."

Yep, there it was. His need to stifle anticipation, excitement, for fear of what could go wrong.

"And how would that happen?" she asked, mostly out of peevishness, because with those few words he'd managed to dampen a bit of her anticipation. More than her own reasoning had been able to do.

"Your heart is so big, and so soft… You've already been hurt enough. I know you. And I worry that you'll fall in love with her and then have to give her up…"

"You're too late," she told him, feeling stronger by the moment. "I've already fallen."

And whether she had to give up that baby in the next room or not, she was going to be blessed by having known her.

Sometimes the chance was worth the risk. The doing worth the pain.

A concept Ben had never seemed able to understand.

"Because we now suspect you were specifically targeted, there's going to be a patrol officer parked here tonight," Ben said. Telling, not asking. "We don't know who the leaver might have been fearing, running from. Or if they saw you take the baby. If you hear anything, need anything, Officer James will be right outside."

As he left, reminding her to lock the door behind him, she slid the dead bolt in place, as she'd have done anyway, and then stood there, struggling with the tears his departure from their home brought her.

Tears for her own broken heart, but for his, as well.

Because she knew him, too. And knew that underneath all his logic, his evidence and statistics, his lonely heart ached.

And his dreams lay in ashes.

Chapter 3

Ben spent the night working, getting people out of bed, following leads, and faced the morning with fatigue and little else to offer the Baby Doe case, as he'd named it on the official police record.

If social services, and the courts, wanted to name the child Ella, in the event family wasn't found, that was on them. It hadn't happened yet.

"Whoa, man, you don't look good," Drake Johnson said, coming into the squad room where all five of the Jasper Gulley detectives had desks. "You been here all night?"

In his perfectly fitting pants, athletic-cut shirt and pristinely knotted tie, the man was far too chipper for Ben's frame of mind.

"I have," he answered, wiping a hand down his face. Thinking about a cup of coffee, strong and black, he listened as the station came to life around him, and the night people called goodbyes. Not wanting to talk to any of them. Not day shift. Night shift. Not Drake, or any of his other fellow detectives.

He knew it was uncalled for, and not real smart, but as the night ended without answers for Baby Doe, he felt as though he'd just failed Jen again. Another day with the infant, weaving her dreams, and it would be that much harder for her to let that baby go.

"She told me about the foster family thing," he said, when Drake appeared beside his desk, setting down a cup of coffee for him. He knew the guy felt like he owed Ben. Ben figured it was the other way around.

"Dare I ask if you managed to keep your mouth shut about it?" came the response. He'd told Drake a thing or two during those dark weeks two years before, after he'd moved out of the house he'd expected to grow old in.

"I had too much else on my mind." Like the fact that being back in that home, with Jen, all he'd wanted to do was put his arm around her, take her upstairs to their bed and, holding her close, lie down and sleep for a month. "She's really taken with Baby Doe," he said. "I have to get this done before she starts thinking she might be able to keep her."

"You know, if it's not this baby, she's going to take in others."

He did know. And had been giving himself an ulcer about it. Jen all alone, dealing with rebellious teenagers. Always seeing them through loving eyes. Expecting the best of them.

Maybe they'd give it to her. Their best. Maybe they wouldn't.

Ben had always known his responsibility to life was to do all he could do. So what did he do when those he loved wouldn't let him do his best?

Why did all the things he *was* doing never seem to be enough? And too much at the same time?

Thoughts for another day.

"I'm heading home to get in a couple hours of sleep," he said, dropping a folder on Drake's desk. As the squad's lead detective, Ben was in charge of giving assignments. "Here's what I've got so far. Look over it. See if you catch something I've missed. Call me if you get anything new.

And check back with the hospital if you wouldn't mind. See if there's anything in the blood report that could lead us to the mother. Any particulars about the trace amounts of drugs in the baby's system… If they're prescription, we could start there. You got to figure the child was born nearby. I've already made calls to all the hospitals between here and Phoenix, looking for any babies born that fit this little one's description. You'll be getting calls back on that, too. At least we can narrow down the follow-ups and maybe give those to Lizzie." The department's tech guru who could find magic in dry dirt. "And when Audrey comes in, will you ask her to do some further canvassing around the neighborhood of the church? See if anyone has surveillance cameras we can get a look at, or if they noticed anyone carrying a black suitcase last night. Or saw someone in the immediate area with a baby…" Uniforms had already done a solid check. But sometimes talking to a plainclothes person, one with more interrogation training, netted new material.

Something Audrey, who'd made detective sooner than any officer in the history of the Jasper Gulley Police Department, was particularly good at. But then, single-handedly raising her hellion brother through his high school years had given her a load of experience.

"Got it. And I'm on it." Drake had already opened the folder Ben had passed over to him, and there was nothing more for Ben to do but go home.

He was in the rental car that had been delivered while his own sedan got a new front end, heading down Main Street, when his hands-free system signaled a text and then read it aloud.

The baby is safe now. Leave it alone. The sterile, computerized female voice hit him like a shotgun blast.

Pulling over to the side of the road, he had his phone out and the messaging app open in seconds, looking for the sender of the message.

He didn't recognize the number but hadn't expected to. It wasn't like it would be in his contacts. But he made note of it, pushing speed dial for Drake.

There was that *safe* word again. Implying the danger that existed.

"Have Lizzie run this number for me," he said, in lieu of hello, and waited while his second-in-command did his bidding and got back to their call.

His night's work hadn't been for naught after all. He'd shaken some leaves off a tree someplace. Now all they had to do was find the tree.

He sat there less than a minute, all systems on high alert. Watching every car that passed, looking into the woods along the side of the road...

The hourly reports he'd had from the officer outside Jen's house had all been benign.

"It's a burner phone." Drake's voice came back on the line. "And it's off. Can't even get a ping out of it. Guy probably dumped it in the trash. But Lizzie's watching it in case it comes back on."

"There's a list in the folder of everyone I contacted..."

"I've got it in front of me."

"The guy has to be connected there somewhere. The warning came specifically to me. My phone. Means he's reacting to my reaching out..."

"I'm on it," Drake said. "Get some rest so you can get back in here."

He could head back in as he was. It wouldn't be the first time he'd worked thirty-six or more hours straight. He'd aged some but had kept himself in top shape.

He also recognized that others could do follow-up while he refilled his personal resources. Telling Drake to call him if anything significant turned up, Ben disconnected.

He'd agreed to rest, but he had one stop to make first.

There was something criminal going on. It was up to him to find out what. The baby was safe, the message had said. As though, if he kept looking, she wouldn't be.

As though she'd been left at the church to remove her from danger? Or his searching would bring her more danger?

That meant the leaver was at least aware of some potentially great risk, if not directly involved in it.

And the leaver had specifically targeted Jen. Knew her routines.

He wasn't quite halfway to his old driveway, on his way to warn Jen about the text, when he got a call from the officer who'd just taken over in front of Jen's house, letting him know that they were on their way to a pediatrician appointment, one that had been set up before she'd left the hospital the night before, and to which Jen had insisted on driving herself. The officer was following her, but she wasn't happy about it.

And she'd be even less happy if Ben showed up on the premises.

If he pushed too hard, she'd just shut him out completely. He'd learned that lesson well.

She had a police escort. He had to be satisfied with that.

Having connected his phone to the rental car, he gave the command to send Jen a text. And then said two words, knowing that her hands-free system would relay his words to her.

Be careful.

Be careful. Not his usual *be safe*. His warning was more than concern. It had merit.

She didn't respond.

In days gone by, Ben might have called.

Would have called.

But those were days gone by.

Be careful. Not *be safe*.

Jenny hated the tension that tightened her entire being as she drove the last couple of miles to the doctor's office with a police car right behind her. Keeping her eye on the road and her surroundings, she fought darts of panic as a car appeared in the lane beside her, keeping exact pace with her, reminding her of the night before. And flooded with relief when the vehicle passed her without inflicting harm through the back window. Which was ludicrous. She had a police car right there.

The overload of emotion was because of Ben. The fear he instilled in her. He meant to keep her aware and safe. But that fear, instead, took the joy out of life.

Ben's words were still reverberating in her mind an hour later as she waited for the elevator that would take her back down to the ground floor of the clinic. After expressly telling the officer she would not accept escort into the doctor's office, which was her right, she'd told him she'd call when she was ready for an escort home. And she would. But she was going to walk the few steps from the front door of the clinic to her car first. Mostly because she was suddenly afraid to do so.

She wasn't going to be stupid. But neither was she going to allow her ex-husband to bring his particularly difficult brand of anxiety back into her life. Whoever had left little Ella wanted her safe. That was clear. As was the fact that since the person had left the baby with Jenny, that person obviously knew Jenny could keep her safe. And Jenny was keeping her safe. She and the leaver were on the same team.

Be careful. Not *be safe.* As though he was telling her there was a particular threat.

Getting off the elevator, she turned toward the outer doors several yards away. Ella, who'd been crying after an injection, was in a swaddling cloth tied to her chest, leaving the empty carrier hanging from Jenny's arm. The child was as safe as she could get. And Jenny had everything under control.

An old Kelly Clarkson song came to her. One that Jenny had begun to relate to toward the end of her marriage. The chorus played through her mind.

It was a song about fear. About the ability of a loved one to instill fear into you until you were afraid to stray too far from the sidewalk.

She'd dismissed her own affinity with the song almost immediately, even back then. The lyrics were about domestic abuse and she'd never, ever even come close to experiencing that insidious disease. And was hugely thankful for that fact.

Ben was overprotective. To the point of making her afraid of shadows sometimes. And stifling her joy. But he'd only and always been gentle in his touch. And in his words, too. She could count on one finger the number of times she'd seen him truly lose his temper.

That one time, she'd stormed out during a fight, had gone for a walk alone at night—to prove to him that she could—and had refused to answer his call on her way around the block. She hadn't stayed out long. Had had her phone with her, and her finger on speed dial. She'd stayed in their neighborhood. Having told him that if he followed her, she was leaving. She hadn't been going to go. She'd just been trying to get through to him. When she'd returned, calmed down, she found him pacing, his phone in hand. He'd seen her, raised his voice. Berating her for not picking up. She'd said he couldn't follow her. She'd said nothing about phoning. His face had turned red. And then he'd pulled her gently to him, with tears in his eyes. And now was not the time to think about that.

Instead, she had a flashback to nineteen years ago. She'd been in that very same building, coming from an appointment with four-year-old Simon. Her mom and dad had still been in town, rather than living out their retirement touring the country in the fancy motorhome they'd bought after they'd sold the home she'd grown up in. She and Ben had just been granted custody of the little boy. Something for which they had in no way been prepared.

And Ben, who'd worked late the night before, was home waiting for them.

What she'd give to have that full house again...

Funny how what you'd thought of at one time as a curse, had actually been a blessing.

She missed Ben every single day. But she didn't miss the fights—the calm conversations with no raised voices, but some gritted teeth, where they were diametrically opposed and couldn't find any middle ground. They'd been fighting for what mattered most—and had been on opposite sides of the battle. Every single one of those arguments had erected another brick on the wall that had been building between them for years.

Their lives were better now, she reminded herself as she moved toward the double doors that would take her out to a parking lot she had no reason to fear. The empty hallway seemed to mock her. The only reason there were no other people around was because she'd taken the earliest appointment of the day.

She might be lonely without Ben, but she also woke up every morning looking for the good in the day. And a lot of times, finding some.

She grieved, but anger didn't live in her home anymore.

The baby had fallen asleep and the comfort of that sweet weight against her brought resolve with it. For however long she had this child, she would teach her to explore her world, not fear it. To see the good that was everywhere, rather than constantly looking for what might hurt her. There would always be boundaries. Safety was paramount. But Ella would not be constricted to the point of having her spirit's circulation cut off.

With that thought, she pushed through the double doors to the outside, her gaze focused on the car she'd parked in the first spot to the right in the L-shaped lot. Just get to the car. Get locked inside, then take Ella out of the swaddling. Call for police escort. And then worry about getting the baby strapped into the car seat.

Her keys in hand, she pushed to unlock the door. Fighting the fear that wanted to take possession of her mind.

Another ten steps and she'd be there. Down off the curb, she glanced behind her, briefly, to make certain there were no cars coming from the opposite part of the L. Heard an engine rev loudly. A big engine. Roaring.

Before she could even compute that it was coming closer, she moved to step out of its path. Caught a brief glimpse of white. A truck. Saw the driver's door open and felt the hard jerk to her shoulder as a big black-gloved hand wrenched the baby carrier off her arm.

The truck never slowed. And Jenny was still standing there in shock, stabbing pain in her shoulder, as she saw the speeding vehicle reach the end of the row, roar toward the exit, the empty carrier flying out to bounce on the pavement.

Shaking, both arms wrapped around the baby in spite of the pain shooting down from her left shoulder, she ran back inside the building.

Thoughts screaming. He'd been waiting for her. Had angrily discarded the carrier seconds after he snatched it.

It hadn't been the carrier he wanted.

But what he'd thought it held.

Someone had just tried to kidnap Ella.

She had to call Ben.

Chapter 4

"I'm here." The words were out of Ben's mouth and he was half standing before he even had his eyes open enough to focus. He'd lain on the couch with his phone in hand. Knew it was the only way he'd sleep.

And knew her ringtone.

"I'm at—" her tone had him running for the door "—the clinic. A man just tried to take Ella…" Car started, he floored the gas on the way down his short drive.

"Find security," he barked, needing to ask questions but not daring to take the time.

"He's already here." The tone didn't sound like Jen. "He dialed 911. I can hear sirens…"

Thank God. She was likely safe for the moment. "I'm still five away. Stay put until I get there." Hearing his urgent tone, he took a breath. "Please." If he drove her away…

The radio hooked to his belt sounded out an all-points bulletin for a white truck driven by a male within five miles of the clinic. Officers were instructed to stop all vehicles fitting the description for a welfare check.

"I'm the lead on the case, Jen. And you're the only witness. The faster I get information the more likely I am to find the guy," he said as he swerved around a curve, watching traffic carefully as his portable bubble swirled above him. Trying to believe that his rate of speed really was just about wanting to question his witness.

Officers were already canvassing the area. She was safe.

And he had to see for himself.

There it was. His biggest fault.

No matter how he reasoned, or pretended, he still couldn't rest unless he knew Jen was alright. Not just alive. And with security.

But really okay.

"Stay on the phone with me?" she asked.

His gut wrenched. "Of course."

He'd never heard her sound so…helpless…before. Not when she'd called him to tell him there'd been an accident, and he'd arrived at the hospital to find his mother's car had been traveling at a low rate of speed on the freeway and had been hit by a semi. Jen had met him at the door. She'd been the one to tell him his mother hadn't survived.

There'd been fear and powerlessness in Jen's voice when she'd called him home to tell him that sixteen-year-old Simon had put in his emancipation papers. But there'd been a sense of strength there, too. Probably because of the anger. Aimed at him. An emotion that had come through loud and clear weeks later when she'd left the voicemail telling him that the boy they'd raised had left Jasper Gulley and wasn't planning to come back…

"I'm here." Pulling into the lot, he sped to the curb at the front door of the large medical building—one that housed every nonhospital medical and dental office in the city. He left the car there and ran into the building.

"We're at the main office."

He knew the place well. Had been attending medical appointments there since the building had been erected twenty-five years before. And let the fire in his veins drive him straight to his ex-wife.

And the infant she'd clearly already taken into her heart.

He saw them in the distance—the child strapped to Jen's chest in one of those carrier things—and filled with a different kind of dread. Fearing that, when he solved the case, and found that child's family, he'd be breaking Jen's heart all over again.

No one made Jenny feel safer than Ben Sanders. She didn't know another human being who lived life as focused on potential dangers, with an eye to preventing them, as he did. Which made him the most prepared human being she'd ever met. Add that to his extensive knowledge of people, of police work, of crime solving—and you had the one man you could trust to be able to keep you alive.

Which was why he'd been the first and only call she'd made after the security officer had met her just inside the clinic.

And why she felt a prick of grateful tears in her eyes as she clung to the sleeping baby and watched her tall, muscled ex-husband approach.

For once, the piercing way his gaze ran over every inch of her didn't rankle. Instead, his completely professional assessment gave her back a semblance of the confidence she'd just lost to a black glove protruding from a white truck.

As he came up to them, he reached out a hand, lightly clasping her upper arm, and leaned forward to kiss her cheek.

Shock ran through her, but she didn't pull back. Didn't call him on the familiarity. Instead, she gave him a tremulous, grateful smile.

She'd berated him for taking all the joy out of life, and

yet, there she was, in trouble, needing him. If she wasn't so frantically lost with no idea what to do, she'd have berated herself for being too hard on him.

"You're sure you're okay?" he asked, his hand leaving her arm, putting a little pressure on that shoulder.

Jenny held back the wince that threatened to shoot across her face. She'd already tested her shoulder for any damage. She had full range of motion. And it only hurt when she applied pressure against the shoulder joint.

She was bruised, not damaged to the point of needing treatment. And wasn't about to turn Ella over to someone else while she was put through unnecessary medical checkups just to be sure.

Not while danger lurked everywhere, and they had no way of knowing from which source it might spring.

"It feels like someone is getting desperate," she said softly, rocking a little from side to side, cradling the baby, while she looked up at Ben. "Whoever left her last night didn't want to be seen. Why else risk arrest for child abandonment when it could have been avoided by simply handing the suitcase to me rather than setting it down yards away?" Ben had probably already established as much the night before.

Jenny had mostly been busy spinning possibilities about a local person not wanting to be seen for fear of retribution—perhaps a young girl whose family didn't know she was pregnant—or some such. Up until that black glove had snapped out at her.

"And rather than going through authorities to get the baby back, someone is now trying to kidnap her from me?"

"I need to know everything you can remember," Ben said, his gaze intense—on Jenny, not the baby—as he failed to join the conversation she'd started.

Starting his own, instead.

Reminding her that they were no longer partners in life. In spite of the speed with which he'd reached her.

And the kiss on her cheek.

Accepting the rightness of his approach, Jenny replayed the scene for Ben, giving him every detail she could recall. Including… "I think he'd been drinking. I caught a whiff of alcohol breath. Or something that reminded me of it…"

"And you're sure you've never seen him before? There was nothing about the man, or the truck, that seemed familiar?"

She wanted there to be. Closed her eyes and tried to go back to the moment exactly as it had been. Then, eyes opening, shook her head. "Just that smell. The alcohol. It happened so fast… The truck, it was a pickup. Big, you know, like a work truck of some kind. That's got a big enough engine to haul a trailer or something. But no back seat…" That last came to her as she stood there meeting Ben's gaze.

He seemed so kind, encouraging, without pressuring her…which made the minutes seem a little easier. And gave her a pang of regret, too. He'd always been that way during times of trouble. How could she have forgotten that?

"But I never really saw him. Just saw his glove. His hand seemed as big as yours…and…there was a patch of skin— at the edge as he jerked the carrier…" She blinked. Looked up at Ben. "He was white," she told him, as though she'd had the information front and center all along. She was that certain.

"What about his face? Any whiskers? Hair color? Length?"

She hated to disappoint him but shook her head. "He came up from behind. I saw the hand, but he'd already driven past by the time I had a chance to look up from the carrier."

"What did you see through the rear window?"

She hadn't looked. She'd been focused on Ella. On getting into the building...

"You saw him throw out the carrier seconds after he snatched it." Ben's tone was soft.

Right. So she'd been looking. And...

"I only saw one head," she said slowly. "Like he was alone... And a cowboy hat."

Which was so common in Jasper Gulley that it hadn't stood out to her at all. Except that... "Do you think he was from here?"

Ben didn't respond to her question. Just said, "Give me a second," and, grabbing his phone, walked away from her.

He didn't look away, though. He'd put enough distance between them to prevent her from hearing his conversation, but she watched him watching her the entire time he was on the phone. Standing in the hallway outside the main security office, she didn't even consider heading back into the office. To sit down and wait.

Instead, she stood there, rocking gently, back and forth, weight on her right leg, then her left, and back again. Needing to keep Ella asleep so that the little girl had no indication of the fear sluicing around her.

To know that while the infant's life was held in the balance, Ella was peacefully unaware of the turmoil. To protect the baby's innocent ability to live without fear for as long as possible.

She'd grown up with a security that set her free to dream. Not worry. Ben hadn't had that luxury.

The serious, intent look on his face as he pocketed his phone and headed back to her had her defenses instantly shooting up. Only to be knocked down by the fear still holding her hostage.

"I'm about to make you mad," he said, looking her straight in the eye.

If they'd still been married, she might have considered the possibility. Since their divorce, she didn't get angry with Ben. She just walked away.

Raising her chin a notch, she stood there.

"I've made arrangements for you and the infant to be taken to a safe house," he said, his tone brooking no refusal. He held her gaze. Didn't blink. "Sara Unger is on her way now, in plain clothes and an unmarked car, to pick you up. As soon as she's certain she isn't being followed, she's going to bring you back to Center Street. The department owns an old house in the middle of the block. It's got alarms on all the windows and doors, all outside glass is unbreakable, and it's fully wired for surveillance, inside and out. If she has any hint that someone is on to her—and she'll take enough nonsense turns to know—we head to plan B."

"The Livingston case." She said the first thing that came to her mind. She'd known nothing about the high-powered mobster who was testifying against the cartel that had killed his family except what she'd seen in the news with the rest of the riveted nation. Until after the televised Phoenix case was through with weeks of testimony, and the man went into witness protection. Simon had heard something at school about Richard Livingston having been in Jasper Gulley, and Ben had admitted that he'd been guarding the man. She'd been hurt. And furious, too. That he'd watch over her and Simon so closely, try to protect them from any potential danger that occurred to him, but put himself in harm's way like that? And not even tell her?

He'd never told her where the house was. She was just guessing.

Ben didn't show any sign of having heard her. He was

watching her, steadily, as though she was already under guard. His feet apart, arms at his sides, the bulge of the gun at his waist visible beneath his shirt. Shoulders squared as though prepared to block any attempt she made to escape.

"Is Sara staying there with me?" she asked, grateful as hell that he'd pulled whatever strings were necessary to protect the baby. Just until he found his answers.

Glad to know that those big strong shoulders were back on her team, in spite of their divorce.

"Officers will trade shifts during the day," he relayed seriously. "I'll be there at night, with someone on patrol outside, and someone else watching the cameras at the station."

She nodded. Flooding with relief. With…more…but she refused to explore that feeling now. "I'll need the baby's things."

"It's best that we get new. If someone's watching your place, we don't want to lead him from there to downtown. Better that he thinks you've left Jasper Gulley. You can order what you need, and I'll send someone to Flagstaff to pick it all up for you."

Wanting to wrap her arms around the man, to hug him to her and hold on, Jenny nodded. Whether Ben was seeing anyone or not, she didn't know. And it didn't matter. He wasn't hers to hug anymore.

In spite of the fact that she still loved him. Had never stopped loving him.

Something she'd told him the day they'd signed the divorce papers.

She loved him, but they weren't good for each other. Were wired too diametrically different and brought harm to those in their midst, when they were together.

She suspected—wanted to believe—that he still loved her, too.

They'd split before the love could turn to hate. His idea. His words. Not hers.

But she hadn't argued.

Simon's departure had made the truth of their union clear to both of them. They failed as a couple to build a home that nurtured family.

But they weren't a couple anymore.

Did she dare hope that, together, they could protect someone else's child when they'd been unable to provide enough emotional and mental sustenance to save the one they'd been given to raise?

Did she have any other viable choice?

"I'll make the list now," she told him, pulling out her phone. "And text it to you." Leaning against the wall, with the baby still asleep against her, Jenny started typing, grateful for the distraction. The need to focus on a practical matter.

To stop looking at her ex-husband as though he was the man of her dreams come to live life with her again.

She knew better. Knew herself better. At the moment, she was in real danger and needed Ben's skills. But when the case was solved, and life returned to normal...

"That's it? You're agreeing to the plan? To going to the safe house?" His question brought her gaze up to his again. He hadn't changed positions. Was still standing guard.

Not to keep her in, she knew. But to keep anyone else from getting to her.

And Ella. The victim in his case.

"Of course, I am," she told him, flashing back to him telling her he was about to make her mad. "I'm grateful for the offer."

His brows rose with what looked like genuine surprise.

And she shook her head. "How could you think I'd do any differently?" she asked him, honestly curious.

Shaking his head, Ben stopped, met her gaze. And held on. "All I ever had to do was suggest a safety measure to you and you'd balk. An argument would be tripping off your tongue before I even had a chance to state my full case…"

His words hit her between the eyes.

And in the gut.

One word sprang to her tongue. *No.* She held it back. Wasn't going to fall back into old habits and patterns.

She no longer had to fight to keep her outlook on life. Or to maintain her ability to live with joy. Not that living alone, living without Ben, had been all that joyful. But it had been a hell of a lot more peaceful. With moments that were filled with smiles.

Mouth open, with her response still hanging there disallowed, Jenny heard his words again, playing through her mind.

And saw something she'd never seen before.

The way her fight to maintain her sense of optimism, to be able to live without fear and the constant anxiety that had threatened to overcome her, must have appeared to him.

As though she was willing to put herself in danger just to not give in to him. To have her way. To win.

"It wasn't about winning," she said aloud then. "I wasn't fighting you, Ben."

He shook his head. "We must have been living in two different houses," he said then. "Living two different lives."

"I was fighting," she said then. "But not you."

He stilled. Frowning. Watching. "What then?"

"I was fighting *for* my ability to be happy."

And there it was.

A truth she'd never seen clearly.

She'd been, still was, deeply in love with Ben Sanders. She just hadn't been happy living with him.

And knew, by the dawning light that seemed to take over his expression, that he hadn't been happy living with her, either.

They were too different. Saw the world through unmatched lenses.

She'd always thought that falling in love, real love, true, lifelong love, meant finding happily ever after.

But for her and Ben, it had done exactly the opposite.

For them, falling in love had been the beginning of the end.

Chapter 5

I was fighting for *my ability to be happy.*

Ben was standing in shock—reeling from Jenny's words, devastated, and yet, seeing a glimmer of light in the darkness, the light of understanding—when his phone rang.

And hers did, as well. They reached for their phones. Simultaneously. As soon as Ben saw Drake's number, his stomach sank.

"What's up?" he asked, phone to his ear, as his gaze remained glued to his ex-wife. She'd answered, as well. A second before he had. Her face had gone pale.

"There was a break-in at the preschool overnight," Drake said. "Jenny's office. The assistant director just called it in."

And then called Jen, Ben surmised, watching the expressions chase themselves across his ex-wife's frowning face. The way her free hand instinctively tightened on the bundle tied to her chest.

"Papers were out of place, like someone was looking for something in particular. Her locked bottom desk drawer had been broken into and the cash box was empty. It was only a few hundred dollars. Petty cash," Drake was relaying, while Jen's face showed him fear, confusion and, to a lesser extent, anger.

"More important to us at the moment is that the perpetrator slashed her desk chair and flipped the desk. The guy was angry."

Because he hadn't found what he was after, Ben surmised, but didn't say aloud. Thanking his next in command for the call, he told Drake to call him when the investigative partnership finished collecting evidence. And to make sure that all fingerprints or anything with any possible DNA attachment that may have been left behind were driven to the lab in Flagstaff with lights and, if necessary, siren blaring, and personally handed to the technician there who was responsible for Jasper Gulley work. He wanted answers as soon as humanly possible.

Jen had hung up just before him. Was staring at him as he gave the last directive.

But before she could say anything, Officer Sara Unger, inarguably one of the best law enforcement personnel in Northern Arizona, radioed that she'd arrived, and Ben quickly walked Jen through the maze of hallways and doors closed to the public to reach a drive-down ramp in the basement for deliveries. Maybe it was overkill, loading Jen and the baby up like boxes of produce, but he didn't give a damn either way.

He'd been following his gut since he was six years old, an only child dealing with a grieving, sensitive, widowed mother. With his father's last words to him that last morning still ringing in his ears. *You're the man of the house until I get back.*

He'd left childhood behind and had become a man at six.

He hadn't even fully grasped what death meant at that point. But he'd caught on quick and had known from that day forward that he'd do whatever it took to keep that horrible, dark irrevocable state from happening to anyone else he cared about. Or die trying.

It was all he knew. The backbone, the framework within which he'd grown up. Protect or die trying.

And his framework had made the love of his life feel as though she'd had to fight for her ability to be happy?

Not sure what in the hell he did with that, other than let it go, Ben made his way through that day a somewhat changed man. It hadn't been him that Jen had had to fight. Him that he'd felt as though she'd grown to hate. Her constant defensiveness, her lack of willingness to listen to reason…they hadn't been because she'd lost faith in him. Or no longer needed or wanted him.

Not to say those things hadn't happened. He was still certain that they had. At least to some extent.

But not because she'd grown to hate him.

She'd had to fight to protect her ability to be happy.

The distinction was miniscule. A blip that wouldn't show up on any radar.

But it stuck with him. A faint freckle on the skin. Something that had appeared, that he'd noticed, that made him a little bit…different than he'd been before it was there.

He carried that small mark with him that evening as he parked a couple of streets over from the safe house, went inside the home of a retired Jasper Gulley detective and was led through the house to the garage to climb into the back of the man's van. And it was with him as the detective's wife, a retired officer, drove him to a take-out place in town, where he climbed into the back seat of a delivery car and was taken to the safe house.

Overkill, to be sure. And yet, a system that had been set up for, yes, Jen had guessed it, the Livingston case. And one Drake, as well as their captain, had suggested using even before Ben could let them know that he'd be using it whether they liked it or not.

If he'd thought about seeking their support, he expected that they'd give it. He just wasn't much of a look-to-others-for-support kind of guy.

He was more the get-it-done man.

The Enforcer, his little brother had once called him. During one of their less brotherly moments.

Jen was in the sunken family room located in the back of the house—with a long strip of windows up high near the ceiling—when he entered the house.

Sara pointed to the room as she let herself out through the secluded back entrance through which he'd come in, before she slid down on the back seat of the delivery car to be taken to another secluded entrance at the station. Sara would enter the building undetected while Johnny was delivering a pizza to the front door. And come out half an hour later to get into her own car still parked in the station's lot.

It was all something he'd have expected to see in some television crime sitcom, and probably had sometime during his childhood. Not a circumstance he'd ever have expected to be a part of life in the small, quiet, secluded mountain town of Jasper Gulley. Nor had he ever thought to be tasked with guarding a mobster, or to be given the opportunity to help bring down a lucrative international cartel.

Things happened and life changed.

And some things didn't change, he had to admit, as Jen watched him walk into the room. The way her gaze slid over him, the look in her eyes—before her defenses had risen so high against him, it had always been that way. Like she wasn't just seeing him but seeing *inside* him. Not the body parts. The heart parts.

Like she accepted what she saw. Understood.

She just hadn't been able to live with it.

So that look…coming at him then, in that moment, with

him wearing his new little freckle… She didn't hate him. She accepted him. Understood him.

Could that be right?

"I've been waiting for a report." Jen's words brought him back to real life. The stuff that was always staring him in the face. The stuff he could see and affect.

He nodded. "I have one," he told her. "And plan to share. Just not over the phone."

Because he needed to be sure that she didn't go off half-cocked on him and jump the safe ship he had her on while he was unable to do anything about it. He'd never ever used physical force with Jen. Or anyone who wasn't a perpetrator under arrest and fighting him. He'd never even blocked her way out of a room or taken her car keys. She'd always been free to do as she felt best.

He'd just needed to be certain that she understood all the risks that came with whatever action she'd been taking.

"I've been at it nonstop all day," he told her then, sitting down in an armchair perpendicular to the couch upon which she was sitting. A portable crib sat on the floor, up against the side of the couch, and Jen had an arm hanging over the end of the couch and down against the inside of the crib's mesh wall.

She was all in. No doubt about that one.

"I needed to be able to discuss things with you…"

He broke off as she nodded. "To make sure I understand the gravity of the situation," she said.

There was no rancor in her tone. And not a hint of the stony-faced expression he'd seen more often than not during the last years of their marriage.

Should they talk about that?

Was he out of his mind? They were living on the edge

of life-threatening danger, for the first time in their lives together, and he was thinking about their broken marriage?

As though he was giving his team a briefing, he told her about the forensics report from Flagstaff. It gave them no leads as to who broke into her office. Church security cameras had been busted, including those angled toward the parking lot. Which meant that someone had to have done that damage before driving onto the lot.

"The cameras were still intact when I found Ella," Jenny pointed out. To which he nodded. Watching her. Feeling a slight lessening in the knot of tension coiling through him.

"Maybe whoever left her had second thoughts. And was trying to find my personal information, or something…and that's who tried to take her this morning. Maybe the mother left her. The father found out. She had second thoughts, told him where she'd dropped off Ella…and he followed me to the clinic this morning, to get her back," she continued.

He'd like that to be all they were looking at. Would love even one minute to live within Jen's optimism.

He wanted to point out the level of anger displayed by the damage done to her office—the split chair with stuffing thrown around the room, the splintered desk. That the force with which the carrier was thrown out of the truck that morning was not conducive to a safe or secure home life for anyone, let alone a newborn baby.

Thought about mentioning that the baby carrier had been disposed of with such strength that an object designed to withstand a car accident had cracked in half.

He didn't want to hear Jen's positive spin on possible explanations for either one of those situations. Didn't have the wherewithal at the moment to debate with her.

The situation wasn't up for debate.

"I received a text this morning. On my personal phone." He met and held her gaze.

Wide-eyed, she seemed to be giving him full focus.

"It said, 'The baby is safe now. Leave it alone.'" He had a spiel to give her on that fact alone. But didn't spit it all over her.

He would. He had to.

But that freckle…made him itch to give Jen a second to breathe first.

He might have to steal her joy, but he didn't have to suffocate her in the process.

Thank God! Jenny had to steel herself to stay seated. Her whole body ached to jump up, throw herself at Ben's feet, clasp her hands over his knees, letting her arms fall to the sides of his legs, and ask him to please abide by the text message.

Like she'd begged him in high school to please do one bungee jump with her. He'd been all about stopping her. Had a whole list of dangers, ranging from whiplash to death, and for what? Less than a minute of a rush?

But he'd gone.

Had laughed out loud during his descent. And had gone a second time.

That was the day she'd fallen deeply, romantically in love with him.

And that was the last time she could remember him giving in to her begging. Maybe because he'd been so into her, and them, that she hadn't had to ask for much of what she'd needed, let alone beg. He'd been so mature, so aware, and took genuine comfort out of providing what she needed and wanted.

Except for when he'd deemed the activity to be too risky.

He'd never prevented her from doing something. But he'd certainly managed to take the joy out of the doing. She'd spend her time looking over her shoulder. Worrying more than participating in life...

Glancing at Ella, Jenny felt like her heart was ripping open. And knew she wanted it open. Wide open. No matter how much it cost. Or hurt.

"Please, Ben. Please adhere to the text. Even if just for a day or two. I'll stay right here, accept all protection, even if I think it's overkill. I'll do exactly as you stipulate. If you'll please just back off on finding out who left the baby. Trust whoever it is to love this little girl enough to protect her. To know that leaving her here with me is her best chance. Trust them to know something you do not and to have made this choice accordingly. Trust her to know that if you push, Ella is going to get hurt." Trust *her*.

As though Jenny knew for certain that the leaver was a woman. She had no way of proving that. No evidence whatsoever to suggest it.

But her heart believed it.

"You have no idea why this baby was left, Ben, or what kind of danger she could be facing, but the person who left her does. Please..." She broke off as tears pricked the backs of her eyes.

Ben wasn't good with her tears. He'd accused her of using them as a ploy, to get at him, during more than one of their fights that last year.

She'd begun to figure out that maybe her tears had made him feel like a failure. Taking away his sense of having any control over the situation.

Or, at the very least, had threatened him, somehow...

"You're assuming that the person who left her did so for the infant's sake," Ben's words sucked some of the hope out of Jenny. But not all. In the past, he'd have immediately shut her down. "What if the child was left so that someone doesn't find out that a young woman just gave birth and had the child taken from her? What if the person who sent that text is out to save his own ass? Not Ella's?"

Jenny swallowed. Leave it to Ben to go to worst-case scenario. Or a worse case, at any rate.

But…she couldn't completely deny the logic in the possibility of his theory.

"The text came from a burner phone, Jen," he said. "One that's been shut off ever since."

"It's not like someone who wants her baby to be well cared for and loved, and knows that some biological caregiver won't give Ella that care and love, would use her own phone to make the call. You and I both know, firsthand, that family members can be abusive, Ben."

The blow was low. And yet…not at all. It was completely, importantly relevant. She and Ben had walked in on his stepfather hitting his mother. Simon had been two. And Ben had made certain that the man never got near his mother—or Simon—again. He'd taken time away from college to help his mother through her divorce and to testify at the trial that had severed the other man's paternal rights.

"If you're right, that means whoever left the baby is likely still living in that situation. You think I should just leave her there?"

Right. She'd picked the wrong scenario, after all. Just not for the reason she'd known.

"What if the mother's a woman no one knows was pregnant?" She tried again, to get Ben to see that a few days of waiting was worth the chance of giving a newborn baby a better life. One that whoever had loved her enough to leave her had wanted for her. "She could be married and love her husband. Or a teenager with her whole life ahead of her, paying for one mistake. Someone too young to be a good mother, or any kind of mother. Maybe she's too overwhelmed to be able to love the baby. She could be someone I know. Who trusts me to love her daughter when she cannot."

That last bit, about trusting her to love a child well... Jenny's heart had recognized it as truth from the first moment she'd given thought to finding Ella.

A truth that rang more strongly with each thing that had happened since. She'd been targeted, just as Ben had said. And the text to get him to leave it all alone... "Just a few days, Ben. Or at least one. Give us twenty-four hours. If nothing else happens..."

"The trail gets colder."

"If nothing else happens then maybe it means that whoever ransacked my office—which happened *before* you got the text—wasn't out to get Ella back—maybe it was unrelated to..."

"The attempt to take her at the clinic came afterward." His quiet interruption hit Jenny just as she was having the same thought.

"So we know whoever is trying to take her isn't the same person who left her," she said, following the thought further. Looking for the leaver to be someone she could trust. Someone who wanted what was best for her child.

And who thought Jenny was it.

Someone who knew her... "If you give it a day or two, maybe the person who left her will reach out to me," she said, believing there was a chance Ben would grant the small request. He was listening. Engaging with her thoughts, not just trying to get her to accept his. "Just as she reached out to you," she added.

"Someone broke into your office, Jen. You can't expect the day care, the church or the Jasper Gulley police to just ignore that crime—"

"I'm not!" She interrupted that time. Desperate to get Ben to be different than he'd been in the past. To see more than just his side of things. "Investigate the break-in. That works. Takes eyes off from the baby that was left. Even if just for a day or two. That's how you buy the time. Just lay off the Ella part. Let child services do what they do when a baby is abandoned."

"They use police resources to attempt to find out the identity of the child."

"Police resources, not their lead detective." When Ben didn't immediately open his mouth, shooting out a response before he'd had time to consider what she'd said, Jenny leaned forward. "Just a day, Ben. Let Ella's appearance pass through the system as it would have had I not been involved. That's all I'm asking. And in exchange, I stay right here, or anywhere you're comfortable with, and follow, to a tee, every safety edict you give me."

"What about the fact that someone tried to snatch the infant from you this morning?" Ben's words were softly spoken, bearing none of his usual unbending tone.

"That's why I stay right here. Hidden. What's the worst anyone can do? Break into my house? Isn't that worth the chance that the dust will settle, the chance the leaver might need to get things under control and ensure Ella's future safety? All I'm asking is that you trust whoever left her with me to have this covered, or to get help if it turns out it isn't. Give her a chance to come to you, at the very least, if she finds out that whatever—likely whomever—led her to leave the baby has somehow found out that she's done so."

Ben continued to meet her gaze. As though her words

were no longer the direct threat to him they'd once seemed to be.

Because he no longer loved her as deeply, as desperately, as he'd once done?

The thought put a little damper on any joy she might find in the day. But didn't change her resolve in the slightest.

"I spent the night putting out feelers, Jen," Ben said. "From hospitals and birthing centers, to birthing hotlines. I contacted police in surrounding districts. Women's shelters who offer pregnancy services or advice. Even the children's home in Satina. I let them all know I was interested in anyone who might have given birth in the past week who could be in some kind of trouble. Someone who may have been on drugs three months ago. Asking for missing persons reports that could fit. And sending a sample of the baby's DNA through the database."

Her heart lurched. He had information! He knew…

And hadn't been eager to tell her. Which meant…

"The only response I got that connected in any way to my night's work was that text this morning. You're right. With an abandoned child, I wouldn't have been involved in Ella's discovery last night. The only way anyone would have known I was on the case was if they somehow got wind of last night's work. My gut's telling me that something criminal is going on here. On a larger scale than a baby left illegally at a church."

"It's possible the leaver didn't know that Arizona safe-haven laws include the necessity of handing the child off to a person. It seems to be pretty common knowledge that churches are safe havens, but the hand-off procedure… You have to go read the actual law to know that part…"

Which meant little to their current discussion. Except,

"Maybe your calls tipped the leaver, or someone known to the leaver, to the illegality of what they'd done. Maybe they were just desperate to get her back so they didn't go to jail. And went about it in a very juvenile series of events."

Considering some of the things Simon had done at fourteen and fifteen, she could buy into the reasoning quite easily.

But then, her heart fully trusted that the leaver knew her. Had chosen her because of knowing her. Which meant they had to be looking at someone there in Jasper Gulley.

Jenny was, and had always been, a hometown girl. Even more so since her parents had spread their wings and had become world travelers, living out of a fancy RV in different states, any time they were in the US.

"One day, Ben. Give us one day."

Us. Her and Ella? Her and Ben? Why had she said us? Jenny shook her head.

And heard Ben say, "And if the man who attempted to kidnap that infant this morning ends up doing harm to the woman who had her? Or to whoever left her, if that's not the same person? If Ella's been kidnapped from a loving family and the kidnapper gets paid and disappears? If we're lucky and the family's plight reaches us here, we do DNA testing and the infant is returned to her family, but the kidnapper, having been successful, likely won't stop there. Depending on why he took the child…"

"The child was left with me. I was targeted. You even said so. Why would someone take a child from a loving family and then just abandon it with someone they don't know? Or even with someone they do know?"

When Ben shook his head, looking more exhausted than

angry, Jenny felt a pang that she hadn't felt in a while. A need to soothe him, to ease his mind. To help him rest.

He took the worries of the world on his shoulders every day.

Had been doing so since he was way too young to know any differently.

"You're right. It's not likely that someone would target you with a baby stolen from a loving family, unless..." Ben stopped. Wiped a hand over his mouth and down his chin, as though clearing away words that he'd almost said. Or ones he wished he hadn't already. "For now, let's go with the first scenario," he continued. "Because it's more likely. For someone to leave a baby with you, without telling you, speaks of desperation. And if this person is in a desperate situation, I can't just sit back and leave her there, Jen."

She'd lost. Spirits dropping to the floor, Jenny glanced at Ella, sleeping so sweetly in her portable crib. Ben wasn't going to heed the warning to protect Ella by leaving the case alone.

Which meant Ella was likely going to be in more danger.

Jenny wanted to grab the baby and leave Ben sitting there in his safe house all alone. She had to fight the urge to run with the baby to some unknown faraway place. But even as she had the thought, she recognized the futility of it.

Because, while her heart knew the truth, that Ella was safest without Ben's perusal of the case, she also recognized the viable possibilities in what he'd said. That him dropping things could put the leaver—in Jenny's mind, the mother—in more danger.

And she couldn't sleep well with that thought, either.

Chapter 6

Ben knew he'd won by the light that went out of Jen's eyes. Waited for her to wheel the portable crib to whichever of the two bedrooms down the hall she'd chosen to occupy for the night.

Figured himself for an hour or two in the chair before getting back to work.

Victory brought relief. But no pleasure beyond that.

Jen wasn't vacating his space.

Glancing over, he saw her watching him.

If she thought she was going to try some new angle to work him…

Because he hadn't been as much of a jackass in his response to her as he had during their marriage…acting like he knew better and refusing to relent when he saw danger present, needing her to see what he saw so that she'd protect herself…

"What?" he asked, needing to get the conversation over so he could attempt to rest. And then get to work. In the past, all the dangers he'd seen in Jen's path, they'd been what-ifs.

In the present…someone had vented their anger all over her office. And had targeted her that morning at the clinic, too. Someone who wanted the infant. And knew Jen had her. Possible loss of life didn't get any more real than that.

He had the job of his life in his lap. Pressing on his shoulders. And pushing at his back.

And he would not fail her.

No matter how upset she got.

"You stopped talking when you mentioned a baby being stolen from a loving family…"

He heard her words. Didn't follow where she was going at all. "Yeah." How had that been a problem for her? He'd dropped the scenario…

"Your eyes… They lost their light…like they always did when you were using a case to try to convince me of the real danger in front of me."

Yeah, he'd done that too much. Brought the job home with him. Drake, the pain in his ass, had pointed the fact out to him one night shortly after Ben's divorce, when he'd been wallowing in more beer than was necessary. He'd learned from his job what could happen to good people. And had thought himself richer for it. More able to protect his own. Had never understood why Jen couldn't partake of the riches…or at least open her mind enough to see the credibility in them.

"I apologize for bringing the job home too often," he said. Because he meant the words. And because he needed her to leave him alone for a few hours.

Leave him in peace.

Because he wasn't going to fight with her again. He'd made himself the promise the day he'd told her he wanted a divorce. Those fights were killing both of them. The divorce… hopefully only killed a part of him, not her.

He'd set her free so she could be happy.

"I don't need an apology, Ben." Her soft words brought his gaze back to her. He didn't get them, either, or the tone.

Where was the spitfire who had enough gumption to stay alive while he caught whoever was after her and the child?

The one who'd stood up to her foot taller, muscular, armed and trained cop husband, and smooshed him down like an ant?

"I want to know about the case…"

His mistake had been bringing too much work home with him. And now she wanted him to talk about the case?

Right, they weren't home.

She *was* work.

With the thought that the truth might help Jen understand his perspective, to trust his knowledge and gut to lead them safely through the fire, he said, "There are three of them, actually," he told her. "Last year, a woman in California had a note left on her door, telling her that her newly deceased younger sister's newborn baby was in danger. At one point, there was some suspicion that the baby, if there was one, might be in Northern Arizona. A nationally renowned firm of experts, Sierra's Web, was working the case, and they called in local police forces for information. I ended up working with the firm."

"Was there a baby? Did you find it?" Jen's gaze was glued to him like he was some kind of high interest television drama crime show. He didn't hate her attention. "Me? No. The firm solved the case in Nevada, but due to my response on that one, they called me a few months later, asking for help in locating one of their partners and an FBI agent who went missing after a failed kidnapping of a newborn from a birthing clinic in Las Sendas." He named the small town not far outside of Phoenix. They'd driven through it once, on their way home from Arizona State University. They'd stopped at the base of the mountain and had sex in the back seat of his old beater. Did she remember?

"So it wasn't really a kidnapping case." No sign of recollection.

"It was," he told her. "The agent had been trying to break up a suspected kidnapping ring for more than six months. Turned out that one arm of the ring was working out of an old, abandoned mining town twenty miles from here into the mountain. I helped with the case, was on the ground for the rescue and have been working to help locate other babies who'd been stolen and sold through illegal adoption proceedings…"

Jen's eyes grew wide. "There was a lobbyist or something at the head of it, right?"

Ben shrugged. Because the case was ongoing, until all babies were found the information wasn't his to share. The important thing for her to know was, "It's possible that this child was one of those babies, Jen. There were many arms of that operation, and no one is sure if they've all been arrested. Maybe one has tried to continue. Or it's a copycat."

"Then why leave the baby with me?"

"Because Agent Michaels is closing in hard, and it's possible that this baby was dumped to avoid discovery."

"You called this agent last night, didn't you?" She wasn't the least bit enthralled with him. Her gaze had turned piercing.

One nod, chin to chest, was all he gave her. He was doing his job.

Bracing himself, he waited for her to berate him. To tell him he was overreacting. Instead, she sat there, studying him. As though, if she watched him long enough, she'd find something she didn't already have.

It wasn't going to happen. The woman had owned him since puberty.

Still, the scrutiny, with him being so tired… He could

only withstand it for so long. "I had to make the call, Jen. I'm officially part of that case."

She nodded.

"The perpetrators are all locals in whatever towns they're working. They're all hiding in plain sight. It's possible that someone here is involved. And that they targeted you because they do know you. Or know of you. One of the ringleaders of the arm of the operation close by was a retired schoolteacher. You didn't have her, but I did— Grace Arnold."

Her eyes widened. She didn't glance at the baby. Just blurted, "Mrs. Arnold was involved?" She stared, as though by watching him she could find a way to make sense of what he was saying. "You said, or I read, that all of the kidnappings were babies taken from birthing centers."

"That's right."

"You called every one in the state last night, didn't you? Or had someone else doing so?" Defensiveness had always been her go to when she was feeling panicked.

"Centers in a six-state radius have been contacted at this point."

"Any kidnapped babies reported?"

She had to know there hadn't been. The infant next to her would have been taken into custody—left with Jen but made part of the official investigation until DNA cleared— if that had been the case. "No," he finally admitted.

"So it doesn't fit the MO of the case."

Method of operation. Had he ever talked to her about anything other than police work in those last difficult years of their marriage? They'd both been so defensive. So shut off. As they'd worked at odds to raise a rebellious teenage boy.

His memory of the time was of him filled with an intense

need to get her to understand that the dangers he'd been try-ing to prevent were real. He'd brought home a lot of proof.

"The methods are changing, Jen," he said quietly. "Those involved, or a copycat, know a lot of what we know and will change practices accordingly. Millions of dollars were involved here. And the ring ran successfully for more than two years before anyone was even on to it. If not for Dr. Lowell's intervention in the kidnapping at the birthing cen-ter, it would still be going strong. Babies were being sold all over the country to rich couples who had issues in their past that made it difficult for them to adopt. Someone who's already crossed the line, who hasn't yet been discovered, would find it difficult not to continue raking in that kind of paycheck. They likely set up a new site on the dark web to find buyers. And will come up with new ways to take babies, too."

"This is all supposition, right?" she asked next. "There's no proof that this Agent Michaels hasn't found all those involved?"

"He's still working the case." He couldn't say more. Not even to Jen. He'd already said too much.

A plea deal, involving a possible unloading of current information, hung in the balance.

"This Sierra's Web…you haven't called them, have you? To work on Ella's case specifically?"

Ben took a deep breath. Weighing what to say. How much to say. If she had any idea of the lengths he'd been taking over the years to watch over his brother…

"You can't call them, Ben!" Jen blurted then, scooting forward to the front of her seat. Glancing over her shoul-der at the sleeping baby and then pinning him with that ur-gent stare that hit him in the gut every time. "You were just warned to drop things, and even if you aren't going to do that, you can't call in a national firm of experts here! There's no telling what will happen! That guy this morning...he was big, determined, bold. We have no idea why he wanted Ella, but the leaver, or whoever sent that text, has to know. Has to know that if you leave it alone, the guy will back down."

"Or the person who sent that text, warning me off, is part of this kidnapping ring and hasn't been caught. He'd know that I'm involved. I helped bring in the remaining crew that we know of that was attached to the schoolteacher."

Mouth open, Jen stared. Met his gaze. "Oh, my God, you've already called Sierra's Web. Have them working on Ella's case! Which is likely going to put her in more danger!"

He would have called. Had wanted to do so. Even knowing it would have to be at his own expense. "No," he shook his head. Because he'd wanted to talk to her first.

A lot of good that had done him.

He looked her in the eye. "They know nothing about this infant. Unless Agent Michaels told them." Michaels was the only one with jurisdiction to involve the private firm in the kidnapping case. The FBI was paying the bill.

Ben's association with Hudson Warner and the rest of the firm had nothing to do with an abandoned newborn. Or a kidnapping ring.

It was far more personal than an unknown baby.

And that was something he hoped Jen would never find out.

Jenny wasn't eager to head into the bedroom. She felt safe enough on the lower level, like in the family room, with the only outside access being the row of windows up near the ceiling.

But she was sitting with Ben, alone, in a home, for the

first time in years. Still on different sides of the fence. And yet, that fence, the baby in her care, held them both captive.

Just as Simon had done.

That night felt different, though. Ben's point of view didn't make her feel as though she couldn't breathe. She wasn't sharing a life with him.

Could walk away.

And, in that moment, didn't want to.

Ella could be waking for a feeding soon. Sometime in the next hour or so. Telling herself that she'd get back to the work she was doing when Ben came in until it was time to prepare the next bottle, Jenny tapped on the screen on her lap, waking it up.

Prepared to ignore her ex-husband, even while she acknowledged that she hoped he stayed in the room with her.

Her plan worked for a bit. Ben had closed his eyes. And, feeling content, she got back to reading responses to the questionnaires she'd sent out shortly after arriving at the safe house. Each one addressed to one of the nine parents in the three-year-old class.

The day care had been closed that day, due to the break-in. All the kids whose families couldn't make arrangements for them were being cared for in the church itself, by day care staff.

Some of her questions netted opinions on that matter. Jenny was just compiling those responses into a separate document to send to Ben, just in case someone said something that struck a chord with him, when she heard a digital sound coming from his direction.

Glancing up, she saw his eyes pop open, seemingly instantly alert, as he pulled a phone out of his shirt pocket.

Touching the screen, he looked at it long enough to read a short message and then strode out, heading up the flight of four stairs to the fully above-ground portion of the house. Seconds later, she heard the rumble of his voice but couldn't make out the words. Forced herself to stay seated. Waited through a silence and then heard him speak again, clear tension in his tone.

Was he talking about Ella? About the baby's case? She had a right to know.

But Ben wasn't her husband anymore. He was the detective on a case in which she was involved. She had to treat him as she would any other member of law enforcement.

With respect, of course—that was a given, even when they'd been fighting every second they'd been together. But also with professional distance.

That one was harder.

Most particularly when she could read the agitation running through his body as he returned, trying to give her an easy nod, as though she'd buy his attempt at reassurance.

The call *had* been about Ella. Or Jenny? Someone had targeted her with the baby drop. Had the person given her name to someone else?

Or was the leaver wanting Ella back?

"What?" she asked when Ben took a seat on the end of the couch on which she sat. Much closer to her than before.

Within reaching distance.

"They found the white truck." He sounded…almost conversational. Not quite. But close.

So maybe she was overreacting.

Not something she'd been guilty of in the past. To the contrary, Ben had always accused her of having her head in the sand in her refusals to accept that the world was a scary place.

"Oh, good," she said, watching him closely. Glad that he

was sharing case information with her as it came in. Not wanting to stem his flow.

When he shook his head, she tensed. "Not good," he told her. Looked her straight in the eye and said, "They found it smashed through our garage door, Jen."

Our. They'd bought the house together. He hadn't lived in it in years. Had signed it over to her as part of the divorce settlement.

And that's what she was thinking about? Ownership of a garage door?

It was easier to grasp than the rest. "Someone ran a truck through the garage door," she stated. Then she figured it out… "To get into the house?"

Oh. *God, no.* Her home, all her belongings, a lifetime worth of memories… A flash of a photo she'd seen of her office that morning passed through her mind.

"No." Ben's word came slowly, but it stopped the panic sluicing through her.

"No?" At first, she wasn't sure she'd heard him correctly.

"Someone, we're assuming the perpetrator who yanked the baby carrier from you this morning, drove it through the garage door, hit your car, which I'd had returned to the house this morning from the clinic parking lot, and then… nothing."

She had no idea what to make of that. Until… "You need the code to the security camera," she figured out. And stopped talking when he shook his head.

"They were inactivated before the truck pulled into the driveway. Shot out with a BB gun."

"Someone deliberately disabled my security cameras, drove his truck through the garage door and then just left?" She was starting to shake inside. Didn't want to hear Ben's take on the situation. She was already scared enough. "He must have been spooked before he got a chance to get in the house," she blurted, her mind running with the scenario.

"It's possible, Jen, but not likely." Ben's words came quietly. "If he wanted in the house, why not park elsewhere and head to your place on foot? Quietly break down the side garage door? It's out of sight of the street. And is the only entrance to the house without a dead bolt." Something he'd been on her about since she'd had the door replaced a few years before due to rotting wood. "Once inside the garage, he could still take his time to break through the door leading into the house without being seen."

"Not everyone is as savvy as you are as to how to commit crimes undetected," she said, not quite at a snap, but close. And then quickly threw out, "I'm sorry, Ben. Truly sorry. You didn't deserve that."

She didn't want to alienate him. At all. Or be at odds with him.

What she wanted was for her ex-husband to reach over, pull her up against his warmth and hold on.

Just until her jitters went away.

Chapter 7

Ben didn't want to tell her the rest. Finding no humor in the fact that during their marriage, his number one priority sometimes had seemed to be telling Jen every bad thing he saw or dealt with so that he could make certain she had the knowledge she'd need to keep herself safe.

Yet, for the first time she was sitting in real, current danger—not some perceived physical hardship that might befall her—and he suddenly wanted to keep the information from her?

To protect her from the pain?

Made so little sense to him that he pushed aside his personal thoughts. Finding them untrustworthy in the current circumstance.

"There's more." He held her gaze, as though by doing so, he could hold her up, too. "The way he crashed through the door, it wasn't a mistake, Jen. He went in far enough to damage your car, to obliterate the door, and then stopped. It wasn't a misplaced foot on the gas. It was a slow, steady, purposeful crunch."

A message.

"He's warning me," she said, seeming to hold completely steady. She'd always been a rock. The confidence with which her parents raised her had helped make her so.

Why hadn't he seen that before? Trusted it more?

Instead of treating her like someone who couldn't take care of herself?

Because he lived on the other side. The answer followed right behind the silent question. How could he spend all day every day with his head fully enmeshed in solving crimes, and then just pretend he wasn't filled with the vile activity that went on in the world? How could he pretend not to see…?

"He's angry," Ben finally responded to her statement. "And probably warning you that he's not going to stop coming after you." He knew she didn't want to hear the fact. Would probably find some other scenario to try to make it disappear. Or at least have to share the stage.

Didn't matter to his case, one way or the other. Someone was targeting the only woman he was ever going to marry. He had a job to do.

"So trace the truck." Her tone, her expression was recalcitrant. She'd know that he'd already have put out the command to do so.

Didn't know that Drake had already done so before calling him.

"It was reported stolen from Yuma three weeks ago."

"Yuma? That's down at the border…"

He knew. And Michaels did, too, now. Ben had called the agent before heading back to Jen.

"I can't tell you what we're involved with here, Jen, but I can guarantee you that it's not some local girl wanting you to love her child because she's afraid to tell her parents she was pregnant. Or someone who's trying to get rid of the result of an unwanted pregnancy."

She sat up then. Closed her laptop. Glanced at the infant on the other side of her and then faced him. "But it doesn't sound like the other case you were talking about," she told him, meeting his gaze straight on. "From what I understood from the little bit in the news, that whole thing was run on the down-low. As a matter of fact, when that one kidnapping went sour, they just went on and kidnapped another baby, right?"

"And tried to get rid of the woman who'd thwarted the first one because they didn't know what she'd seen. Maybe this guy thinks you can identify him."

Ben saw the fear in her gaze and his heart sank. She wasn't going to accept his very real, valid, and threatening theory.

At least not without a fight.

"Maybe he's the father of the child the woman gave up to me."

"In a stolen truck?"

"He has anger issues," Jen said, more because she had to fight her fight than because she was convinced of what she was saying. She couldn't give in to fear. "Clearly, he's not father of the year material, or why would the mother give her up like she did? In secret?"

"It's more likely that someone got wind of the sale, that someone chickened out and tried to stop it from happening. Or maybe whoever took the baby was seen, someone got the baby back, disposed of it quickly, to keep those in charge of the operation from finding out. Or that the baby they took wasn't the right one. This one didn't fit the order, and they needed to dispose of it quickly and get the right one in time to make the drop-off. That first kidnapping, the one that Dr. Lowell thwarted…the kidnapper who made the mistake was shot dead in cold blood the very next day."

Okay, she hadn't read that part. But looking in Ben's eyes, she knew he was telling her the truth. Even as she suspected he was trying to scare her into submission to whatever plan he had in mind to keep her safe.

She could have told him he needn't have bothered. She was all in. As long as she got to care for Ella until they figured out what was going on. Someone had to do it. She was the one who'd been chosen. And she was already in danger. Why put anyone else in that situation?

Unless… "You aren't about to tell me that I'm supposed to hand over Ella and run for the hills, are you? You aren't shipping me off to Paris or Timbuktu with some kind of protective team, to keep me safe until this is resolved."

Ben's soft, half-hearted chuckle shocked her. The sadness in his eyes was a surprise, too. Though not a welcome one. He shook his head. "No, Jen, I know you better than that. And I need you here."

She stiffened. "So you can keep an eye on me. Keep me under lock and key." The idea wasn't unwelcome at that moment. She just needed to find a way to save face—for her own sanity—before she complied.

"No, so you can take care of the infant and be here for us to question when we start to home in on this guy. We know whoever left the baby targeted you. We don't know why. There's likely going to be something that turns up during our investigation that will mean nothing to me but could be an eye-opener to you that helps us crack things wide open. I suspect you're being scared off in an effort to ensure that you don't do that. It's not like the whole town doesn't know our history. You trying to get me to back off…"

Jenny's mouth fell open. She closed it. Immediately. But continued to stare at Ben. And then, when she couldn't deal with the rest of it, focused on the shocking part and said, "You want my help?"

Why the idea had her fighting tears, she had no idea.

She put her emotionalism down to the events of the past twenty-four hours. And the uncertain hours ahead.

Not to any healing needed as a result of their marriage fallout. She'd dealt with all of that. Had moved on to a happier state.

Ben's slow nod, up and down, short movements, again and again, a rocking motion, was the only answer she got.

So Jen nodded, too.

She was getting what she wanted.

Under the circumstances.

At least somewhat.

As long as she didn't think of all of the things she wanted that she wasn't getting.

Like a minute in her ex-husband's arms.

The second Jenny finished feeding the baby and said that she was going to lie down to get some rest before the infant woke again, Ben jumped up and wheeled the portable crib to the room she'd chosen. If he was being obvious in his need to have her out of the room, to have time apart from her, so be it.

He had a job to do. And couldn't do it with her sitting there judging him. Or pulling at him not to do what he knew had to be done. She wasn't his wife. She was a case.

Her life—and the infant's—depended on him getting it right.

He wasn't good husband or father material. He'd accepted that.

He *was* a good cop. A detective who'd solved, or helped solve, more cases than any other small-town detective in the state. One whose expertise was sought after.

Sitting there, phone in hand, he ran down a mental list of his credentials, not because he got off on how great he was. To the contrary. He did it to remind himself that making the call he was about to make was the right choice in the given situation.

Because the man in him who still loved his ex-wife felt bad for doing so.

If he let personal emotions get in the way of the job, he had to take himself off the case. And there was no way in hell he was going to leave Jen's safety to anyone else.

He'd spent most of his life prepared to jump in front of bullets for the woman.

Someone was targeting her. Might be a hidden arm of the kidnapping ring Agent Michaels and Dr. Lowell had brought down. Michaels was certain there was one.

Or it could be someone else. For reasons unknown. Ben wasn't losing sight of that fact—though his gut pointed to the monied operation.

Still…he dialed Michaels. The agent, who'd relocated to Phoenix, was out of the office a lot more than he'd ever been now that he and the doctor had hooked up—but Scott Michaels was still committed to the job. And would want the call. As he'd assured Ben the night before.

Unlike Ben, who'd fallen for an optimistic child life specialist who lived in a beautiful world Ben had never known, Michaels's wife—a partner in Sierra's Web—was one of *them*. A person who'd suffered greatly and found peace and a curious brand of happiness in eradicating danger, one small step at a time.

According to Michaels, he and Dorian had found much more than that, in each other. The agent had tried selling Ben on the possibility of seeing the darkness but being able to walk in light, as well, but Ben wasn't buying it.

He'd believed once.

And had been burned worse than ever when it all fell apart.

He knew better. There were some people who were born into a good world where bad things happened, but beauty still reigned. And others who never got to feel real beauty full-out.

His life with Jen had taught him that those two types of people should never mix.

A thought that had solidified one night when she'd been telling him about one of her classes that day. Something about how people's ability to give and seek love was instilled, created, during the childhood years. Before puberty.

He'd loved. And been loved. And loved Jen deeply. Just as he'd loved his mother and little brother.

But if the theory worked for love, it worked for other emotions, too. Like happiness. His inability to believe in happily ever after had been instilled since his early childhood. While Jen had been blessed with a mammoth capacity to see the good in everything.

All things that he'd realized too late. But knowing helped him push the speed dial button as he stood and walked up the short flight of stairs to the front of the house to assure the privacy of his conversation.

He needed Jen to work with him, not defend against him. And while he was not going to lie to her—never had—he knew there were some things he couldn't tell her—to bring the job to a successful conclusion.

In the past, he'd learned too late that his lack of sharing had been a problem. For the marriage.

In the present, there was no marriage.

Detectives didn't tell their victims all the facts of the case.

"I've got the truck," he said as soon as Michaels picked up. "Stolen from Yuma. Three weeks ago."

"Damn."

Yuma. The site of the unsolved kidnapping. Michaels believed that, for a chance to see daylight again, his "general" had confessed to the national syndicate he'd run, stealing and selling babies for illegal adoptions, but that there was someone he'd protected.

Maybe a family member. Or lover.

Someone who'd been involved enough to know how to go into business for himself. Or herself.

The Yuma kidnapping had happened after the general's arrest.

Fit the same MO.

And Sierra's Web had found a listing on a dark website that, while different than the general's coding, had been similar enough to match a parameter search.

"We got no fingerprints or fibers," he continued. And then admitted the perplexing part. "The guy drove the truck through my ex-wife's garage and left it there." He told Michaels, without being asked, about nothing being disturbed or stolen, other than the garage door and her car. "Why not push it over the mountain? Why not dispose of it like others were disposed of?" he asked then, referring to the general's men who'd made the mistakes that had allowed Michaels to solve the case. That piece had been bothering the hell out of him all evening. Making him edgier than he liked to be. "Why leave it there for us to find?"

"It's personal."

Yeah, that's what he'd known. Had suspected it the night before but had told himself he was being too negative. Assuming the worst.

"Because of me," he said then. "I'm the one who made the arrests. Who clued you in on my old schoolteacher, Grace Arnold, and brought in this entire prong of the operation. Now whoever the general left behind is going after my family."

"Where's the truck now?"

"In custody. I'm assuming you're going to want your people going over it."

Michaels rattled off the address where the truck should land. And Ben asked a question born from the conversation the two men had had the night before. "If we go with the theory that we didn't get everyone up here...there was someone in the cell left behind...why not just go after me? Why involve a baby? And my wife?"

"If he did his homework, he knows that the only way to hurt you bad is through her." Michaels's comments came softly. "I know that just from the little searching I did," the agent continued. "You live in a small town, man. With a small-town newspaper that's gone digital..."

Right.

"And... I might have heard a thing or two through Sierra's Web, too," Michaels admitted.

He'd given the agency the right to give Michaels any information he needed on Ben, back when the agent had been recovering from a gunshot wound and had needed help in the area and Ben had volunteered.

Because there'd been some Northern Arizona small-town dirty cops involved in the operation. It had been one of the reasons Ben had volunteered to help. And probably the only reason Michaels had vetted him so carefully.

"You also think this guy might be someone we know." Ben guessed what he knew was coming.

"The idea is on my radar."

"You got the list I sent." Of everyone Ben could think of who'd have it in for him.

"I did. Sierra's Web is on it." That information eased

Ben's mind some. The firm had the resources to make miracles happen almost daily.

"I'm bothered about the infant," Ben said then. "What if the mother really is someone who was desperate, for whatever reason, to secretly find her baby a good home? Someone who knows Jen. Doesn't make sense to me that one of the general's leftovers would go to the trouble of kidnapping just to get at me. Why not just go after Jen?"

"If he was one of the kidnappers, stealing babies is his skill. And if he's done his research, he's going to know that he can squeeze you until it hurts so bad you're bleeding with it, by having the two of you pitted against each other while she's in danger. And one google of Jen's name and you get that she's a perennial mother whose only regret is not having a child of her own."

He'd told Jen not to talk to that reporter. He'd been proud of the state child life specialist award she'd won. But some things should be kept private.

"The public statement you made on the department's Facebook page after the divorce makes me cringe at the moment," Michaels said.

Jasper Gulley was a small town. Where they'd both grown up. Had careers. He'd taken responsibility for the divorce. Saying that all acrimony came from him, from his job. That Jen had been right to fight back and claim her right to see the world as a beautiful place.

Grief had driven him into the mistake.

That and his never-ending need to protect his wife.

Along with a six pack.

He'd taken the post down the next morning.

By then it had already been shared more than a hundred times.

He'd sent requests to have them all removed. Good luck with that one. Shares had been shared.

And shared…

He hadn't posted on social media since.

Years later, was his mistake playing right into the hands of a man out to make him suffer?

By making Jen's world as ugly as his own?

Still, he shook his head. Looked toward the ceiling. Needing to keep Jen's beliefs on the table at all times. To allow the less ugly world to exist. "I can't imagine someone is so hell-bent on revenge that he'd be willing to give up the money that baby would bring on the market," he said aloud.

Even as his mind came up with a couple of scenarios.

The jerk took the wrong baby. Had to quickly dispose of it. And was twisted enough, angry enough to use it to bring the utmost pain to the man who'd stolen his army from him.

By giving it to Jen. Letting their agony play out. And if, eventually, the baby Jen fell in love with turned out to belong to someone else, there'd be the added heartache of taking it away from her.

"Could be he meant all along to get the child back, which would explain the attempted kidnapping this morning. Maybe he hoped to shoot you up with pain *and* make the sale. He's cocky enough to steal babies from birthing centers, he'd be fairly confident he could get one from a single woman. Could also be the sale fell through," Michaels said slowly. And then, with urgency, "Or… I've got to get Sierra's Web on her socials," he said. "I need every username and password she's currently implementing and any she's had in the past. This guy could be framing her, Sanders. Could have her on the dark web as a buyer…"

The thought sent chills to Ben's bones. The text he'd

received, telling him to leave it alone. Would ensure that he didn't.

A conflict that would keep him and Jen at odds. Leading to him believing her guilty of such a heinous crime?

She'd said her only regret was not being a mother. Had recently applied to foster...

Could someone really be so twisted?

Could he afford not to pursue the possibility?

"This is more than a safe harbor incident, Detective." Scott Michaels's tone came softer, more personal. "Whatever is going on, whether it has ties to the general's operation or not, it's bad. It seems pretty clear that whoever is behind it has had some experience in the criminal world. He's managed to get our attention without leaving a single clue as to his identity. From the slashes on your tires last night, the attempted kidnapping this morning, the burner phone text warning you off. And now, with the truck crash...it's clear, in-your-face anger. He's escalating, daring you to find him, and you can count on it getting worse until you do. Get me those usernames." Michaels clicked off.

Ben nodded to the darkness around him. Recognizing the truth with every nerve in his being.

And went to wake up Jen.

Come hell or high water, he was getting her usernames and passwords.

Even if it meant she never spoke to him again.

Chapter 8

Feeling strangely content, hardly believing what a great conversation she and Ben had just had—not the content, but the way they'd been able to share with each other without walls and defenses—Jenny drifted off to sleep shortly after climbing into bed.

Only to be awakened what seemed like seconds later by a soft knock on her bedroom door, followed by, "Jen?"

Ben.

Shooting straight up from the pillows, hand going to the neckline of the T-shirt she'd put on with the flannel sleep shorts, she checked to see that Ella was there, threw her legs over the edge of the bed and opened the door.

Eyes wide, she quickly glanced at Ben, looked back at the sleeping baby and then met his gaze fully. He hadn't changed out of the beige pants and brown dress shirt with beige and brown tie—his self-imposed daily uniform since he'd made detective—he'd had on when he'd arrived at the safe house that night.

The colors changed. Beige and Brown. Grey and black. Always with the pants lighter colored than the shirt and a tie to match both.

Something she'd found endearing once upon a time. And homed in on when she saw the steely look in his eyes.

She wasn't going to like what was coming. He knew it. And intended to make it happen anyway.

"What?" she asked, the contentment with which she'd gone to sleep seeping out of the edges of her heart.

"I need all of your usernames and passwords." It clearly wasn't a request. Most clearly. And yet…his tone… Did it hold a hint of apology?

Or sorrow?

There was something there she didn't recognize…

"Why?" she asked, not sure she cared. The ask was simple enough. It would only take her a minute at the most to send the list she kept on her computer to his phone.

When he hesitated, her heart started to pound harder. She recognized the sensation. Felt the claustrophobic anger Ben's protectiveness had instilled in her during the last year that Simon had lived with them.

The year that Ben had insisted Simon get a full-time job over the summer rather than hang out and get into trouble, which had prompted their smart and charming child to develop skills at a body shop that allowed him to make enough money to take them to court to emancipate from them.

"I need to check your followers and commenters for anything that might raise a flag as to the infant's identity. See if there's anyone who seems to be watching your posts and look at ways they comment. Like, perhaps, a mother looking for someone with whom to leave her baby. And I need to make certain you haven't been hacked."

Lizzie Baldwin must be working on the case. The Jasper Gulley Police Department's tech whiz. The late-in-life baby sister of a woman Jen had graduated high school with. Marian, the sister, had long since married and moved away. But Lizzie had stuck around.

With a nod, she told Ben she'd send them right away,

and when he thanked her and backed up, she quickly shut the door.

He'd glanced down. Had seen her bare legs.

He'd always had a thing for her legs.

She'd noticed his quick intake of breath.

And they couldn't have any of that going on. At all. Period. Not even in thought.

Knowing that he'd be sending the file to his techie, Jenny emailed her list to Ben's email and then texted him to let him know she'd done so.

Then turned off the light and got back into bed.

Forcing herself not to think about the burst of heat in her husband's eyes. *Ex*-husband.

Sex had never been a problem for them. To the contrary, even after twenty years of marriage, and living within angry silences much of the time, she and Ben had always been able to find each other in bed. And to love each other while doing so.

But they weren't married anymore.

Which could make sex a problem.

If they let it. She wasn't going to. He didn't know she'd seen his glance. Or the response to it. She'd forget it ever happened. And make sure there was no cause for it to happen again.

Problem solved.

Ben sent the list to Agent Michaels. The agent had jurisdiction with Sierra's Web where the kidnapping case was concerned, and the current theory—that someone was framing Jen as an illegal baby buyer—was his bailiwick. And then he sent them to Lizzie Baldwin, too, to see if, by chance, anything popped up as suspicious in followers, likes or conversations.

Someone who could have been looking at her as a possible safe haven for her baby.

Who then—or what—changed her mind?

Because if it was a father who'd found out, or parents or boyfriend or some other relative who wanted the child, they wouldn't have had to steal it. Ben put the nix on that theory. Just hadn't seen the point in the argument.

Anyone else with the rights to the child, even someone who was incarcerated and wouldn't be granted permanent custody, could still claim the infant. And pursue custody or visitation through family services and the courts.

Same went for a mother who might have changed her mind—though there'd be that little charge of abandonment to deal with, he allowed. And then pushed it aside. He wasn't there to judge a desperate woman's choice.

Only to identify the woman. Find her.

And locate whoever was threatening Jen and trying to steal the child, before the suspect got hold of either one of them.

Closing his laptop, Ben pulled the lever to bring up the footrest on his chair, pushed back until he was in a near reclining position, laid his head back and closed his eyes to a vision of Jen's long legs. As he'd seen them that night. And in visions of them wrapped around him, too.

If that's what it took to get himself out of the darkness long enough to get some rest, he was all for it.

Cold shower in the morning—or a dozen of them—be damned...

He awoke with a start. What was that?

Pushing the footrest of the chair down as he reached for his phone, Ben stood, his eyes taking in the peaceful empty space around him as he woke up, fully conscious, and, on his way to Jen's bedroom, glanced at his screen.

Drake was calling.

It was three minutes past four in the morning.

"Someone's watching your place," his second-in-command said with lots of urgency and no preamble. "Patrol has seen the same black sedan three times tonight. Didn't think about it at first. The third time, ten minutes ago, they called it in. They didn't get the plate. The car sped up and turned as soon as they turned onto your street. I had the officers check your security lights and cameras. Both were disabled by what looks like Bee Bee gun shots. We're running make and model of the car, as best as the officer could describe it. Two door. Newer. No sunroof. Emblem in the middle of the trunk, not off to either side."

The list of features narrowed down manufacturers some. Not enough.

"Blaine noticed the emblem the second time he saw it," Drake continued, naming one of their newer patrol officers. A recruit from the academy in Phoenix. "Said it was too dark to see a plate. Likely it was missing or covered with mud." Not all that unusual in the Northern Arizona mountain town. It had rained hard twice in the past week.

In the living room upstairs, Ben had his phone on speaker long enough to check his home camera app. And saw nothing. Looked at the app's timestamp for most recent transmission. "The cameras have been out since seven eighteen last night," he reported.

"I've got four guys on the ground," Drake said. "I'll let you know what they report back."

His guess was there wouldn't be much *to* report. Not to him. The news was already out. Whoever was looking for him now knew he hadn't gone home.

They could have just checked the parking lot at the station to find out that he'd spent the night at the office. A not uncommon occurrence for him.

Or for his car. It had been left at the station every single night he'd taken night duty on the Livingston case.

Unless the perpetrator wasn't from Jasper Gulley. Didn't know his habits as well as he'd seemed to know Jen's.

Or knew him well enough to have figured out that his car at the station could have been left there on purpose. To make it look as though he'd been there as a cover that let him slip away undetected.

Any potential explanation that sprang to mind was possible. Which meant, for safety's sake, he had to go with the most threatening. To be prepared for worst-case scenario.

He had to assume that whoever was angry with Jen, and had told him to leave the case alone, could be prepared to take him out to make certain that he did as commanded.

Telling Drake that he was going to be staying in the safe house full-time—to go into the emergency mode that was set up during the Livingston case—and that he'd still be heading up the case from there, he hung up.

And paced, his mind whirring through facts, ways they fit together, things he was missing, while he waited to hear back from someone.

Michaels. Drake. Or anyone else who had his number.

With waking up every two to three hours to feed the baby—and the fact that she had an officer babysitter in the house— Jenny stayed in bed until after nine Thursday morning. Dozing, and then working on her laptop.

In addition to her normal financial, promotional, safety and educational duties, she had a serious problem in her three-year-old class that wasn't going to wait for law enforcement to figure out how she could safely take Ella home. All but one questionnaire had been returned. The family that hadn't responded was the one least known to Jenny. A mother who was always harried. Several children. Lived outside town, kept to themselves. The father was gone a lot. A road worker. Or truck driver. She wasn't sure which. Had heard both. The three-year-old, Oliver, was at the preschool on a scholarship awarded by random drawing.

And the teacher was Katy, a single woman living in town since her college graduation. She had recently taken in her high school freshman sister from her mom and stepfather in Tucson. The girl had been in trouble. They figured getting her into a small-town setting would help. Jenny wasn't sure if it had or not. But the upheaval appeared to be affecting Katy's attention in the classroom. All reports pointed to lack of structured learning, of organization. Several mentioned Oliver's failure to follow direction with no apparent consequences.

Jenny didn't like to pry into people's personal lives, preferring to leave her door open and to listen with care and compassion when others came to her. Until a situation got out of hand, as it had in the three-year-old class.

She had to meet with Katy. Sooner rather than later. She wanted to do so in person but couldn't wait another day. Scheduling an online meeting with the woman during Katy's lunch break, Jenny had just set her phone down and reached for the formula, gallon jug of spring water and bottle—planning to warm the formula in the plugged-in portable warmer on the nightstand—when her phone buzzed a text.

Katy. She was sure. She ignored it while she measured and poured. Shook. Put the bottle in the warmer. Then she picked up her phone.

Jenny had grown fond of Katy. Extremely fond.

But she couldn't back down. Or let compassion blind her to the plight of a classroom of children at one of the most critical developmental ages.

So, resigned, she picked up the phone. Tapped her message icon.

And stared.

Get your man under control. Her life depends on it. The words were followed by a praying hands emoji.

Full sentences. An emoji emitting emotion. Begging.

Jenny thought the sender must be female.

She'd taken a class on texting as part of her preparation for foster parenting. Had wanted to be fully on top of every situation so she wouldn't fail whoever came into her home. One of many classes she'd attended and podcasts she'd watched. She'd failed at motherhood once. Wasn't going to do so again.

The class had been to help her learn teens' texting habits. There were emojis included in the lessons. Who used them when and what they meant. Things like cucumbers and eggplants with sexual connotations. Warning signs that would help if you were raising someone who could be being groomed over social media...

None of which mattered right then.

Shaking, she was halfway to the door, seeking out whoever had relieved Ben that morning, when she stopped. Any cop outside her door was working for Ben.

And Ben would immediately have Jenny's phone checked, find out who texted and do everything he could to bring the person in.

He'd push, rather than heed the warning.

And maybe that's what they needed.

Her entire being cried out at the thought.

Because of Ella.

All the woman on the other end of that text wanted was for Ella to be safe and loved.

Pacing, sweating, turning off the bottle warmer since Ella was still sound asleep, Jenny tried to find reason. To figure out her best choice.

Ella's life hung in the balance. And what happened next all depended on Jenny.

She stared at her phone. Wishing she could see through the waves of technology to the sender's face. Not for identity discovery, but to see into the woman's eyes. To know her suffering. And her heart.

The sender obviously knew what danger was out there, trying to get at Jenny. And so knew how best to keep Ella safe from it. If Ben would just back off, even for a day, as the woman had asked, the guy probably would not have crashed the truck into the garage. Once his anger faded, he was going to fade away. At least to the point of reason. It's the only thing that made sense. The only reason the woman would be asking…

The leaver—Jenny felt certain that was who was texting, or at least the person who was behind Ella's abandonment—had tried Ben first. The morning before. He'd called in the FBI.

And the burner phone had been trashed.

Hands shaking, she glanced again at her phone. Had a sense that the woman was right there. At her fingertips.

What if she could help them all?

Help Ben find out who Ella was and why she'd been left—at least enough for him to quit worrying about a hidden cell of a now defunct kidnapping ring—and help the woman and Ella, too, by calming Ben down enough to let the case play out in child services. Those people were trained to deal with overwrought familial emotions.

Dealt with them every day. Mostly with good results.

As opposed to Ben's hunting, which was clearly only escalating already growing anger and panic.

With the message app open, staring up at her, Jenny felt pressure at her back. Urging her to act—right then before the woman was no longer free to respond. Or threw the phone away.

If she hadn't already.

As she turned to glance at the door, she felt a wrench on her sore shoulder. Reminding her of the very near kidnapping outside the clinic the morning before.

Because Ben had ignored his early morning warning to back off?

One last glance over at the sleeping baby and then at the message—sent from the newborn's mother?

I'm trying. Help me. Give me something. Anything. Are you okay? She typed. And hit Send before she could change her mind.

Ella's first little waking cry sounded before she had a chance to fret over a nonresponse. And start to worry about having sent the text at all. Wondering, too late, if she'd put her and Ella and their protective duty in danger by sending a text from her location.

She had location off, she reminded herself, as she settled against the pillows propped up on the headboard of the bed, with the baby in one arm, the bottle in the other hand and her phone on the bed beside her.

Eyes still closed, Ella's little lips hungrily latched on to the nipple Jenny offered her, and the breathing, sucking, swallowing rhythm that followed—a process already heartrendingly familiar after just a day and a half of feedings—calmed Jenny immediately.

She'd promised to do all she could to see that Ella was safe and loved.

She'd done so.

Was doing so.

And would do so, as new information and challenges presented themselves.

Smiling as the baby opened her eyes—a pale blue that might or might not change in coming weeks—Jenny made certain that Ella saw happiness shining back at her.

And heard her phone vibrate against the mattress.

She held the bottle in place with the hand of the arm holding the baby and reached down to touch the screen.

I'm fine. For now.

Jenny's heart lurched. Her throat tightened.

For now? she typed as quickly as she could with one hand. While gently rocking the baby she fed. Needing Ella to feel comfort, in spite of Jenny's growing by the second tension.

He's angry. He'll calm down.

Okay. But... When he calms down? Can everything be resolved? If it was a family issue...

She and Ben knew all about anger that sizzled, calmed and re-sizzled. But their anger had never even hinted at escalating to violence of any kind. Or anything else illegal.

He's got a lucrative business going and isn't going to blow it all. The response made sense to her. And pointed straight at family court for resolution.

And, of course, Ben would need to press charges for the attempted kidnapping the morning before, the damage to her garage. His car repairs. Hopefully, depending on the way it played out, the abandonment charges could be dropped.

How much time do you need? she typed, heart pounding so hard she feared that it would upset Ella.

The baby, still sucking with gusto, didn't seem to mind. Maybe the heartbeat reminded her of the womb?

Jenny thought again about her phone being pingable or something from a nearby tower. Not exact location but...

Forever. Just get him to drop it.

Forever! Forever? So, Ella really could be hers permanently?

Forever. Meaning, no culpability? No charges for everything the man had already done? Meaning, he'd be free to continue to thwart his anger at those who angered him? Including the woman on the other end of the text? No way.

But if she could buy the woman some time. Give the man time to calm down as the woman had asked...

Let me help you, she typed, just as quickly as she'd been doing.

Ella's mouth let go of the nipple. The baby was staring up at her. Jenny instantly smiled, put the baby on the bed and talked nonstop, in a soft cheery voice, as she changed Ella and then held her up to her chest, patting her back.

The morning before it had taken Jenny twenty minutes to get the baby back to sleep. As opposed to nighttime wakings when Ella had to be changed before feeding because the baby fell asleep while she was eating.

They were already establishing a routine. Jenny was learning the infant's schedule and needs. A beautiful, wonderful, very good thing.

In the midst of...

Glancing at her phone for the fifteenth or so time since she'd set it down, Jenny finally lay the sleeping baby down.

Half an hour had passed with no response.

She had to accept that she probably wasn't going to get one. At least not then. Could be that the other woman's privacy had been interrupted. By whatever means. She might text back later.

She might not.

Leaving Jenny with some excruciatingly difficult decisions to make.

Chapter 9

By ten o'clock Thursday morning, Ben was getting truly concerned about Jen. Not just bouncing around various things that could be going on behind that closed door, but starting to think she had a headache or something.

Had someone found a way into the nearly impossible to breach home? The thought drove him to her door.

Jen had always been up at dawn. Even during the summer when light hit Arizona before 5:00 a.m.

He'd heard water in pipes rushing toward her vicinity a few hours earlier. Had figured she'd been taking a shower in the bathroom attached to her room. And then nothing.

Not even a brief trip to the kitchen.

Rapping his knuckles lightly, not wanting to disturb the infant, he called, "Jen?"

The door flew open. Jen's face marred with fear, she stared up at him. "Ben? What's wrong? What happened?"

Frowning, he watched her. Had the tension gotten to her? Real danger instead of just his warnings of what could be...

"That's what I'm here to find out. You haven't been out of your room..."

But she was dressed in black denim capri pants and a white sleeveless blouse showing him more tanned skin and outlining beautiful breasts that he didn't need to see.

Clothes that had been picked up in Flagstaff for her, based on the list she'd written up.

Her hair was up in a haphazard bun. She had on makeup. And showed no signs of injury.

"What are you doing here?" she asked then, dropping her hand from the door handle as she wrapped both arms around her middle. "You were supposed to be relieved at six."

Exactly what he'd been waiting all morning to talk to her about. That and a few other things she wasn't going to like.

"We've changed protocols," he told her. But he was finding it more difficult to see her as a victim and himself as lead detective on the case, with her bed in full view behind her. And the pajamas he'd seen her wearing the night before on the pillow closest to the portable crib.

He couldn't see the infant through the bed's mattress. He assumed she was sleeping.

Jen would be all over everything if there was a problem with the baby. Which was why he was counting on her. Completely.

Jen was frowning up at him, still hugging her middle. A defensive position he recognized only too well.

Obviously, she'd figured out that he came bearing news that was going to shoot her defenses sky-high.

Best to just get it over with—something else he'd learned from the past—but not there. He didn't relish having a door shut in his face, and locked, before he'd delivered all his directives.

"Can you bring your computer and come out to the sitting room?" he asked, turning to head back down the hall before she could argue the point. She'd follow. Because she needed to know what he was up to.

He'd learned that about her, too.

And felt like a louse using the weakness against her.

"Ben?" Her voice called out to him. He didn't turn. He couldn't take her on in a bedroom.

But he stopped walking away. "What?" he asked, his back to her.

"Would you mind wheeling the playpen? You said I need my computer, too, and I also have a critical online meeting in less than an hour."

How the woman could make him feel like a screwup with just a few words, Ben would never know. Or why, after all the years of knowing her, he was suddenly feeling like he didn't know her at all, Ben couldn't say. He turned, though, and silently did what he'd just told himself he would not do.

He entered Jen's bedroom, with her in it.

And then, with his gaze only on the top bars of the crib, until he could see more of it and keep his gaze there, he quickly did as she'd asked, as he'd normally have done in any other circumstance and wheeled the portable crib out of the room for her.

Jenny had been counting on getting through the rest of the day before seeing Ben again. Her phone, in the back pocket of her pants, burned against her butt. Because of the sleeping screen hiding text messages that had been searing through her mind ever since she'd engaged in them.

Somehow, she had to get Ben to back down.

She couldn't tell him about the texts.

But on the off chance that telling might give him the clue to getting them out of danger sooner—rather than waiting for an angry man to calm down—she had to tell him.

What if not telling him solidified Ella's safe, loving future, but got her mother killed? Was that right? Could Jenny just sit back and trust the grown woman, letting her sacrifice her own life, albeit knowingly, without at least trying to save both mother and child?

If the texter even was Ella's biological parent. Could be an aunt.

A friend.

Or someone working with the kidnapping ring? Trying to trap her?

Mrs. Arnold had been involved in the original case. One of Ben's teachers. She could only imagine how that had all gone down. Finding major crime going on right underneath his nose.

It had all been long after their divorce.

When they'd been married, he'd gone so overboard warning her of all the dangers in their safe little town, she'd started to blow them off just to find any joy in life.

But he'd become a sought-after detective. Highly respected. Because he was one of the best at what he did.

He parked the crib. Came toward her with a cup of coffee as she took her seat on the couch from the day before.

She took the cup in both hands, lifted it to her mouth. More to hide a minute longer than because she needed any caffeine.

"I can't believe you made it until almost lunchtime without coffee," he said, taking a seat on the other end of the couch, rather than across the room as he had the night before.

Because he knew she was keeping secrets from him?

What the hell? He wasn't her husband anymore. She didn't owe him anything.

He *was* the lead detective on a case in which she was immediately involved. If she wanted him to help her, she had to tell him what she knew.

Was he spot-on in his assessment?

Unless…she trusted him to keep her safe, during the interim that the leaver had requested, but also knew him to act as though the worst was happening, when he had no proof that it was. Just in case. In the current situation, aggressive prevention measures could cause more danger, not lessen it.

Those measures could cost people their lives. But if she kept her secret and managed to talk him into lying low, then, hopefully, the case would solve itself.

The attempted kidnapper, the garage smasher, would disappear. Maybe the mother would, too. Maybe that was for the best.

It was the reason that safe harbor laws had been put into effect to begin with.

Trying to rein in her speeding thoughts, she took another sip of coffee before lowering the cup. "I have a small coffee maker in my room," she told him. "It was on my list. Along with coffee. And some breakfast bars, too. With the baby waking me up every few hours…" She let the rest of the sentence hang unsaid.

And seemed to regain her senses a bit, too. Thought about what he'd said when he'd suddenly shocked her by appearing at her door when she'd had him firmly ensconced in the day's work at the station. "You said there are changed protocols?"

Ben's brown-eyed gaze was serious and straight on as he turned to face her and nodded. She waited for more. Too conflicted about what she knew that he didn't. Needing to hear what he had to say, in case it influenced the choices she was making in any way. Making them clearer, she hoped.

"Someone has been watching my bungalow," he told her, adding that his own security measures had been disarmed as hers had been. "They're looking for me," he continued, "which means I can't come and go from the safe house without a high risk of exposing its location."

Her heart dropped. "So…you waited to tell me that, and then you're leaving?" Butterflies swarmed in her belly. A dozen swarms of nervous ones. She might not agree with Ben's worst-case scenario outlook on life, but there was no one on earth with whom she'd feel safer right then. Sitting in the vortex of danger.

"No." His shake of head eased her tension some. He was coming back then? "I'm not leaving at all," he told her. Sending shards of sensation through her. Good. Bad. Relief. Dread.

That was her and Ben. Couldn't live with him. Felt emptier in a life without him.

"We had a plan set up in the event that the safe house was compromised during the Livingston trial. My car, the rental at the moment, will be driven in the dark by Billingsly, who is my size and shape, to my home, and then, after a brief stop, he'll come out with a suitcase and head out of town. He'll be followed, for safety procedures of course. He'll drive to the Phoenix airport and then, through a series of pass offs, will lose any trail, change clothes and by daylight be waking up in his own home. My rental will remain at the airport until further notice. The phone I'd been using is turned off. I always travel with a couple of burners. I'll check my phone once a day, just enough to see if anything has come through, but only keep it on a couple of seconds. Someone would have to be physically watching the line to know that it went on, but the signal is scrambled so they won't be able to tell from where."

Shivering, Jenny stared. All that effort. All those precautions. She'd known the Livingston case was huge. She had no idea the amount of risk involved for Ben. She stared at him, feeling tears at the back of her eyes. And toughened up.

Thinking of the implications of Ben's home being watched in light of the text messages she'd received. And sent.

The current situation—him staying out of sight—it played right into her hands, didn't it? Maybe she wouldn't even have to ask him to back off…it would all just happen… The perpetrators would never be found and things could calm down long enough for child services to make a determination in Ella's case.

Or Ben and the teams involved would find out whoever was behind the recent string of events.

It wouldn't be that simple, she knew. Even if the danger dissipated, attempts had to be made to find the leaver, since the child hadn't been handed off to a person. Maybe, once the angry jerk calmed down, that father, or whoever *he* was, would come forward calmly to claim Ella.

There'd be an investigation, with all eyes on him. His anger would come to light, even if she had to expose it herself. One way or another they'd get the guy. But didn't they have a better chance if he calmed down? The texter seemed certain he would.

Because experience had taught her as much?

It made more sense not to tell Ben right away. So why did she feel so knotted up about keeping things from him?

Residual feelings from their marriage vows? Promises that no longer existed?

Or were her instincts trying to get past years of defenses and let herself see that she and Ben and Ella were deeply into Ben's world, and she needed to trust him implicitly? On everything.

He didn't say anything about her social accounts. She didn't ask.

Maybe Lizzie hadn't had time to go through them all yet.

More likely, they'd found nothing. It had been one of Ben's just-in-case procedural calls.

"I'm assuming you've heard nothing regarding Ella's identity?" she asked when the need to tell him about the texts, the battle waging inside her, was tightening her throat.

His brief headshake was a relief. For Ella. For the mother. And for her silence, too.

"Surely, if there'd been a kidnapping, either for the ring or a domestic situation, that would have been reported, right?"

His shrug took a little bit of the wind out of her sails. "Michaels has people searching nationally, but with the truck having been stolen in Yuma, there could be recruits down there. She could have come from over the border."

Ella wasn't Hispanic. But white people lived in Mexico.

"It could also be a situation where a woman agreed to birth a child and give it up for sale and then changed her mind. There was a case involving a prominent lawyer that broke in Phoenix a few years ago. The guy hired women, usually without families close by, to get pregnant and have babies. He'd house them, see to their medical care, pay them and take the babies after they were born. If a member of the ring caught wind of that, that member could have decided to go in business for himself. Hiring women to have the babies and then paying them off upon delivery. We can't be certain of anything at this point. Except that Michaels is convinced that he's found more sales on the dark web. Which was what sparked his entire kidnapping ring investigation all those months ago."

Fear shot through Jenny. That last scenario…it could fit. A mother falling in love with her baby during pregnancy, not wanting to sell the child…wanting them to go to a home she trusted. She could have found Jenny on the internet. Or through someone in town.

Maybe the mother had given up the baby, taken the money and then had stolen her own baby back...

She was thinking like Ben.

And yet, she kind of understood how...if you were trying to figure out who'd done what, you'd have to put yourself in every imaginable situation...

Bottom line—she had to go with what she believed. To trust her own mind. She believed that someone had chosen her specifically to keep Ella safe. And that the leaver desperately needed Ben to back off.

She knew that she didn't have any way to judge the real circumstance because she had no idea what it was.

And she was certain that the person who knew the situation was begging for Ben to let things go. That someone had cared about Ella enough to potentially risk her life, and definitely her freedom, by leaving Ella with Jenny.

The leaver and Jenny wanted the same thing. For Ella to be loved and safe.

She also knew, as her phone buzzed against her butt, that she had an important meeting in ten minutes and had to get set up and ready for it.

Maybe the diversion would give her the brief space she needed to see clearly where Ella and the texts were concerned.

Standing, she asked Ben if he minded if she used the kitchen table. He'd spread out on one end. She could work on the other. She needed all performance sheets and questionnaires at hand in case Katy got defensive.

And maybe, a small part of her wanted her ex-husband to see *her* at work. To find out, firsthand, that Jenny didn't walk through life with her head in the clouds, as he'd accused her on more than one occasion. That, just because she chose to see the best in everyone until proven differently, she still recognized and dealt with problems when they arose.

Besides, if Ella awoke, she'd need someone to feed her. The little one had lungs that didn't quit when she was hungry. As Jenny had discovered during the first eight hours of her and Ella's association.

Telling Ben how to prepare the formula, just in case, she saw him frown but nod. And she opened her computer to start her difficult call.

Glad that he was there.

Stay asleep. Ben's one glance in the direction of the mesh siding through which the infant could be seen was as commanding as he could make it. And it would do no good, he knew that.

A detective, no matter how good he might be at his job, had zero ability to control the natural sleeping schedule of newborns.

So he turned to something he could control. The various reports flowing in.

While he'd chosen to stay in one place for the time being, the second they had a name and a possible location for the guy targeting Jen and probably him, he'd be out of there. On a hunt of his own. With an army of people watching over Jen and the infant. He had to be where he was most effective at all times.

Lizzie had found little on Jen's socials. Some people read her posts but didn't comment. She was following up on every one of them, but had already checked their profiles. They were all legitimate and the practice of liking but not commenting, or reading and not reacting, was common and not ringing any alarm bells.

Michaels hadn't heard back from the Sierra's Web team yet on that score. Their dive was going a lot deeper—far beyond accounts and into data that couldn't be seen unless you knew where and how to look.

Ben's own team had been following up with individual obstetrician offices—starting with Northern Arizona, then Yuma, and then every place in between, checking to see if any of them had treated any patients who didn't stay with them through birth. Or any who'd been due to give birth at the clinic but hadn't followed through.

So far, nothing on that end, either.

Blood drawn from the baby had brought no identification hits. Matching DNA wasn't in the system.

The one lead they had was an alternator on the stolen truck. It had been installed after the theft, and Michaels was tracing its origin. He'd traced the serial number to a supplier that serviced both Yuma and Tucson.

Ben's mood had lifted some as soon as he'd received that news. A truck part could solve the whole case before the day was through. He already had transportation and protection lined up in the event he needed to make a quick exit.

"He needs further testing, but the father won't hear of it and the mother does as he says. She's overwhelmed out there with no money and so many kids…"

Katy, one of Jen's preschool teachers, was talking about a troublemaker in class. Three years old and already labeled…

But as the teacher outlined behaviors, Ben's attention perked up. Not because of the case, but the kid… Three years old and the level of understanding and observations that came out of his mouth.

"I once had a professor tell me that the prisons are filled with geniuses," he heard Jen say softly. "Because it's more of a challenge to be bad than to be good. To lead, rather than follow the rules. And we also know, acting out is sometimes the only way littles know how to get attention in a situation they can't resolve themselves."

Ben listened to his wife—his ex-wife—speak and felt pride. He told himself to move on. Her business meeting had nothing to do with the case. Or him.

As he thought about getting up to leave the room, he remembered the crib. And sat down in the armchair he'd ended up sleeping in the night before. On and off. He could see the top of the crib from there, but not the contents. And he could hear if the infant stirred. A big *if* he hoped didn't happen.

He heard Jen mention a plan, in spite of his efforts to tune out her conversation. Some details were discussed to challenge the three-year-old troublemaker. And to better distract him in the classroom so that he didn't create distractions. Jen was going to find money for testing for the toddler and talk to the mother about the process, as they couldn't move forward without parental consent.

"So tell me about things at home." Jen's change of tone caught him. Instead of being on an even playing field, two professionals working through a situation to find the best solution, she suddenly sounded like a boss. A concerned one.

"They're much better," said Katy. "I know I haven't been at the top of my game the past six months, but I swear, I've got things under control." The woman sounded like she was begging to keep her job.

And it hit him, the meeting, scheduled when Jen was in a safe house… She'd been considering having to let the teacher go. Yet…her approach of building the other woman's confidence and giving her the benefit of the doubt enough to let her show herself…

Jen had believed in Katy enough to give her a second chance when clearly, there'd been more than just one troublesome student going on.

He listened to the other woman speak about the fourteen-year-old sister, Molly, who'd come to live with her, about her mother and stepfather being at their wit's end. The girl had fallen into a wrong crowd, believed herself to be in love with a seventeen-year-old who'd been in some trouble and was acting like she was his property.

"She's doing so much better now," Katy said. "She hasn't talked about Dale at all lately. In the past week or so, it's like she's a new person. She's hanging with me constantly, wants to cook and watch movies. Is talking about going to college. Ever since she moved here she'd been wearing baggy sweats and grungy dark T-shirts that were two sizes too big for her, and suddenly, she's in leggings and shirts that look more like what girls her age are wearing…"

Ben put the footrest down so abruptly, he heard stirring from the side of the couch. Held his breath. And when no other sounds hit him, he stood up.

Striding over to get a look at Jen's computer screen, without being in view of the camera, he saw Katy's last name on the screen as one of the meeting attendees. Jen glanced at him. He raised a brow, pointed to the name, showed her his phone with Drake's text box showing, and when she nodded, sent a quick text to Drake to look into Katy Wickens's sister, Molly. To get back to him ASAP.

And chomped at the bit until Jen ended the meeting.

"Did you catch that?" he asked, pumped, ready to pursue… needing to get the case solved.

Jen closed her laptop. "What?" she asked, as she headed

straight over to peek in the crib and then take a seat on the couch next to it.

Crossing the room in front of her, Ben couldn't sit down. He wasn't a stationary guy. And being locked into rooms with Jen was proving far more challenging than he'd have ever thought it would be. Adding in an infant, who she was clearly allowing herself to think of as her own, added tension he wasn't handling all that well.

"That girl, Molly. Fourteen. Older, controlling boyfriend who's trouble. She was wearing baggy clothes, then not. As though she'd been hiding a weight gain, and then lost it. Is suddenly doing better, hanging with her sister…heading out into the future rather than moping alone in her room…"

Jen was frowning, her tone almost defensive as she said, "Of course I caught it. I care about Katy. I paid attention to every word. And am happy for her." Her brow cleared as her eyes opened wide.

And Ben, taking a seat on the edge of the couch next to her, nodded.

"You think Molly…"

Grabbing his phone, he pulled up the list of names Lizzie had texted him to show Jen. The one that contained people who didn't follow her, or react to her posts, but who read all of them.

"Molly Mitchell." Jen picked it out at once. Different fathers, different last names.

He was nodding.

And she took the new-to-her phone he was handing her.

Chapter 10

Jenny didn't call Katy first. Ben had given her the choice to handle reaching out to her employee, but she had to reach her assistant director, Heather, to make certain that Katy's class was covered, before alerting the teacher.

And because she had to wait for confirmation that someone would be with the class, Jenny was left to sit with the silence in the safe house. To sit with her own sense of shock. Ben had had her believing they could be dealing with some maniacal people, when, in truth, it looked like she was hidden away in a safe house over a seventeen-year-old boy?

Most people didn't have immediate safe house access, nor constant phone pinging.

Or any pinging at all.

Unless location was on.

And permission was given.

But Ben…he'd jumped in with both feet, using all the powerful tools at his disposable. Scaring her half to death…

Unable to resolve her Ben issues, she glanced at the baby. And was swamped with conflicting and overpowering emotions all over again.

Katy would take Ella—likely rename her.

And that was all good. As long as the baby was safe and loved.

They had to get the boy, first.

Molly had come from Tucson. That's where the controlling, bad-news kid was from.

And where Simon had moved when he'd been almost the same age. Right after he'd emancipated.

She'd never been to the city. But, that day she hated it.

Had Molly been the one she was texting with that morning? Adrenaline running through her, she jumped as her second in command texted that Katy was free, freeing Jenny from her own pit of hell.

But what Jenny had to say was clearly too much for Katy. Most particularly when Ella woke up and started to cry. And the pre-school teacher heard her in the background.

The woman agreed to speak to Ben.

Jenny tended to the baby and was feeding her a bottle of formula when she found Ben up in the living room, still on the phone.

With Katy or not, she wasn't sure.

"Molly *was* pregnant," he said the second he disconnected the call. "By the guy in Tucson, Rinaldi Germantown. Kid's had a couple of priors, has clear anger issues and is in the wind."

It was as though he thought if he threw things at her quickly enough, they'd bounce off her, rather than penetrate and knock her down. Jenny fell onto the closest armchair, perched there, mouth open, managing to keep the nipple in Ella's mouth.

"So that's it? It's over?" she asked, too shocked to feel much of anything, thoughts flying in every direction. Ella wasn't hers. The baby was going to be well loved by a child development specialist. Not that she'd been told Katy would keep her.

As soon as they caught the Germantown kid, Ella could go home.

Molly would be safe.

And she and Ben would go back to speaking only if they happened to run into each other in the grocery store. Which had been the last time they'd spoken, three months prior to her finding Ella outside her door at the church.

It took her a second to focus on Ben's shaking head. "Molly insists that she didn't leave a baby anywhere," he said. "Katy video called her with me on the line. She says she was pregnant, which was why she'd gained weight and had been wearing the sweats and big T-shirts, but she lost the child, in the bathroom at Katy's house, a couple of weeks ago. And that Rinaldi has moved on. He's got a new girlfriend. But when Drake tried to reach him, there was no answer. I just got off the phone with his parents. They said they haven't seen or heard from him in almost a week. Which, apparently, isn't all that unusual."

Her chest feeling weighted, Jenny sat while her entire system slowed down. And energy seemed to seep away. "You think Molly's lying. And Rinaldi is here."

Shaking his head, Ben said, "I don't know what I think right now. Except that I have leads to follow, and I have to see where they take me."

He sounded so... Ben. Practical. Looking at facts. As though nothing bothered him overly much.

She had, once upon a time. Bothered him. Raised emotions in him. In the bedroom, but in situations that had raised huge levels of frustration, too. Ben's form of anger. Quiet sense of losing control of a situation that boiled over into words, walls and his eventual checking out.

Where had all that passion gone?

"Katy is taking Molly to the clinic. We'll see what comes

from that. If she gave birth more than a week ago, we'll know. It'll take a bit longer for the DNA results to come back. Someone will drive Molly's sample to Flagstaff this afternoon."

He glanced away as he finished. And without thinking, Jenny said, "What aren't you telling me?"

When had she figured out that Ben wouldn't look at her when he didn't want any more questions from her? Had she always known?

Had she instinctively asked more, just to rile him, because they'd been at war? She was scared? Maybe she felt threatened when their love didn't seem to be enough...

"The stolen truck, there's a possible link to it and Tucson." He talked about an alternator. Likely from Tucson or Yuma.

Made more sense to her that Yuma was the source, since the truck had originally come from there. But Ben... He had to follow through on every possibility.

Something she actually respected the hell out of him for. She'd never had to worry about him jumping to the wrong conclusions.

And Jenny knew she had to tell him about the text conversation she'd had that morning. And the possibility that it could be easily traced to Molly.

He was no longer going to trust her.

She'd lose his respect...if she hadn't lost every speck of it already.

Neither of which could matter—except to her heart, privately, inside where love for Ben Sanders still burned.

A baby's life, and her and Ben's because of that child, were at stake.

Looking up at him, she tried to find words. Thought about starting with an apology. Immediately rejected that. Stick to the facts. Ben liked the facts.

Motivation. That was it. Tell him why she hadn't told him about the texts. Explain her thought process.

Past behavior. It had never worked. He hadn't cared about reasons or whys. He'd cared about results. Choices made to prevent risk. Or minimize danger. Period.

He was pacing. She stared.

Couldn't bear to bring his disappointed glare in her direction.

Pulled out her phone. Opened the message app with one hand, reached it out toward him and said, "You need to read this."

And then, taking the baby's bottle back with that same hand, rocking her as Ella emptied the last of the bottle and drifted back to sleep, Jenny waited for the next axe to fall.

Ben read. Sent dual texts to Drake and Michaels, forwarding the entire conversation and asking them to follow up on the restricted number's activity, most importantly for its location when it was communicating with Jen. He didn't sit. He paced. Waiting for the initial surge of disappointment, hurt, frustration to pass, for his head to clear. And then, hating to have to do it, he gave Jen her phone back. Or, rather, set it on the small table beside her chair, saying, "If you want me to stay on this case, you need to turn this phone off and keep it off."

He hated sounding like an ass. No other words came to him to get his point across.

"Not everyone has the capability of pinging phones, or tracking them without permission," she said. He heard the defensive note.

Figured she'd already pegged him for his response before he'd even delivered it.

She'd have to have known there was a possibility she

could have been traced and, deeming it slight, had kept her phone on.

Her choice.

As was his to walk away from the case.

Did she also know he could never do that? Turn his back on her in danger?

She knew he could leave.

He'd proven that.

"If you'd let me know when the texting was happening, even just texted me at the same time to clue me in, I could have had your phone traced during the connection and possibly determined a location. At the very least, I could have narrowed down the tower it was connecting to and have a location within a few miles radius."

It was more of an explanation than he'd have given in the past.

He hadn't been at his best back then. He'd since come to understand that there were times when explaining himself in more detail brought better results.

"Ben?"

On his way to the far wall for the umpteenth time, Ben swung around at Jen's soft call. She had her phone in her hand. Was holding it toward him.

Looking him straight in the eye.

He got her message loud and clear. Not only was she agreeing to keep the phone off, in order to keep him there, but she wasn't even asking him to trust her to do it. She was making certain he didn't leave because of her misstep.

"You can turn it on and off as you deem fit, to see if anything else comes in."

She was *listening* to him. *Trusting* him. As he took the phone, he wanted to swoop down and kiss her. Just to see if she'd kiss him back.

"Rinaldi Germantown," he blurted instead, almost desperately, it seemed to him. Getting himself back on track. "Drake and Michaels are working together, sending his photo across all law enforcement contacts, naming him as a person of interest in a kidnapping."

"How can you do that at this point, with no proof? He might be completely innocent."

"We can bring him in for questioning."

Was she really challenging him over the fate of a seventeen-year-old when a baby's life was at stake?

Ben knew better.

She seemed as off-kilter as he suddenly. Because of him?

Was she experiencing some of the same awareness of him as he was of her? The thought made him a little hard.

She'd said, many times, that she'd always love him. He'd figured it was her way of spreading kindness. Was it possible she really did still feel…things for him?

Surely he'd killed all that for her. Or they had together, with their continuous energy-depleting arguments. Their inability to merge views that were poles apart.

His love for her had managed to survive through it, but he was much less sensitive than she was. Didn't take everything to heart.

Only the stuff that mattered most.

And what mattered was getting his butt on his computer, signing in with the scrambled and secure identity that had been created for him during the Livingston case, and following leads.

Not lusting after his ex-wife.

Chapter 11

Jenny couldn't get the texts, or the woman who'd sent them, out of her mind. Over the next couple of hours, she imagined the distraught mother in situation after situation, having sacrificed herself for the safety of her child.

Ben wasn't backing down.

And Jenny couldn't just do *nothing*. Somehow, she had to reach out to the woman. To find a way to help her.

Without risking Ella's life or well-being in any way.

Which mostly left her climbing walls, sliding back down and climbing them again. She was getting nowhere.

She'd made them both chef salads for lunch. His with vegetables, eggs and meats sliced and arranged in separate patches around the bowl. Hers diced and all mixed in together.

A week's worth of groceries, at least, more with dried foods, had been in the kitchen when she'd arrived at the house.

Jenny didn't have any intention of lying low for that long.

Studying her own social media accounts, looking for anything that might stand out to her took a while. She turned to preschool files next. Going through every child's family history, parent-teacher meeting reports, her own notes…

If Molly was telling the truth and it turned out that Ella wasn't hers, where did that leave them?

"How often can we turn my phone on?" she asked Ben from her seat on the couch next to the crib. She'd shut her laptop but hadn't closed any files as he came back downstairs. He'd been at the table for much of the time since they'd retreated to their own workspaces but had stepped away briefly.

Presumably to take a phone call.

"I just did," he told her, pulling the cell out of his back pocket and handing it to her. "There's been no activity." Taking the phone, she set it on the couch. He'd told her what she needed to know. But it felt better, having it there beside her. Even turned off.

As though she'd unconsciously know if she was being contacted.

"The texts came from a burner phone. Impossible to tell where it was during submission."

When he sat down next to the phone, close enough on the couch that she could smell his aftershave, Jenny took a long slow breath. Inhaling the familiar scent. Finding a quick second of peace.

Until, on the edge of the couch, with his elbows on his thighs, he turned to look at her and said, "I just got off the phone with Molly's doctor. Katy gave her permission to speak openly with me. Molly *was* pregnant. Various hormone levels indicate that she was likely pregnant when she arrived in Jasper Gulley, but that she lost the baby at least two months ago. There was no indication that she gave birth to a baby more than a pound or two."

So the girl *had* been lying. Slightly. Her timeline was off.

"And Rinaldi?" she asked.

"He doesn't have a new girlfriend. He'd been in foster care. His mother got clean, and he moved home with her."

A bit of a potential happy ending was nice. Would have been even nicer if Molly had been clued in on that piece.

Didn't help whoever was out there in trouble because of Ella, either.

Or her and Ben and Ella.

It did help, though, seeing Ben's work firsthand. Experiencing it with him.

"The doctor told me something else," he said then, and based on his serious expression, his tone, she braced herself.

"She knows of a woman, down in Yuma, who has an ob-gyn practice, but who also offers prenatal and birthing services off the books, for free, to women who can't afford proper care."

"I'm guessing that's illegal?"

"There are some gray areas, but overall, yes. Medical professionals are required to keep records." His glance at her was firm. "I've sent the information to Michaels. This could be why two agencies and a private firm with security clearance can't find any record of a lost pregnancy or baby unaccounted for in Arizona and all adjoining states in the past month."

She hadn't realized they were searching that far back. And then it hit her...

"You think this doctor in Yuma could have delivered Ella..." Horror struck through her. Leaving her nerves shaking from the inside out. Ben could be right. Ella could have been stolen...could be a pawn in a despicable godawful game.

"I think it could be this doctor or someone like her. We know the white truck came from there. That child was either delivered by a doctor who isn't telling us the truth about a pregnancy that didn't follow through to birth, with no request for records to be sent. Or a woman gave birth at home, after having no prenatal care, managed to tend to the umbilical cord and the baby professionally, and then either had the baby taken from her, or willingly gave the child up. To you. Or to whoever was in the chain that gave it to you."

"She gave it up to me," Jenny said, remaining firm on that one. He had cop instincts. She had motherly ones. "That was her on the text message this morning. Or it was someone close to her that gave Ella to me at the mother's behest." It was possible the woman hadn't been able to travel. Most particularly if she gave birth without medical help.

Ben didn't argue. But he glanced away.

"Why text me, if not out of concern for Ella? Why risk getting caught?"

"To get me to back off."

Right. That was obvious. "Why care whether you do or not if not out of concern for the baby's safety?"

His glance at her then was almost an eye roll. "To protect the operation."

Her muscles tightened into knots. Ella might have been intended as a safe harbor baby, which would make her eligible for adoption very shortly, with Jenny's name first on the list and her credentials already established. With a father, or other male figure in her life, not happy about the choice.

Or the baby, who was officially abandoned since she wasn't handed off, could be part of something far bigger. And more menacing.

An arm of a child trafficking ring that, until a few months before, had been operating right there in their mountains.

Her mind was one track. Ella.

Ben's had to be on the case as a whole.

Different perspectives but working toward the same end. She hoped.

Seeing him differently than she had in the past.
Even if they still didn't see eye to eye.

Ben's phone buzzed against his hip. Without even a
glance at Jen—something that was starting to distract him
from the job he knew he had to do even if she didn't like
it—he climbed the stairs and walked to the far corner of
the living room to talk to his second-in-command.

"Jeb over at the funeral home just called for you, man."
Drake's low tone was foreboding.

"Who died?"

"He said he had to speak directly to you."

Feeling like he'd just swallowed a bowl of rocks, Ben
asked the other man to patch him through. And waited,
keeping a firm hold on his imagination, and reminding himself that he could be certain it wasn't Jen. He had no other
family. But there were plenty of people in town he'd known
all his life. And he'd agreed to be executor of a few estates.

"Benjamin?" Jeb's croaky tones gave him a jolt, coming
so loudly out of the silence. And calling him by his given
name. Something only a handful of people in town could
get away with. And usually didn't do.

"What's up, Jeb?" he asked, keeping his tone calm.
Knowing that was the way to start sending the sensation
to the rest of his body. Some tricks he'd learned so young,
they were ingrained. As much a part of him as his hands
and feet.

"Your mom's grave, son," the seventy-something man
said. "Someone did a number on the headstone. It's broke
clear in half. The flowerpot's broke, too, and all the flow-
ers broken and smooshed into the ground..."

Ben's heart thudded. In spite of his calm. His ability to
home in on facts.

His need to stay focused.

Asking Jeb not to touch anything, he ended that call and then asked, "Drake, you still there?" His phone showed him another caller. But with no contacts on the burner...

"Yeah."

"You heard?"

"I did, and I'm sorry. I'm on my way over right now. I'll get pictures and have Larry meet me there."

Larry Simpson. Their sole officer with forensics training.

"This guy's not letting up, man," Drake said then, sounds of a car starting in the background. "He knows enough about you to hit you where it counts."

"Tell me something I don't know." Ben wasn't buying into the drama. He was getting pissed.

"Something real bad going on that he wants you off the case this badly."

"Might be a reason to show myself to him," Ben said then, the idea building like an avalanche inside him. "We can't sit here forever, waiting to find him. And other than an alternator, which could have come from anywhere in Tucson or Yuma and all points in between, we're pushing forty-eight hours in and bubkes. He wants me. We're going to give him me. Time to end this thing."

"You know that's exactly what he's hoping for, right? Why else make it so personal? Unless to draw you out."

He got that. As well as the fact that the perp had the advantage. He knew Ben, was on a hunt for him, but Ben had no idea who he was.

"So we have to tread carefully," he said then, not even considering backing down. His mother's grave! "The plan has to be solid, well thought out, with multiple brains working it. Put the entire team on it," he said.

"And if you're outvoted four to one?"

"My vote wins." He was the boss.

"Got it."

Walking to the steps, leading down to the family room, getting a glimpse of Jen on the couch, feeding the baby—assuring himself all was well—Ben said, "I want it done today." Disconnecting when Drake said he'd hit him back.

Drake could hit him all he wanted. Ben was not going to let the perp escalate any further. There was no telling what, or who, he'd go after next. To make Ben pay.

The list was too long. Didn't bear thinking about.

Starting with Jen.

What if the baby was all a ruse somehow? Not that he had any instant answers for how that would work. But what if…?

Anyone wanting to get at Ben could figure out Jen was his weak spot with very little effort. And then a dive on her socials would easily show a way to get her complete involvement. In a way that would likely contradict Ben.

That thought crystalized as Ben stood behind the curtain in the living room, looking out onto a street he used to ride his bike along.

It wouldn't take much digging to know that Ben's divorce was the worst, most painful experience in his life. Just a casual question asked around town would likely give that up.

So could the whole thing be payback? Someone who was off-kilter enough to steal babies and sell them would not react normally to having his source cut off. Grace Arnold's secret son, a highly revered political lobbyist, the general had been taken down with the rest of the multiarmed, multistate kidnapping ring.

But what if there was someone else?

The best way to hurt Ben, to squeeze him before obliterating life right before his eyes, would be to pit him and Jen against each other. And then kill her. And, again, everyone knew their bone of contention had been Simon. Raising the recalcitrant kid. Grace might have even had Simon in class.

A child had torn apart his and Jen's fairy-tale marriage. And now they were brought together again, with their lives in the balance, because of a child she'd probably already fallen in love with.

A child she'd already put her name down to keep, if it worked out that she could…

Maybe he was seeing dangers that weren't there.

If the perpetrator had a legitimate claim to the infant, he could prove so and let the courts decide whether or not he got her back. After he paid for the crimes he'd committed in the past two days.

And if he didn't…

Ben would get him.

Period.

Jenny could hear Ben pacing. She'd changed Ella. Had finished feeding her, and then played with her for a bit since the baby was staring straight at her. She sang happy little toddler songs, moved the little one's hands and feet in time with the rhythm. Counted her toes, one by one. Raised her hands over her head and made eyes-wide-open funny faces.

By the time Ella's eyes started to blink with less briskness, she lifted the baby up to her chest and rocked her. Talking softly. Reciting a story she'd memorized years before. About a moon and going to sleep.

She held Ella for a few minutes after she was fully asleep. Taking solace from the soft, warm, trusting weight, and then, glancing in the direction of the living room, she pulled her computer back onto her lap. She needed to turn on her phone. To check for possible contact. Had promised herself she wouldn't do so without Ben present.

Because she wasn't a cop. Didn't think like a cop. And she was in the middle of a cop's case.

And because she didn't want to risk losing his trust again.

They'd argued enough in the past to divorce, but she'd always trusted him. And believed he'd always trusted her, too.

She'd never lied to him or gone behind his back. She just hadn't followed his protocols. Unless she'd given specific indication that she would.

Screen on, browser open, Jenny clicked on the first social icon on her taskbar. She had posts scheduled for every Thursday of the month. They'd publish from her account, through her computer at work.

Giving no indication to her current location.

But, maybe, if they were lucky, she'd get some kind of response?

In the midst of traumatic events, she'd forgotten all about them, until she'd been feeding Ella minutes before. And thinking about needing to turn on her phone.

Just because the woman had used an untraceable phone, didn't mean it wasn't still in her possession. She could be someone who couldn't afford a registered phone plan.

When waiting for Ben to return grew nerve-racking, she'd focused on ways the woman who'd texted her earlier in the day might try to reach out, other than text.

Had thought of social media. And remembered her posts.

She couldn't respond. Not overtly, anyway. But she could make up a name, grab a free email address from somewhere, open up a new account.

She had to do something. Jenny had never been a sit-around-and-let-others-get-the-job-done kind of person.

And the Wi-Fi at the safe house was scrambled all over. No one would be able to trace it back to her.

If that woman was out there, her life at risk, and Jenny could do something to help...

She'd looked at one site, had just seen that the post had published, when Ben came down the stairs. "You ready for a phone check?"

It was as though the man had radar that could tell the second Jenny started to feel the least bit uncomfortable about not leaving him with full control in the current situation.

"Yes," she told him, grabbing up the cell and turning it on.

If she was letting the past interfere with her thinking... letting her automatic defenses against Ben's sense of danger blind her to current situations...

Phone on, she touched to open the lock screen. "There's nothing," she reported, trying to keep her spirits from dropping down to her toes. She'd been so hoping...

"Give it a minute," Ben told her, walking to the table and glancing at his computer screen. "Might take a second to catch up..."

She waited.

"Okay, turn it off," Ben said then, looking up from the screen. Had he been timing them? A literal minute?

"Still nothing," she told him. Hugely disappointed, in spite of her admonitions to the contrary. She was about to turn her screen to him, to let him see another letdown—nothing that looked at all out of place on her socials, no responses that could be deemed anything other than what they were—when he came and sat on the couch. Closer to her than he'd been before.

It was like, each time he joined her, he moved in a little more.

She didn't hate the closeness.

Wished she could reach up and wipe the frown lines from his forehead. Find a way to make him smile.

It had been so long since she'd heard Ben's hearty laugh. The sound used to turn her on every time. Weird, maybe, but that reaction had been a sign to her that he was it for her.

And she still believed that.

Chapter 12

Needing to somehow reach the man she'd lost, Jenny watched as Ben scrolled on his phone for a second, then held it out to her. "My mom's grave site was vandalized."

One glance and she turned away. Passing the phone back to him, fighting tears. "What the hell...?" she started. Had to stop.

The day she'd stood with Ben, little Simon at her side, holding her hand, as they laid his mother to rest...was the first time she'd ever seen her lover cry.

And the last.

"I don't..." She shook her head.

"He's letting me know that he's not going to stop." Ben's tone held little emotion as he shoved the phone back into his pocket. If you didn't count the hard-core determination emanating from him. "I have to go after him, Jen. It's the only way to make this stop."

"No." One word. Said so harshly her throat hurt with the release.

"I can't just sit here while he's out there, trying to make me pay. Today was a grave site. What if it's Jeb next? Or Mrs. Hunter?" The woman who cleaned for him. "Or Preacher Tobias?"

The one who'd married them.

"Or a child?"

Horror froze her thoughts. Was he actually suggesting the perp would pick an innocent little one off the streets of Jasper Gulley just to squeeze Ben tighter?

Could she go along with that thought? Even for a minute?

"Please, Ben," she said softly. "Let's just give it a little time. At least until morning." Then, desperate to move on, ahead and away from his disastrous suggestion—and any minute chances that he could be right about potential consequences—she turned her computer toward him.

Explained about the forgotten prescheduled posts.

Wanted him to get engrossed in them—at least long enough to distract them from the emotional cliff they were about to go over. To study her accounts, instead. Do what he did, notice what he noticed, and clear them.

He glanced at them. And then straight at her. "I've got people watching those accounts twenty-four seven right now," he said. As though she'd known that his request for access had come with a full-time babysitter. "That's another thing I need to talk to you about."

If he was about to tell her that she had to erase her accounts…that she couldn't be on the internet anymore because of the dangers that lurked there…

In that moment, she might have complied. Even knowing it was overkill. She wanted to help him. To solve the current case, of course, but more.

She wanted him to smile again.

She used to be great at making the man smile.

Instead, at forty-two, he was already getting lines on his face where there shouldn't be any. Frown lines. Studied lines. He'd left her and seemed to have forgotten how to find any joy at all.

"I gave Agent Michaels permission to give your social

information to Sierra's Web. Their IT experts are the best anywhere, and if there was anyone using your information on the dark web, from which the kidnapping ring operated, we needed to know about it."

If he was about to try to convince her she was involved with the ring, even inadvertently...

"There's the possibility that whoever is behind the events of the past couple of days are out to get me—we're thinking someone leftover in this arm of the operation. Did you know that Grace Arnold had a son? She used her maiden name on the birth certificate. Grace Evart."

"Wait, Colin Evart, the lobbyist. That was Grace's son?" A piece of information that most definitely had been kept from the news reports.

He nodded. Held her gaze, his brown eyes serious and solemn. "For all we know there could have been another child—who is now an adult. And left behind."

Talk about webs getting tangled into unrecognizable shapes. Jenny wasn't even sure she recognized herself as she sat there, full-time caretaker of a newborn baby, alone in a safe house with her ex-husband and said infant, fearing for her life...

With interstate child trafficking on the table.

"Hudson Warner, Sierra's Web's tech partner, has had his team on your accounts all day. They found a woman with a username registered to a public IP address in Phoenix has been all over your accounts. And not just liking or commenting. Or visiting your pages. She's done some behind-the-scenes location searches and accessed your credit card information, too."

Jenny's hiss of breath burned her throat. Made her cough. And brought tears to her eyes.

Or at least gave her the excuse to let them fall.

* * *

He hadn't wanted to take away her joy. But if scaring Jen with hard truths kept her safe, then he'd zap her of happiness every time.

She'd smile again. As soon as the case was solved and the danger past. It was just who she was—a person able to find the good everywhere no matter the stench it might be buried in.

He loved that about her. Had been a happier person, even with the fights, with her in his life. Her enthusiasm and ability to find hope and joy in mundane places had been contagious.

Or at least had rubbed off on him when they'd shared the same home.

There was no light in the frightened eyes she turned to him. "My credit card information? I check the account every Monday. There haven't been any unknown charges…"

A wave of…goodness…swept through him. She still checked her accounts every week. Just like he'd insisted they do.

He almost smiled at her as he said, "You didn't respond to the phishing emails sent that would have given them your expiration date and security code, and you changed your password shortly after the hack had happened."

She nodded, still looking slightly sick to her stomach. "I never respond to that stuff, you know that. And I still change passwords at least once a month."

She said it as though he'd assume she'd continue with all the safety measures he'd insisted upon when they'd shared accounts. "I figured those measures were one of the first things you'd rid yourself of when you were free," he let slip, instead of keeping his mind firmly where it needed to be. On the plan he had to lay out for her.

His plan to leave her once again.

Her face scrunched, in a way endearingly familiar to him, as she said, "I complained about them too much, huh?" she asked. Then, completely serious, shook her head and met his gaze. "I was suffocating, Bennie. Some of the precautions, they made a lot of sense. But the others…somehow over the years, and the battles, they all got lumped together. I hated having to do any of them. But still always did, and do, the ones that made sense to me."

He swallowed. Hard. Warmth, need, welled up inside him. Heading to the point of no return. He saw it coming. Had to fight it.

The case.

"The woman in Phoenix—she's a fake. No person in any database with her name, address or photo. No birth certificate.

"Someone made up a fake profile. And used a public computer. So there's no way to trace who it was.

"Sierra's Web is still trying," he said softly. "There might be security camera footage at or around the computer's location. If they can find an image that shows up repeatedly, matching the times that the profile was used, they might be able to do facial recognition."

"Or she could be someone I know." Jen's gaze was straight on. Blank. Complete lack of…anything. He was speaking one professional to another.

He should be gratified. Thankful. She was finally taking him verbatim. Open to every word he said, every warning.

Sadness engulfed him. For the second it took him to tamp it down. Bury it in the grave his mind had made at six years of age.

He'd been doing it his whole life. He could do it again.

And again and again and again. As many times as it took

to help make the world a safer, happier place for all of those who believed and could see such things.

"I'm thinking this might be the person who texted you today, too," he said to that end.

Jen's sudden straightening, the widening of her eyes, the way her whole face seemed to light up shocked him. "This might be it, Ben!" she said, losing him. Because what he homed in on was the change back to what she'd been calling him since the fights had consumed more of their time together than the loving had. *Ben.* Not, *Bennie.*

"If they can identify her, then we can find her. Help her! Get the father, or whoever is threatening her—and us. This could all be over!"

Ben, and others, were pretty certain they were dealing with part of the mostly defunct child trafficking ring. Or a copycat. Most likely male. Texting in more of a female tone. Anyone could go out on the internet and read pages of studies done—academic and otherwise—about typical differences between male and female texters. And then emulate them.

Gearing up to tell her so—that no one on the case still believed they were just dealing with a domestic situation— hating to reinstate the unscalable walls between him and Jen during his last few hours there with her, Ben felt his phone vibrate against his butt. Pulled it out and, clicking to answer, immediately stood, heading upstairs.

Jen could follow him. Listen in. He knew she wouldn't.

And for a second there, he wished she would.

Bennie? Had she really said that?

What was happening to her? Surely she wasn't falling back into all of her old habits and ways. Not only having to watch for Ben's overprotectiveness, but her bone-deep love for him, too?

Except…she'd seen a look in his eyes, more than once, that day. Starting in her bedroom when he'd come to check on her…

Senses honed, warmth buzzing through her veins, Jenny entertained the idea that Ben was falling for her all over again, too. That the love she'd known as a teenager that they'd always shared was coming out of hiding. The first chance they'd given it to do so since the divorce.

His looks…the way he talked with her, rather than at her…

She wasn't just dreaming that stuff up.

And…he'd said he was going to leave. With a plan that sounded like putting himself on a hook as bait.

Talk about walking straight into danger. Not taking precautions…

She had to stop him.

The thought brought her up against a mental brick wall. She couldn't even get him to take a day's break to give the leaver a chance to solve her situation, since she seemed to think she could. How could she convince Ben to back down on his plan to get the guy and end the case?

Unless…she talked to him in his language, his world… pointing out all the dangers he'd be walking into.

Which meant she was going to have to think like him. Figure out dangers that would likely never surface. Give him such a plateful of them he'd see that he couldn't possibly protect himself against all of them. At least not without a lot of time and planning.

Which would give the leaver a chance to end things peacefully.

With the least damage, shorter jail time and no lives lost.

And in so doing, she could buy them another day or two together. Because…maybe…had this time been given to them for another reason? To give them a chance to find each other again?

Yeah, the guy who'd been attacking them was angry. She'd even go so far as to say he had anger issues and needed counseling. Didn't make him a killer. A child trafficker.

He was damaging property, clearly taunting Ben with that last hellacious outburst. But if he had time to calm down, to get past the initial searing pain of having his child taken from him, get himself back to the point where he could see and listen to reason…

Ella had only been asleep a little more than half an hour when Jenny heard Ben's footsteps on the stairs. They should think about having dinner.

More salad was fine with her. But Ben…he'd always been a big eater.

And then, afterward, when Ella was fed and sleeping again…maybe…could they possibly…

Wetness was pooling, unbelievably, as the love of her life entered the room. Fourteen or forty, didn't much matter. He did it to her.

Though, forty-two looked a whole lot manlier, sexier than fourteen had…

Until she raised her glance to Ben's completely straight face. The steely glint in his eyes. As soon as she met his gaze he said, "Another sale just hit on the dark web. Sierra's Web has compared technical signatures and has traced funding to the same money transfer protocol. We've either got an arm still out there, or we're dealing with a copycat."

He didn't sit. And didn't hold her gaze for long.

Throat suddenly dry, she watched him move from one

end of the long room to the other. Rubbing his thumb and forefinger of one hand together, as though he could whisk up some genie dust.

A nervous habit? Something newly acquired, that was for sure.

Jenny stared at that hand. Watching the movement. It was something she could let sink in as she tried to make sense of the rest.

Make sense of…not accept.

A child trafficking ring? In her quiet, plebian life? A stolen baby in her possession? Just did not compute. There'd been no sign. No hint, even.

And she could not deny what she'd just heard. An FBI agent, a firm of experts, Ben…all highly respected, capable, powerful human beings who took on the world's evil every single day of their lives—all felt certain the kidnapping ring was involved.

"I have to go, Jen." Ben's soft words, the intense tone, drew her gaze back to him. He'd stopped moving. Was standing only feet from her, his gaze boring into her. "This is our only real lead. This guy doesn't think like we do, or live in a world where decency rules. Or even exists. Grace could have another son we don't know about. Or someone else who was living off the ring, involved in the operation, was left behind." He started pacing again, talking more like a lecturer trying to instill the importance of something into his class. "There were prongs of the ring in multiple states, arrests made across the country. But Colin and Grace were from here. Stands to reason that there were more players here." He turned to face her again and then sat right next to her on the couch, looked her in the eye and said, "The takedown was here, Jen. I was the first officer on the scene to reach Scott Michaels after Chuck McKellips, Grace Arnold's underling, shot him. I applied a tourniquet, saved Michaels' life. And he went on to crack the case. If not for me, there'd have been a mess to clean up, but Colin, Grace, they'd have brushed off and moved on…"

He could have been bragging. Trying to get her to see how great he was, in some pre-divorce need to get her to see that his seemingly constant warnings were warranted.

But she didn't get that impression at all. His gaze implored her. As though his need for her to understand wasn't about him at all.

Or rather, about him being right.

He didn't need her to agree.

He was asking her to understand.

Throat tight, eyes moist, she nodded.

And then, knowing that he was leaving, that she might never see him again, she did what she had to do.

Sliding her arms up and around his neck, she pushed him over on the couch, planted her lips, open-mouthed and hungry, on his and climbed his body.

Chapter 13

Ben's mouth opened and he joined with Jen as though the world was ending. Only for a second. He had to stop before things got out of hand. Couldn't do anything that she stood to probably later regret.

But...oh, *God*...those soft lips. That tongue.

His arms slid around her, holding her steady so she didn't fall off the couch. And then, just held on. Tight. Pressing her to him so he could feel every inch of her again.

The pelvic bone that perfectly fit his groin. Those hips that were so slim and hid hard, toned muscles.

Ribs that his fingers could reach around to find the soft sides of her breasts.

One kiss was all he had. All he could allow. And for that kiss, he lost himself. Taking everything he could take. Giving her every ounce of everything good about him.

His fingertips found home at the softness of the sides of her breasts. Moving over them, getting all he could, he sucked on her tongue and soaked up the tender cushion that had always been Jen's welcome.

No matter what life brought, she'd been that for him. The tender cushion of hope and happiness upon which he could rest his weary head.

Or...find...a piece of ecstasy. Still kissing him, she was

moving her pelvis against him. His penis so hard he ached, he sank into the bliss of having her stroke it the way she'd learned to do.

Heard the familiar growl in her throat.

She wanted more. He did, too.

Jen led with her heart. It was his job to see that they didn't do anything that would come back at them later. Come between them.

He had to…

Jen's hand had left his neck, requiring him to prevent them from falling. Still keeping her lips active on his, allowing only enough break for air, she braced herself with an arm on his chest and unfastened her blouse with the other hand. She'd always craved his chest hair against her nipples.

He could give her that pleasure and still maintain control. It wasn't like she was going to be imprisoning his hardness with them.

Continuing to hold her steady with both arms, he teased her lips with his tongue in the way she liked, as she unfastened his shirt, too.

And then, as she lowered herself down, he braced himself. Prepared to withstand the oh-so-sweet torture.

"Please… Bennie…" The words were whispered in between licks and kisses on his lips. "Let go…" She nipped his lower lip and then sucked it up into her mouth. "Love me…" She licked that same lip. "You're the only one who knows how…"

With that, her hand grabbed his crotch, squeezed.

And his hips rose to her request.

Jenny wasn't going to stop. She knew Ben's sexual triggers and would hit every single one of them if that's what it took to help him let go.

On fire for the first time in the two years since their divorce, she was driven by the fire pushing at her crotch from the inside out, and from her heart, too.

His lips, his hands on the sides of her breasts, his hardness—they told her what she needed to know.

Letting go of thought, she let nature—and hunger—guide her. Keeping his body so busy, so enflamed, that his mind would have little chance to get a word in edgewise.

His body, the tender way his hands moved and the urgent ways of his tongue and lips—they all told her the truth that was guiding her. Over and over.

She had his pants undone, and her hand was moving on his penis before she attempted to get her own pants down. Was panting, shaking with need, sweating…and her hand kept slipping on the button at her waistband.

Emotional intensity at its peak, she almost cried out, but as the sound built in her throat, she felt Bennie's hand leave her back. Felt a bolt of fear, until, a second later, those capable, big, warm fingers were taking care of the situation. He pushed her pants over her butt, too, using a foot to get them down her legs and off.

Then, before she could do the same for him, he'd rolled her to the side, continued to kiss her as his hands devoured her breasts. Fingers brushing over the tips of her nipples again and again.

She writhed. Pressed her hips toward him, rode his hip hard. Kissed him hard. Shoved his pants over his hips. And with a quick jerk of her foot, got his pants down.

There might not be another chance.

Extreme passion, egged on by desperation, drove her.

He was leaving.

And she couldn't let him go without showing him the

exquisite joy that life held. To give him hope for a future filled with as much good as bad. With her or not.

To give him reason to make it back.

Ben ignited, flew out of the realm of reality when his penis entered Jen. He knew the place, recognized the glorious fit, the feel of her walls clenching against him, and couldn't get enough. Had to pull out just to be able to push in again. Farther. Climbing higher and higher with each thrust. And when he reached the top, spilling over as he glided around in euphoria, and then floated slowly in the nether land, he kept his lips pressed to hers.

Ready to hang on. To keep it alive. Go again.

And crashed to earth as he heard his phone vibrate.

He pulled out slowly, painfully, and then, holding his pants to his hips with one hand, reached for his phone with the other.

He hadn't used a condom. He had them, always, changed out regularly, right there in his wallet.

The phone call was brief, Drake letting him know all details had been finalized. The plan was a go. And it glued his feet firmly back on the hard ground of reality.

Rustling behind him, the sound of a zipper, told him that Jen was back on earth with him.

He needed a moment before facing her. Figured she might need one, too.

He headed to the bathroom, and then the room that held his go bag, and pulled out a clean pair of pants and underwear. He stepped into them. Buttoned his shirt, leaving it untucked.

He'd regret what had just happened. He was sure of it.

The loss of control had been weak. Instead of protecting her, he'd joined her in...

Shaking his head, Ben headed back toward the front room, expecting to see Jen's door closed and to find her and the baby's crib missing from their living area.

The baby would be waking soon. Jen would need dinner. He could fix it.

And use its delivery as an excuse to...

She was still out front. Dressed, crumpled, but there. In the kitchen, actually, with a pot of water on the stove and a box of spaghetti beside it. Ground beef was cooking in a pan on the burner behind it.

He had no idea why he preferred the Italian dish over any other. But every birthday, when she'd asked him what he wanted for dinner, he'd chosen spaghetti. In the early days, she'd made it for him. As time wore on, they'd drive as far as Phoenix to try out a new version at a different restaurant.

Sometimes she'd presented him with a package deal—dinner and a hotel room. With her to unwrap.

Taking a deep breath, holding his focus firmly on the moment, not the distant or most recent past, he leaned against the archway leading into the small cooking area. "That was Drake. The plan is a go. I leave just before dawn. An officer from Sage is picking me up out back where we were let off. Another one will be entering this house as I go out. Her name is Bessie. From there I'll be driven to Globe-Miami, to the mine, where, at shift change, I'll climb into another vehicle. I'll be taken to the Phoenix airport, to a private entrance at terminal three, and from there will walk out as any other passenger, get in my rental car and drive home."

He kept his tone as light as he could. Trying to meet her where she lived. To reach her. And to let her know that he wasn't rushing off on a suicide mission.

Protections were firmly in place. Overprotections, probably. But until they knew the scope of the mission, they had to think as high up as the powerful politician they'd taken down.

Possibly higher.

When Jen reached for the box of spaghetti without any indication she'd heard him, he took note from the straightness of her shoulders and continued, "I'll have unmarked agents in vehicles directly in front of and behind me," he told her. "Both flying in from Nevada—a favor to Michaels who worked in that office for years—and walking out with me to my car. They have cars parked near enough to mine to keep an eye on me at all times."

Her nod, though brief, told him what he needed to know.

She'd accepted what had to be.

Ben was sounding as though he was chatting about a golf outing he'd been invited to attend.

Maybe to him, all of life's activities ranked as one and the same. Not good or bad. Fun or Work. Just the next thing happening in a lifetime of happenings.

She couldn't help the thought. Didn't really believe it.

But didn't get him, either.

Shuddering, trying not to cry, Jenny broke apart pieces of the ground beef with a spatula. Lifting pieces of meat. Turning them. Hoping that the movement camouflaged her hand's shaking.

She nodded. It was the best she could give him. Didn't trust herself to speak.

"And, of course, I'll have my gun in my waistband, and another one strapped to my ankle." He kept talking, when what she needed was for him to go sit and be quiet until dinner was ready.

Maybe by then she'd have herself together enough to sit with him. If not, she'd take her dinner to her room.

He was acting as though a list of precautions would camouflage the fact that if he managed to draw out some killer, that man's chances of success were a whole lot better than Ben's would be.

If he thought he was making things any easier, offering some kind of reassurance, he was failing miserably.

With every word Ben spoke, Jenny's spirit died a little more.

Because she knew the probability was high that he would die during the execution of his bold and dangerous plan.

Just as she was fully aware that there was no way she was going to change his mind. It was already made up. Didn't matter what she said, he was going to go walking into a death trap.

The realization didn't change much. She couldn't get a word out in that moment if she tried. Breathing was presenting a challenge.

She broke spaghetti, dropped it into the pan of boiling water. Hanging on to the activity as though it was rocket science. Fully aware that if she didn't distract herself, she could end up a weak pile of flesh on the floor. Crying. Begging.

Being wrenched from life's supreme high to its deepest low in the space of minutes had sapped her of any strength she'd had left.

If it hadn't been for the baby sleeping in the corner, she'd be a weeping lump in the bed at the moment.

Crack! The loud sound made her jump. Jenny froze. *Crack.* It came again. From somewhere outside the house. Like…hail against the window. Except just one piece…

She flew around as it sounded a third time. Straight into

a head-on gaze with Ben, before he said, "Get in the corner with the baby. Stay there and stay down."

He'd no sooner said the words than he was rushing toward the stairs as she ran for the crib, and an even louder thud, followed by another sound closer by.

Above them.

Someone was breaking into the house!?

"Get the baby. Come now," Ben said softly. Menace in his words. Not directed at her but telling her that there was no time to hesitate. Grabbing up Ella as gently as she could at mock speed, she held the baby to her chest as she ran.

"Get into the tub and stay there," Ben said at the door of her room. "It's a tiled stall and there are no windows in there. Don't come out for any reason until I or another Jasper Gulley police officer tells you to. I mean it, Jen. No one. For any reason."

She was already climbing in. Holding Ella to her chest. "Take this." Ben scooted his ankle pistol across the tiled floor.

"Do not hesitate, even for a second, if you need to use it," he said softly, and then was gone.

No, *take care*. Or, *I love you.*

Be careful, she sent after him.

As she lay there, shivering, gently laying the still-sleeping baby on the floor, leaning over her like a shield, cuddling Ella up to her chest, she had one thought, repeating over and over.

Ben hadn't said he loved her.

But he also hadn't said goodbye.

Ben's phone had been vibrating before he'd had Jen stashed in her bathroom. He picked up as soon as he was in the hall, gun in hand, heading for the back room.

"You all okay in there?" Lindley, the officer in charge outside, asked, his voice clipped.

"Fine." Ben's tone was short. "Three shots. Two at the front windows, a third on the roof, back of the house," he bit out. "Did you see anything?"

"No, sir. Just heard the sounds. We've got everyone on duty already here, searching the area. And the captain's called others out of bed. We'll get this guy."

Ben wasn't so sure. Whoever was after them…the guy was good. Likely professional. A hired gun, or someone on the inside of the kidnapping ring with training. Two crooked cops had been killed during the takedown. Officer Andy Daniels, an associate of Chuck McKellips, and then a female officer who'd fallen in love with Colin Evart, only to be tricked into assisting when the locals screwed up.

There could be more dirty cops.

On his own police force?

Of most concern at the moment—the house had been compromised.

And Jen and the infant were in immediate danger. Maybe even from just outside the house. From one of his own.

Checking his room quickly, seeing the brand-new crack in the ceiling, he dialed Drake as he made his way quickly through the rest of the house.

"He knows where we are," he said grimly as soon as his second-in-command picked up. "We've got a mole."

"The captain's already on it," Drake assured him. "I'm on my way over."

He'd cleared the downstairs, moved up the four stairs to the living area. Couldn't see the glass through the curtains but knew the divots would be there.

"We've got to get them out of here. His next shot might

not be just a bullet." It could be some kind of explosive at the roof.

Upstairs was clear. Heading back down, Ben turned off the stove.

"He shot at the glass first," Drake's tone wasn't as urgent as Ben expected. "He didn't know it was bulletproof."

Right. Ben shook his head. He should have caught that right off. And hadn't.

Because the woman he'd just made love to, the only woman he'd ever loved, was in danger. He couldn't let himself lapse again. And just in case... "You're lead as of now," he told Drake. "No way I'm not working this, but..."

"I got your back, man. Right now, we need to figure out how to make you all disappear."

"Not me," Ben asserted, brooking no argument. "I'm still coming out. It's the surest way to make this guy show himself."

"And if he takes a sniper shot at you?"

Wiping a hand down his face, Ben stared at the wall on the other side of Jen's bathroom. The wall holding the couch he and Jen had just laid on such a short time ago. Minutes before the cracking sounds.

Those three short bursts had changed everything.

The perp had escalated beyond just a warning point.

Unless...

"He knows we're in here and didn't try to penetrate," he said slowly. "So what if he did know about the bulletproof glass? And is still just sending a warning?"

"You can't possibly want to wait this out..."

"Hell no, I'm not suggesting that. But right now, me being in hiding is clearly keeping him agitated. So I come out. Stay at the station. Let's show him I'm back to work. He wants me? Let's make him good and mad, draw him out..."

"And if one of our own is involved, a mole, he's more likely to be exposed, as well..." Drake's tone was thoughtful.

"It might not be the best move, but can you think of a better one?" Ben asked then, not taking his eyes off the wall in front of him. As though he could see through it.

And hold on to the frightened gaze he knew waited just beyond it.

"And Jenny and the baby?"

"They stay there, too. At least for the night. In protective custody. Tomorrow, we move them out of state."

Or upstate.

The thought occurred to him. The cabin they used to go to when Simon was a kid. Ben's father had first taken him there when he was little. Had taught him to fish. And to climb trees—a secret from four-year-old Ben's mother. Ben had taught Simon to fish.

Set on fifty acres in the Northern Arizona wilderness, the cabin was the perfect hiding place. He'd purchased it a couple of years before. Had been slowly renovating it.

And had cameras set up around the perimeter because... that's the kind of thing a cautious guy like him did.

No one knew about the cabin. Not even Drake.

It had been his hideaway after the divorce. A place where he was as free as he'd ever be.

A place to run away when the pain of missing Jen got too bad, though he'd never admit that to anyone but himself...

"We've got the transport van," Drake was saying. "It has bulletproof glass. I'm heading back for it now. Telling no one but the captain. I'll head straight your way after that. Let you know when I'm close."

Ben didn't want to think about one of his own brothers or sisters on the force stabbing him. But who else would have known about him and Jen at the safe house?

He was heading into her room, to fill her in on their immediate plans, when it hit him.

The Livingston case. Several Northern Arizona small-town forces had been called in to assist over the months-long case.

And one of them had been home to the officer gone rogue in the kidnapping ring. Chuck McKellips's friend. Andy Daniels.

Daniels was dead, but what if he hadn't been the only dirty cop in that town?

He put in an urgent call to Michaels. One ring, hang up. Call again.

"Yeah?" The man had clearly been asleep.

"We've been compromised. Andy Daniels. Possible second leak in his orbit."

"I'm on it," Michaels sounded fully awake. And clicked off without another word.

Ben called his captain next. Filled him in with a single curt sentence. He finished with, "If it's him, he'll want the newborn and need me and Jen to disappear."

And if he was right, and the kidnapping ring was connected, as they'd thought all along, they might not just be dealing with an escalating junior member of the group.

They could be facing off with someone as trained as Ben and his fellow officers were. Someone who knew how they'd think, and therefore would know how to manipulate their moves.

Someone who wasn't escalating, but who was biding his time.

Someone who wouldn't miss when he took his real shot.

And if he was a friend of Daniels's, they were dealing with a highly trained, credentialed individual who had a personal vendetta against Ben, too, since Ben had been the one who shot the rogue cop.

"Get yourself and Jenny and the baby safely to the station, Sanders," Captain Olivera said. "I'll take it from there."

With a nod, Ben shoved his phone into his back pocket. And went to force his ex-wife to trust him with her life. Hoping like hell that she didn't argue.

Chapter 14

Ben wasn't telling her all that he knew. With her bag on her shoulder and Ella clutched to her chest, she stood at the ready by the armored door that opened up to the ramp in the back of the house where she'd first entered the building. The van would be arriving momentarily to whisk them away.

She knew that much.

With the Jasper Gulley police force swarming the house, their cars' lights sending swirls of red all over the area, and spotlights and flashlights covering the yard and the neighborhood, their van would blend in. A part of the menagerie of officers, in vehicles and on foot, casing the entire area.

Or so Ben had told her.

He hadn't looked her in the eye as he'd barked out his instructions.

Hadn't met her gaze at all since he'd slid out of her just an hour before.

If there'd been a man after them—Ben wasn't saying but that much was pretty clear—he'd likely have hightailed out of the area or risked getting caught.

Certainly he wouldn't be standing around watching the police van arrive and leave.

"The spaghetti," she said, shivering as they awaited the

call from Drake Johnson. She glommed on the missed dinner. It was in her realm of reality.

"Stove's off. Clean-up crew will get it."

She nodded. Felt his heat directly behind her. Wanted to take the one little step back that would touch her body to his. But didn't. The walls had been erected between them again.

She hadn't put them there.

Ella was waking up. She'd prepared a bottle in the bathroom. Had it ready. Focused on the baby, things she could affect, things that were in her current world that felt good, as they stood there waiting.

And tried to pretend that she didn't desperately need Ben's touch in that moment. Just a hand on her shoulder, a knee against hers. Something that would give her more strength.

Something that told her their lovemaking had meant something to him. That it hadn't just been a desperate moment.

Or a fond farewell.

Ben's phone buzzed. She was practically close enough to feel the vibration against his hip.

She heard the rustle as he reached for the device. Very specifically did not turn around. She was walking into a dark unknown. With Ella. And didn't need any more drama crawling up her spine.

"Come with me." Ben's sudden words shot through her like sparks to her nerves. Scaring her, and surging her into movement, too. She hadn't even completely swung around before he grabbed her hand, pulling her with him.

"What's going on?" she had to ask. Wasn't ready to hear the answer.

Needed to know.

Didn't want to know.

"Drake just texted from an unknown number," he said swiftly, moving them through the house, past her bedroom, heading toward a closet at the end of the hall?

He was going to stash her there. In a closet. In the dark!

"What'd he say?" She *had* to know.

"DJ2, a code only he and I know. Set up during Livingston. Telling me it's him."

He'd opened the closet door, but instead of shoving her inside, he reached for something on the wall. A small cover over a digital panel. Like a home security system pad. Ella let out one short whine. And then another.

Jenny bobbed the baby. Rubbed her back. Kissed the top of her head. Started to pray as she watched Ben start to type into the keypad.

"Change of plans. He's picking us up here," he said as the back wall slid aside to show an odd-looking door. Flat. Steel.

Ben's hand grabbed hers again as he went through first. And then, giving her a slight but definite yank, he pushed her in front of him, along with the baby she held and the bags she wore on her shoulders, into a black sedan through the opened rear passenger door. She caught a glimpse of stucco on the outside of the steel door as it closed behind them while Ben, in the car beside her, used his body to shove her over even as she scrambled to make room for him. As the door closed behind him, he pushed her face down toward the seat.

His own resting against her hip.

As they shot forward, Ella started to cry.

The cries could get them killed. Ben tugged at the black satchel pressing against his rib cage. Reaching inside for the bottle he'd seen Jen slide there as he was pulling them from the bathroom. Fingers wrapped around the still-warm cylinder shape, he took it out and found the hungry mouth in a matter of seconds.

He continued to hold the bottle because Jen didn't. Her arms, sheltering the baby, were trapped by a car seat and baggage.

"I disconnected the radio on this thing," Drake said as the car took a second turn away from the safe house. Following the distance mentally, Ben tensed. They weren't heading back to the station. That second turn, too soon…

He catalogued the rise and fall of Jen's chest with every breath she took. He could feel them against his left shoulder. Took strength from their rhythm.

And from the slight tug against his hand with every swallow of milk the infant took.

Waiting for bullets. His next in command, his friend, could be shot at any second. The car could crash. He held tight to the gun resting at the edge of the seat, underneath his left thigh. Pointing at the floor.

Marked another turn on the mental route. A right one. No stop, first.

"Change of plans," Drake said then, his words more bites than cadence. "Captain's orders."

Ben had just spoken to the captain.

Every muscle in his body ready to spring, he paid attention with every sense, every thought.

Jen breathed. The baby suckled. Swallowed.

Life.

He'd give his to preserve theirs. The knowing was just there.

"In a few minutes, I'm going to be pulling over," Drake

continued, speaking as though doing so in between focusing on other things.

Watching to see if they were being followed, Ben translated.

Making certain they weren't heading into a trap.

"You're to disappear. Get yourself somewhere. Stay there."

He felt the heart pounding harder against him. Rhythms getting lost in long breaths. Shorter ones.

His gut one big knot of rock, he laid there half on top of Jen, prepared to take on whatever came at him.

She would not die on his watch.

He'd made himself the promise the first time he'd kissed her.

Had felt the impossibility of the task ever since. So many things were out of his control...

Illness, a reckless driver, her choices, flying bullets...

"There's ammo in the glove box. Two burners and a wad of cash in the console. Some supplies in the trunk..."

His brain catalogued every piece of information. Filed it.

"Do not contact us. Call Sierra's Web. Period."

And...he got it.

The department had been compromised. Any contact with them could get him and Jen killed.

But he had to know...

"What did he find?" The captain. Drake would know what he meant.

"A bug on the van I was about to use to pick you up."

And there he had it. He was being sold out by one of his own.

Lips tight, Ben took the hit without a blink. The guy who'd sold his soul would pay for having done so. Sooner or later.

At the moment, Ben had to stay focused. Moving enough

to free Jen's hand, he switched the bottle from his fingers to hers.

The car stopped. "Now," Drake said, opening the driver's door just enough to slide quickly out to the ground as Ben, growling at Jen to stay down, made like a snake getting over the seat. The door beside him shut before he was sitting upright.

And the second his foot met the gas, he pushed it to the floor.

Jenny hoped the precautions were overkill. She had to stay calm. Steady. Babies could sense tension and fear, and she had to do her best not to start Ella's life out exposed to the evils of the world. They existed.

She knew that.

Just chose not to dwell on them.

Even while she dealt with them. With the baby finished eating, she settled the two of them together lying across the back seat, Ella up against her chest, strapping them in as best she could. Herself at the waist. The baby with the strap by her chest but twisted around until she managed to keep herself out of that one. If there was an accident, the newborn could be crushed.

Might happen anyway, but she'd done her best with what she had.

And there were no bullets flying at them.

When she was sure Ella was back to sleep, she said firmly, she hoped, from her bed behind him, "I need to know what's going on."

She didn't flinch as she heard about a traitor in Jasper Gulley. Her first instinct—to find another explanation—was zapped when she connected Ben's words with the thing

Drake had said about a bug on the van. Someone they lived with every day was out to get them?

But her heart lifted a tad anyway. "This means this whole thing, Ella's being left, the attempted kidnapping, my garage, your mother's grave, the house tonight…they aren't connected to the kidnapping ring." She spoke to the back of his head, barely visible in the darkness.

Wouldn't let herself worry about where they might be going as the car lurched and turned. It had to be at least eight, maybe nine o'clock.

They hadn't had dinner.

And Ben seemed to be driving up into the mountains that surrounded Jasper Gulley on all sides. His only other option, outside of town, would have been to drive down.

Phoenix was down there. Surely the fifth-largest city in the United States would offer them protection and ample hiding places.

He hadn't responded.

"Ben." Her tone, serious and with none of her usual familiarity when she addressed him, couldn't be helped. "I need to know what's going on. I trust you to do all you can to keep us safe. I'm not going to argue with your choices…" She paused on a cringe as she heard the words come out. She wouldn't argue, but she might suggest heading down the hill, not up. Once she knew what he knew. And she couldn't get to that point without giving him a convincing reason to confide in her. "I can't help if I don't know what I'm up against." Complete and utter truth.

Like it or not—they were in the life-and-death situation together.

More…there was no one else she'd rather have with her in such a situation. No one. Ben's constant awareness of the dangers inherent in every move around him was their best chance of making it out of their current hell alive.

"Let me get where we're going." His answer came a full minute or two later. "I need my full focus right now," he added after another few seconds. "Then we'll talk."

She wanted to ask where they were going.

But as she considered what he'd just said, she understood how important his last statement had been. He was fighting demons in the dark on a winding mountain road that could be perilous in broad daylight.

He sure as hell didn't need her, or her opinions, distracting him.

She wanted to tell him she loved him. That if they didn't make it out alive, she was glad to be spending her last minutes with him.

She settled for a quiet, "Thank you."

And spent the next hour blinking as little as possible as she stared at the back of her ex-husband's big broad shoulders and steady head.

Thinking about his body inside her, loving her, as it had been just a couple of hours before.

She had his seed in her, a part of him.

And from that she drew strength.

Chapter 15

Glancing at the familiar ground around him, the forest of evergreen trees, the dirt path that led to a desert rock and dirt prairie over which he'd soon be crossing, Ben breathed his first deep breath since standing in the safe house kitchen with Jen and hearing shots sound.

His first thought had been that he'd made an error for which he'd never recover—having allowed himself to be distracted by Jen's touch to the point of someone managing to enter the safe house without him knowing.

Making love to Jen might very well turn out to be an error from which he'd never recover, but him having sex had had nothing to do with the house being compromised.

Nor it being shot at.

Armed officers, placed out of sight, guarding the house hadn't seen the shooter. There was no way, from inside the house, he could have.

Once he reached the few acres of mostly rock prairie that served as a driveway to the cabin, accounting for six camouflaged security cameras in place, he grabbed one of the new burner phones and used it to tap into the scrambled service he knew he'd be able to access. From there, he turned on the cameras.

"We're off-road," Jen said then, as though she'd been

waiting for a sign that she could disturb his concentration. Apparently, his use of the phone while driving had served as that sign.

"You can sit up," he told her, with a brief glance in the rearview mirror. Stupid as hell to even care about her reaction, but there it was.

Her mouth dropping open in the shadows behind him, the widened eyes were…nice.

"Are we at the cabin?" she asked him, her tone higher than normal. The lines on her face softening. With a glance down at the seat, she sat fully, scooting forward, her hands on the back of the console between him and the other front seat. "But…how?"

The note in her voice…akin to wonder. Gave him a surge similar to what he'd felt…other times with Jen. When the joy that had emanated from her had seemed to rub off on him.

"I bought it after the divorce," he said. And then wished he'd left off the last part.

"I can't believe it!" Her tone clearly held pleasure. The mention of the divorce was apparently not a factor. "We're at the cabin?" And then, with an obvious injection of tension, "Who else knows about this?"

His life, one where danger lurked around every corner and in plain sight, too, was clearly rubbing off on her.

He'd left her to stop that from happening.

"No one," he assured her. Taking what small amount of satisfaction he could from being able to do so.

"You bought it and no one knows?"

"I bought it, and fifty acres, from the estate of the guy who used to rent it out to us. Paid cash. The property is recorded in my name, but because I'm in law enforcement

I was able to keep the information hidden. It's not on the internet, or in usual databases."

The place was rustic. Ran off generators and a well. Ben's father, the adventurer, had met the owner, an older guy, at a white-water rapids fishing tournament, and had been invited up for cross-country snowshoeing. Ben had been two the first time his father had taken him on a summer trip to the cabin.

And when his mother had died, leaving Ben and Jen legal guardians of four-year-old, fatherless Simon, Ben had started renting the cabin for a week every summer. The three of them would hike and fish in the tributary that ran off from the Verde River, traversing rock face that made it impossible for boaters to pass through. Which meant it, along with a lot of the Verde River, had never attracted tourists, or become a recreation spot.

For several years, the cabin had been their haven. Their happy place, Jen had called it.

They'd have campfires and make s'mores. Ben taught Simon how to climb trees.

Until the five-year-old had fallen and broken an arm...

By the time Simon was eleven, cabin vacations had turned from vacation fun to battleground as Simon insisted on freedom to roam, and Ben had refused to let the boy go off on his own. Bears roamed freely in Northern Arizona. Jen had pointed out—several times, with growing frustration—that Simon knew what to do if he saw a bear. And that black bears, the only species in Arizona, were not known to be aggressive and rarely attacked humans.

Ben had felt completely sideswiped. Couldn't believe that Jen would risk an eleven-year-old boy keeping his cool enough to take safety measures if he came face-to-face with a bear on his own. Had been…hurt…that she'd taken sides against him.

They'd quit renting the cabin the next year.

"It's been…twelve years since I was here," Jen said from behind him as he slowed more, drawing close to the log and stone building.

He'd thought many times about telling her he'd bought the place. Had pictured her up there again.

And at the moment, he couldn't give a second to reminiscing. Still in the car, with the motor running, he put in a call to Hudson Warner, the Sierra's Web partner with whom he'd worked during the takedown of the kidnapping ring. After saving Michaels's life.

And later, too, when he'd hired the firm personally…

Warner picked up on the first ring. "You parked?" Almost ten on a Thursday night… The man worked all hours when he had a life-threatening case.

"Stopped. Checking in first." Ben's gaze continued to roam the shadows around him. The clearing, and the cameras farther out, would make it difficult but not impossible for an intruder to get to them.

He'd learned the hard way. Nothing was impossible. His divorce had proven that to him once and for all.

He could practically feel Jen's breath at his neck as he sat there, outside the front door. Adding a tension he didn't need.

"You sure you weren't followed?"

"No one in front, behind or above, last twenty-five miles. Two passers. Both trucks. One red, one black. Red was two women. Black a man and a woman."

"Noted," Warner said. In case something happened, he'd given their investigation a starting point.

"You were right," the tech expert continued. "Daniels

had a younger brother. Cody. Twenty-three. Been acting up, some bar fights, making threats on his socials since his brother was killed. Spent four years in the military. Been out a year. Says Daniels was innocent. He's MIA. We're pulling up financials now. And there's one more thing."

Ben listened as Warner gave him the last bit of haunting information. His insides becoming a block of ice. Couldn't respond, or even fully compute until he was fully frozen. Warner didn't wait for a response. Just kept right on talking, the professional he was. "You sure your location is secure? No one knows where you are and it's not anyplace anyone knows you'd go?"

"Absolutely." The choice had been clear.

He still didn't feel good about it.

Couldn't think of one place on earth where he'd know Jen was safe. Everything could be breached. That night's shooting was a case in point.

"Stay put and check in every hour."

No request for his location. Or a phone number.

He'd known there wouldn't be.

Couldn't take a chance on having it on anyone's radar.

He'd rest easier that way, too.

Even knowing that it meant there was no way anyone would be rushing in to save his ass if he screwed this one up.

Jen's life, and the baby's, were all on him. In his favor, no one had as much meat in the game as he did.

He just hoped to God she continued to work with him. Not against him.

One thing was for sure. When she found out how he'd known Warner's contact information, not having had a chance to look it up since Drake told him Sierra's Web was his only contact, she was going to wish she'd never made love with him again. Would hate being trapped up there with him.

She might have thought he'd changed since their divorce. But he hadn't.

Just the day before she'd begged him not to call Sierra's Web.

What she hadn't known was that he'd already done so. Months ago.

With a sleeping Ella in her arms, Jenny walked around inside the cabin, taking it all in, as Ben—who'd already given the place a thorough, professional, gun-in-hand check— brought things in from the car.

Her two duffels. The one he'd had along with the folded little crib.

Several canvas bags she was assuming had been in the trunk.

She didn't see the ammunition, cash or other phone, but she knew him well enough to know that at least some of the money and bullets were on his person.

She'd bet a month's pay that he'd also left some in the car. Just in case.

Though probably not in the glove box. First place a perp would look.

The thought brought her back to focus. What, she was starting to think like Ben?

Hadn't she always? At least in the beginning. Later, living in the battles…she'd maybe lost sight of his perspective a bit. In the desperate fight to save her own.

And her own view was to find pleasure in a place that didn't look like it had changed much at all. Some new flooring and paint. Different couch and chairs. Same big wooden table for eating. Probably some new mattresses. But the headboards were the same. Same toilet and shower stall. Different countertop.

She'd liked the old one better. The yellow Formica, while showing age, had brightened up the little room.

Memories swamped her. Ben surprising her with a visit in the small shower one night after Simon was in bed.

The time Simon had been so angry with Ben he'd put a dead gopher in the toilet and flushed…flooding the room and out to the hall.

She shook her head.

Walked out into the front room, rocking Ella lightly as she moved. Saw Ben setting up the portable crib and remembered him on the floor with Simon, playing with a new set of superhero figurines. Talking about their powers…

As soon as the crib was set, she laid the baby down and headed to the kitchen portion of the main room. Looked through bags on the table. Put things away.

Taking up the old routine.

The thought stopped her. They needed to eat. That's why she had to find out what provisions there were.

Except that…she didn't. Ben was reaching into a cupboard, pulling out cans of soup. "These will do for tonight," he said. Adding a box of crackers and a jar of peanut butter to the table.

As though he owned the place.

The thought brought her up short. They weren't in a vacation rental. Weren't even there together because they'd wanted to be.

But she'd wanted them to be.

"The place looks great," she told him as she got out a pan, found the can opener right where it used to be and started the old stove. "You've kept it pretty much just as it was."

"It's got all new plumbing and electric," he told her. "A

new, bigger pump in the well. And two much better generators, with an inground gas tank an acre away, in the rocks, so there's no worry about explosion."

All things he'd said he'd do if he owned the place—sitting right there at that table. Pretty much every time they'd been up.

Not that either one of them made mention of an actual memory up there. Just as they weren't talking about what they'd done on the couch at the safe house a few hours before.

When dinner was ready, she took her normal seat. He took his. And talked about flooring as they ate. But the second the few dishes were done and he asked her to have a seat, she knew her time of procrastination was done.

Frankly, she needed it done.

While she didn't go through life searching out dangers, she'd never been one to blind herself to them when they were in her path. She'd just chosen to assess, make appropriate decisions and move on toward the light.

There was always a chance something would go wrong. Just as there would always be things in life outside of her control.

Chance.

That had been her and Ben's downfall.

He couldn't stand to leave anything up to chance. And he'd been fighting a losing battle.

There'd been a wildfire a few years back that had killed several people. Because the wind had changed drastically in a two-minute span. Nothing anyone could have done. Life and death had been a matter of chance.

And yet…sitting there with Ben, with Ella sleeping contentedly, Jenny knew that if she'd been there with anyone else, she wouldn't have consumed two bowls of soup and a plate of peanut butter slathered crackers. She'd have forced down what she had to, to maintain strength.

The difference was she trusted Ben to have seen to all dangers he could and knew the rest was…up to chance. And that was the point where she found things to enjoy in the moment.

A healthy, sleeping newborn.

A good memory.

A peanut butter cracker.

But first, she had to know what they were up against. To arm herself with potential tasks she'd have to complete, to help Ben in case chance took a wrong turn on them.

And still, before sitting, she took a walk over to the crib. Looked in on the sleeping baby. Took comfort from the sweet, innocent slumber.

Life as it was meant to be.

Back at the table, she chose the chair across from her normal one. Ben, as usual, sat at the head. Because it had a full view of the door—and any potential danger that might try to enter.

The knowledge warmed her.

As had their lovemaking earlier that night. So much.

"We have a mole in our operation," he started. And, at first, Jenny thought he meant there was a critter under the cabin. A groundhog had dug his way under once and…

She stopped herself. Ben wasn't looking her in the eye. And his grim expression didn't speak of a recalcitrant little wild animal. Drake had said that there'd been a bug on the van. Also not a living creature.

She'd hoped the kidnapper had managed to sneak onto the station's parking lot…a fluke of luck that was far-fetched thinking. But still…

One of Ben's own turning on him was unthinkable. Even

he'd never mentioned such a possibility. Her heart hurt for him. Pushing at her to let him know he wasn't alone.

"Do you know who?" she asked, praying that he'd look at her. That she could tell him without the words they weren't speaking that he was a good man. A good cop. The best.

That she still loved him and always would.

"We have a lead." His tone didn't show any relief. "One of the men involved in the kidnapping ring. I shot him. He was a cop in Briar." The small town closest to the abandoned mine encampment out of which the operation had been running.

She didn't want to hear any more. Absorbed every word anyway. And then some. "But if he's been dead for months, he can't be your lead."

"He had a brother. Just got out of the military the year before Andy Daniels died. He'd have the training for the type of sniper shooting we saw tonight. And would have been privy to Daniels's friends and fellow officers. You know how the police wrap our arms around families of our fallen..."

Frowning, her heart dropping, she stared at him. He still wasn't meeting her gaze. Instead, his focus seemed to be on the front door of the windowless building. "Even families of dirty cops?" she asked, and then, without waiting for an answer—as Ben wouldn't be telling her about it if it wasn't already considered pertinent information by those on the case—she said aloud, "This brother, he's after you?"

Ben shrugged. "He's a lead. We've been looking for someone who might have known enough about the inside workings of the ring to continue, or to start a copycat business. If he had access to contacts, potential clients..."

His words dropped off. And Jenny couldn't look away from him.

Ella.

He was about to her tell her that the sweet baby girl had a loving and heartbroken mama whose milk would be fully in…needing to feed her.

But the kidnapping ring wouldn't have had anything to do with Livingston. And the safe house…

"Daniels worked the Livingston case with us," Ben said, as though reading her mind. Something out of place in that moment.

But not in the past.

She shook her head. It was too much.

Coincidence, right?

Except how did she explain the safe house being compromised?

And the texts to her? The woman?

Could she have played right into this… Daniels's hand?

Shaking, filling with horror at the possibility, Jenny couldn't just sit there without Ben meeting her gaze. There was no more room for running. For hiding. For walls.

She needed him right there with her. One hundred percent.

It was the only way for her to see a way out for them. Working together.

Grabbing his arm with one hand and his chin with the other, she turned his face to her. "Tell me what you aren't saying, Ben, please. I can't help if I don't know."

He turned to her then, and she almost wished he hadn't. The look in those brown eyes was lacking in warmth. There was no light. Just grim death.

They were going to die?

Had he died inside already?

"What's going on?" she asked, giving him every ounce of heart she had. Flowing over him with all she was worth. "Whatever it is, we can get through it," she said in an almost whisper. The kind that had carried her promises to him since high school.

"My first contact with Sierra's Web wasn't tonight," he said, maintaining eye contact. As though he'd heard that part of her silent request, at least.

More likely, he'd heard all of it. He just wasn't joining her on the Bennie and Jen bench.

She'd begged him not to call. But… "You listened to your instincts, Ben. I'd have expected nothing less. And as it turns out, you were right."

He shook his head, leaned forward, his gaze boring into hers. "I called them months ago, Jen. After I met Hudson Warner, working the kidnapping case with Michaels."

She nodded. Encouraging him to trust her to help him. So he hadn't told her every aspect of the case two days ago. It hadn't been as pertinent then as it was now.

"I hired them, personally," he said, still staring into her as though she was supposed to get a different translation than her brain was giving her.

Personally. *Personally?*

Sick to her stomach, scared to death, open-mouthed she stared at him. "Someone's been after you ever since. This Daniels guy. The brother. That's how you knew when this happened…" Her throat dried up on her and she swallowed. "Your life's been on the line for months and you didn't even call?"

As if that mattered.

But it did. It did matter. To her. So much. And…

"I hired them to keep track of Simon."

The world stopped spinning. For a brief second, Jenny was floating. Numb. And then her brain played Ben's last words again.

The one thing she'd asked him to do, the only thing she'd

wanted out of their divorce, was to stay away from Simon. The only way that boy, now grown into a man, was ever going to come back to them was if they did as he asked and left him alone. Simon had to be able to come back on his terms.

Jenny stood. Had to get away from the table. From Ben.

His deceit…didn't have anything to do with current danger. But it had everything to do with them.

She'd been ready to ask him to try again. Concocting a pretty story about them conquering evil together and living with Ella happily ever after.

She'd needed to believe in the good that could come from bad. To have faith that finding Ella on her doorstep hadn't only been part of a horrible event. She'd believed love was giving her and Ben a second chance. And the baby a first one.

And once again, chance was breaking her heart.

Chapter 16

Ben knew the second he lost her. The light left her eyes. The mirror into her heart replaced by tempered glass. A sight all too familiar to him during the last years of their marriage.

He'd known it was coming. And he understood why. He'd agreed, in a moment of weakness, to let Simon go. In one of the last conversations he and Jen had had during their marriage. He would have promised just about anything to see the peace come over her. In her face, but in a relaxation of her body, too. Instead of being ready to fight, she'd been his friend again.

He watched her stiff back as she stood, facing the baby crib he'd placed over by the end of the couch as she'd asked him to do. He told himself to let it go.

And then shook his head.

"I tried, Jen," he said softly, needing her to know, when all that mattered at the moment was keeping them alive.

But if his life was written differently, if he did all he could and it wasn't enough…he needed her to know. "I just love him so much. I kept thinking of the last promise I made to Mom, that I'd always watch over him. After a couple of months filled with mostly sleepless nights, worrying about him…" And her, but that wasn't pertinent to the moment. "… I just got up one day and drove to Tucson."

When she spun around, he expected darts of anger to come shooting at him from those so expressive eyes. And words of recrimination to be spit upon him. "You what?" She sank down to a chair at the opposite end of the table. "You said you contacted Sierra's Web a few months ago…"

He nodded. And gave up fighting her. And himself. He was who he was. And who he'd always be. A man who couldn't rest if he wasn't watching out for others. Most particularly, his family.

"When he left—which was before we ever spoke about divorce—I did what I had to and found out that he was living with his biological father in Tucson."

He felt Jenny's hissed intake of breath all the way down the table. "He was emancipated, legally allowed to go, but he was still just a sixteen-year-old kid, Jen. You know what happens to most kids on the street?"

"He had skills, a job in Phoenix. A way to support himself. Which is why the judge allowed the emancipation," she said, as though, all those years later, it could make a difference.

"He was sixteen," he reiterated. Because he'd been sixteen once, too, and knew how hormones had driven so many of his choices. And knew, too, that Simon had been a bit naive in the ways of the world. Like Jen, he saw the good in everything first.

Jen frowned. "And he didn't show up at the job in Phoenix?" She couldn't seem to grasp the fact.

"He did," he told her, though not sure why it mattered. "But a couple of weeks later, he moved to Tucson."

"He texted me," she told him then, glancing up enough that their eyes met briefly. "From Phoenix. Told me he was sorry, but that he had to go. Just wanted me to know he was at his job, he liked it, had the rented room he'd already arranged and was doing fine…"

For a second, Ben was angry at Jen. Truly, bone-deep mad. If he'd known that…

What? He might not have worried so much those first weeks, but he'd have still kept tabs.

And he'd given his wife no openings to tell him anything. He'd been locked away in his own hell, unable to share it with her.

"Please tell me that Bruce didn't…" Jen's plea dropped off midsentence.

But Ben knew where she'd been going. Bruce Connors had lost all rights to his son—after Ben's testimony in court his junior year in college—for hitting Ben's mother. He and Jen had walked in one weekend to surprise the family, to find his mother bleeding and in tears. And Simon gone.

Bruce had taken him. To punish Ben's mom.

And an hour later, when he returned, Ben had the Jasper Gulley Police Department waiting for him.

"Not that I know of," Ben said half a minute after she'd quit talking. "But Simon was big enough to take him on by then." He gave her the rest. "Bruce did well for himself. He had a successful garage, a dozen employees, and since Simon had trained as a mechanic…"

"He found Bruce before he ever left home," Jen said then, staring at Ben. "He'd planned the whole thing."

"That's my take, but I've never been able to verify it." They were spending critical time in the past, when they should be preparing for all eventualities in the event their current hiding place was compromised. But he was building up to that. "I did find that while Bruce ran a good business, a couple of the guys working for him were shady. In and out of jail for small stuff. Hanging with guys who'd done prison time. So that day I drove to Tucson, it was to try to talk Simon into coming home. The result was an unofficial restraining order against me. If I went near him again, he'd file for a formal one."

"Which would effectively end your career."

He nodded.

"That's why you hired Sierra's Web..."

He'd like it to be that nice and clean. "I hired them because I'd found evidence that Simon had gambling problems. They'd started out small, in the back of his dad's shop after hours." He wasn't looking at Jen anymore. Couldn't bear to take in any more of the heartbreak he was inadvertently causing her.

"He ended up in Vegas, doing pretty well at cards a couple of years ago. For a while. Last fall, he got himself into trouble with a big-time bookie. Bruce bailed him out, took him back at the shop. Then, several months ago, I heard that he was back in Vegas. And that's when I hired Sierra's Web."

He sent her a brief glance. Couldn't make out the look in her eyes. Noted the tension around her lips. The slump of her shoulders. "I had the thought that if I knew he was in trouble and had details, if he was arrested, I could go bail him out. Get him all the help I could..."

And that's what lay on the table between them, still. He looked at her. She looked back.

And he knew she knew.

Jenny had thought she knew everything there was to know about breathing through a shattered heart.

She hadn't.

Sitting at that table, she was cold. And then hot. Outside

herself. And far too deeply in. Pain was everywhere. In every thought. Everywhere she looked. Ben. Simon.

She wanted out of the cabin.

Away.

And knew that she had to sit right there and take whatever was coming. She'd made as many life choices as Ben had. Far more than Simon.

They'd led her to that moment.

"If you're about to tell me that Simon is somehow connected to this kidnapping thing..." Jenny tried for a tough tone. Though she sounded more like she was begging, on the verge of tears. She made herself look straight at Ben, though. And keep looking.

Whatever had gone wrong between them, and in their family, was on both of them.

"What we know for sure is that Cody Daniels was on Simon's baseball team in junior high. And that the two had contact when Simon lived in Vegas."

"Vegas is where this whole kidnapping thing started, right?" She kept looking at him. As though she was holding on. Couldn't let go.

"Colin Evart, the mastermind behind the kidnapping ring, the general, grew up there. His wife and kids still have a home there."

"And we both know that Simon had a lot of anger directed at you." She saw him flinch. Hated that she'd been so harsh with him. Hadn't meant to hurt him. But pushed on because she had to. "And since you're the cop who shot Cody's brother..."

The way he sat there, watching her, letting her piece it all together, was new. Empowering in a sad and desperate kind of way. Like she was catching up with him, was able to, because she'd become like him.

Seeing the worst, not looking for the best.

Words left her at that point. She didn't know what to say or do. Just sat there, absorbing her worst nightmare, unable to wake herself up.

Until minutes later, when she said, "You honestly believe that Simon would be involved in kidnapping babies and selling them?"

Which didn't explain Ella. She'd purposely been avoiding that entire train. And couldn't wrap her mind around going there yet.

"No." Ben's statement, said with such authority, so unequivocally, gave her heart a strong jolt. She stared at him, breathing him in like a lifeline as he said, "Simon may be hardheaded and obstinate. He might refuse to listen to reason…"

"… Like his big brother?" she interrupted, tripping over herself to bring a note of normalcy to the situation. To hang on to the invisible thread of hope Ben had just given her.

Ben's nod, the upward lift of both hands, could have been acknowledgment. And then, with his eyes boring dead into hers, he said, "But he's not capable of hurting babies."

He glanced at the cupboard by the stove. Nodded that way. And she remembered…

"The baby skunk."

Their last time at the cabin, in the midst of all the fighting, eleven-year-old Simon had called out for Ben, tears in his voice. He'd found a baby skunk, bleeding from a cut, with what likely had been part of the parent close by. Ben had filled a box with sheets, gone to town to buy supplies, and, teaching Simon as they went along the process, he showed his little brother how to do all they could to nurse the skunk back to health. At the end of that week, they'd had to let him go. But they'd at least left the wild creature fully recovered, with the best chance to fend for himself.

"Doesn't mean he's out of the woods, Jen." Ben's words were a warning. And seemed like a promise that she wasn't going into the day ahead alone. "He needed money, huge amounts of it. His dad couldn't bail him out a second time."

"Sierra's Web's been watching him," she remembered aloud that he'd told her that. For the past months. Since the ring had been supposedly shut down.

"Yes."

"What do you know that you aren't telling me?"

"They've found no trace of him, or his old model SUV, since he gassed up in Vegas a little less than two weeks ago. One of Michaels's agents visited Simon's father in Tucson, and he hadn't heard from him in months. Phone records show that the two of them haven't conversed since Simon went back to Vegas."

Her mind was sharp. Good with math. And was telling her what she didn't want to know.

Simon had disappeared right around the time Ella had been born. Just before a kidnapping had to happen to make the sale Michaels had seen on the internet.

Try as she might, Jenny could not find one good spin to put on that one.

The infant woke up, grabbing Jen's attention away from one of the most honest and open conversations she and Ben had had in years. Ben was almost glad for the reprieve. She bathed the little one, saying something about the umbilical cord, but mostly engaging in baby talk with the newborn in her care.

It wasn't that she was cutting him out. He chose not to look directly at the child. She was a case. And when her biological parents were identified, she would be returned to them.

He would give his life to keep her safe until then.

After a walk around the cabin's perimeter, Ben used the time to get his computer signed into the scrambled network he'd tapped into through the burner phone. Service was sketchy. Didn't matter how good the technology he carried with him might be, his devices still depended on towers through which to transmit. There were none on his fifty acres.

He usually got better service at night, when there was lower usage overall. Was counting on the fact as he went to work with what he'd been told. And combined it with what he knew.

Simon owed a large sum of money to a powerful man who, though he'd been arrested many times, always managed to escape charges. Simon had hooked up with Cody Daniels, whose brother had had a way to make large sums of money.

Simon blamed Ben for his life's failures.

He needed to look at it all with a clear, level head. To be ready.

If he got any chance with his little brother at all—he could bet there'd only be one of them. He needed Jen prepared.

She'd fed the infant. Had gone into the shower.

He opened the file he'd been compiling on his brother ever since Simon had left almost seven years before. Focused on that, keeping his mind off the water sluicing down over his ex-wife's sexy form. Sexier at forty-one than she'd been at twenty, he now knew.

And…he blinked. Saw the screen in front of him. Scrolled. Forced himself to take in what the pages, the various reports, the photos, were showing him. Simon had been unraveling ever since he'd left home. He'd get it together for a month. Several months. And then be on another downhill slide. He'd left his father's home within a year. Went back a time or two, getting bailed out, and then would leave again.

The kid had always thought that he knew better than anyone else.

Like his big brother...

Jen's words hit him again. Not due to any mean-spirited vibes in their delivery. But because she was right. At least in terms of how he'd dealt with his family.

His mother had been relying on him since he was six years old for her emotional sustenance. He'd learned way too young how to think outside himself. Feeling a sense of failure anytime his mother cried. Which had been often. And when he'd left for college, finally taking his life back from the circumstances that had essentially robbed it from him, his mom had ended up with Bruce. Simon's father.

So, yeah, when he'd married the love of his life and they'd had Simon deposited on them, he'd been driven to keep them safe. It was the only way he knew how to live.

And more particularly, to love.

At forty-two, he knew better than to think that would ever change.

But, he didn't know better than anyone else. Had never thought he did. To the contrary, he'd always been watching for what he didn't know. Couldn't do. Trying to prevent both from hurting those he loved.

No way he was going to fail Jen. Or Simon.

He'd thought.

And he'd done exactly that.

An irony, to be sure.

But he was his father's son. No way he'd give up. Or refuse to face the challenge in front of him.

Hearing the bathroom door open, he knew he was going to take on the danger facing them with all he had. And if there was any mercy in life at all, he was going to succeed.

Jen's soft steps, in the flip flops she'd had on at the safe house, sounded across from him. He didn't look up.

"Simon knows about this place. He could find us here."

She was right. That was the plan. And she'd just saved him from having to break it to her.

He looked up at her, noted the wet hair, combed but hanging down around her, the sweatshirt and jeans he'd never seen before. "He might," he said. "And if he does, I need you to follow my lead, Jen." For once, she had to take his side. And that's where he got cold sweats. Every time he'd run through the plan over the past hour.

"He needs tough love, reality right now. Encouraging him to fly, to hope it will all come out right isn't going to help him at this point. I don't believe he has anything to do with the kidnapping of that infant, but he could be the carrier."

"The carrier?"

"He delivers the baby to the new family who purchased it. They have money, want a child and for whatever reason don't qualify for adoption. That's the profile of every one of the families Michaels found." She'd taken a seat, not next to him, but not at the far end of the table, either. Just right there in the middle.

Where she'd always been when it came to him and his little brother.

"Simon's job would, on the surface, be a celebratory time. Giving a family their new baby. An errand performed in a wealthy, warm setting, with everyone happy. He's a good-looking guy, clean-cut, well educated and is comfortable, at home even, in glitzy society."

Jen frowned. "Glitzy society? We weren't glitzy. And, owning and running a garage, I can't imagine Bruce ever got that way. How do you know that?"

Opening the photo folder in Simon's file, Ben turned his computer around so she could see it, too. Then started to click. The screen filled with photo after photo of Simon through the past five years. Longer hair, shorter, whiskers, clean-shaven, but always in high fashion clothes, sometimes even tuxes, in luxurious settings. On the deck of a yacht. Nightclubs. A lanai of a private country club sipping champagne in the sunshine.

"Oh, my God." Jen's hushed tone stabbed at Ben. He'd known for years. All behind her back.

"I can help him, Jen. I can speak to the prosecutor, the judge. I can pull some strings. And agree to take him to my place on house arrest or give whatever other support he might need to keep him safe in prison. But he has to accept my help. And he's not going to do that if you give him hope of another option."

"I just… I can't believe…"

"We're out of time, Jen. And he's out of other options."

Jen's gaze had been fully focused on the screen, as though she could somehow turn back time to let her be on scene where the photos were taken. To have been a part of Simon's life still.

To maybe help shape some of the choices.

"There'd been a time when you might have been successful, guiding him to better decisions, if I'd just supported you." He hadn't planned on the words. Hadn't even said them consciously to himself.

But the truth of them seemed to bounce off the walls around them, a loud proclamation.

Jen looked over at him. Met his gaze. Not with love. But he detected no hate, either. "You *want* him to come here," she said.

He nodded.

And watched as Jen's eyes filled with tears.

Chapter 17

Jenny hurt from the inside out. So much.

Aching with regret.

And something so much more. Ben's *if I'd just supported you* just kept ripping her. She'd cried. Begged. Spewed angry words. To try to get him to give her just that.

Yet…he'd been right, too. Simon had needed a firm hand. Something that Ben couldn't provide in any meaningful way without her support.

She tore her gaze away from his. Needing to run, with nowhere to go.

"Simon isn't going to hurt you or the baby, Jen."

The words brought her gaze back to his. "I know." She nodded. And then, with clearer vision, looked at him. "He left her with me," she said. "Instead of delivering her to the family, he left her with me. He knew that I'd love her as if she was my own." As she'd done with Simon.

But there was more. Her gaze sharpened, and she leaned closer to Ben, his brown eyes steady as they stayed with hers. "And he knew you'd do all it took to keep her safe," she said.

Ben shrugged. "Simon's only hope is if I can get his testimony on record, literally." He held up his cell phone. "And get him to come in with me, to turn himself in. Any other way I see this going down will likely end up getting him killed."

The lump in her throat wouldn't swallow away. It just hung there, making it hard for her to speak. Blinking away the tears that wouldn't be held back, she nodded.

And knew something else he wasn't actually putting into words. Ella. She looked over at the crib. Couldn't stop looking, as her chin trembled.

The *infant*. Had a family of her own. One who was probably devastated. Desperate to get her back.

"When Evart was running things…" Ben's slow words, coming to a stop, brought her attention back to him. His eyes seemed to be awash with understanding.

Like they'd been in high school. And during the first years of their marriage. Before they'd suddenly found themselves grieving Ben's mother and becoming unexpected parents to a precocious four-year-old boy.

They'd been so young. Too young to take on all that. Had put off having a child of their own. And Simon… he'd had a mind of his own even then. Had spent the first four years of his life learning that if he threw a fit, he'd get what he wanted.

She'd told him no. As had Ben. They'd both maintained the stance. She'd just done so with kindness and distraction. Ben's way had been…firmer. He'd never struck the boy. Not even close. Or raised his voice to him, for that matter. He'd just been an unrelenting wall.

Ben's cough brought her attention back to him. He'd been saying something…

"When Evart was running things," he started again, "many of the babies were taken from women who'd already legally given them up," he said. "Some of those adoptive families were still available and eager to take the children when Michaels was finally able to match them up. Others had adopted another baby by that time and new families waiting for a child took the ones who'd been kidnapped."

She nodded. Was glad to know those details. Her heart gave thanks for all those families. And her own ache intensified. The only chance she and Ben had had was Simon. After Simon had left, he'd wanted them to finally start a family of their own. She'd been thirty-four, would be thirty-five before the baby was born. Not as young as she'd have liked, but still well within childbearing years.

But her heart had been so beaten by then. The fighting… Simon's desertion. She hadn't wanted to risk it happening all over again.

Mouth open, she stared at him.

"What?" he asked.

"After Simon…you wanted to have a baby."

He nodded. Shrugged. "I get that it probably would have ended up the same."

She shook her head, couldn't get sidetracked. Wouldn't let herself be distracted. "*You* believed, Ben. *I was* focused on the danger and denied us the chance…"

Shocked, Jenny sat there, completely lost. And when Ben slid his hand across the table, palm up, reaching out to her, she took it.

And held on.

As he felt Jen's soft fingers slide into his, Ben knew he had to give her hope. Even if it got dashed, hope was what would see her through the difficult hours or, God forbid, days immediately in front of them. That was her coping device. He'd finally understood.

Just as his was looking for ways to avoid danger, and in

the event that wasn't possible, ways to mitigate it. To successfully navigate it.

All of which was nice to know but wasn't going to save any lives.

Somehow, life had brought them to that point. Danger was coming. No matter what either one of them tried to do to avoid it. Or how they coped with its nearing.

Jen was still sitting with him. Had taken his hand.

She'd signed on.

Had just doubled his chance of success where his little brother was concerned. And he had to at least give her all the facts. And let her draw her own conclusions.

"The doctor in Yuma. From what I've been able to find on her through my own internet research, she tends to a lot of runaways. Indigent women. Statistics show that many of them turn to drugs. And to sex to pay for their drugs. We know that the...baby —" he nodded toward the crib but didn't let himself land there "—had trace evidence of opiates in her system." Jen's lips parted, trembled a little, and he finished with, "It's possible that she's going to end up a ward of the state, Jen."

Which meant that Jen could possibly end up with her little girl after all. Assuming all things fell into the best of all places given the circumstances.

He could think of many obstacles to that happening. Some possibly further fetched. Many, spot-on. But he figured Jen could, too. If she chose to go that route. She was a smart woman. Something he'd always known. And maybe, in his overprotectiveness, had lost sight of.

Letting go of his hand, she pulled back. Crossed her arms over her chest, chin up.

Ben braced himself.

"Tell me what problems you have with the idea of Simon leaving Ella in my care."

"What?" He'd thought talk about the sex they'd had was coming up, or more about Simon's possible imminent advent upon them. She'd have stipulations he'd have to comply with to get her cooperation.

"I can't think of any," she said. "So, tell me."

He wanted to be able to do so. Only because he knew how badly she hurt when her hopes were dashed.

But trying to protect her from dashed hopes, as well as foreseeable possibilities of physical danger, had ruined his marriage.

Worse, it had caused Jen to have to fight for the right to make her own choices. To fight for the joy that had always effervesced out of her.

Looking her in the eye, he raised his brows and said, "Honestly? I can't think of any. He picked up the baby for the drop the day after the kidnapping, as always happened. Different people in different places for each leg of the operation. He was intending to make the money he needed to get his bookie's strong-arm guy off his back. But when he held the infant, he couldn't do it. It all fits his profile—as can be seen in those reports." He nodded to his laptop. "He also couldn't return her, so he did the only thing Simon would do. He brought her to the one place he knew she'd be safe."

Jen's eyes brimmed again, but tears didn't fall as she said, "And the one place where he knew justice would be served," she said. "His warnings to both of us for you to drop the case. He was scared," she said. "Panicking about what he'd done. He not only had a bookie at his back, but whoever he'd double-crossed, as well. But ultimately, he wanted you to do right by that baby."

Ben wanted to believe she was right. Couldn't come up

with any quick and obvious hole in her story. Maybe because he didn't want to. Didn't try hard enough.

Because there was something far more important staring at them.

"We have a twenty-three-year-old out there, in trouble with the law, running for his life. With at least one and probably two evil men at his back…"

Jen nodded. "I know." Her eyes filled again. She blinked the tears away. Still hugging herself.

He wanted to let it end there. To leave it at that.

But… "Either of those entities could be following him," he told her what had hit him when Warner had told him the news about Simon's association with Cody Daniels just as they'd arrived. "He might lead them straight here."

And if they didn't remain there for him to find them, he'd loose his best chance of staying alive.

Jen didn't flinch. But he saw her arms tighten around her middle. He told her about the cameras he had set up. The various places he had guns stashed around and outside the cabin. He talked about a small, buried propane tank an acre from the building, at a rock formation that they'd always used as a landmark in the past. And told her how to set it safely on fire, if necessary, to buy herself some time. And he told her about the old Jeep he had stashed just over the hill on the opposite side of the cabin.

All overkill. He cringed inside with every word that came out of him. Yeah, he'd spent years renovating the property he'd bought. And he'd also spent part of that time giving the property every precaution he could think of in case anyone he put away ever found him there.

He'd just needed to feel that one place on earth was completely fail proof, safe.

When in reality, no place really was.

Jen didn't react much as he spoke. Just sat there, taking it all in. Nodding every now and then. Never said a word, until he'd finished his instructions. Then asked, "Do you think both of them were involved on the attacks on us?"

"Hard to say, but doubtful. What does a bookie want with a stolen kid on his hands? And he certainly wouldn't want Simon dead. There'd be no money in that."

"Unless they'd written off what he owed them and wanted to use him to set an example."

He wanted to smile when she came out with that one. Just couldn't find any humor inside him. "That's mostly in the movies," he told her. "But it does happen."

And was already on the table with Ben.

"So who tried to kidnap Ella outside the clinic?" she asked next. But one look at her and he figured she knew.

"You tell me."

She sighed. Dropped her arms and stood. "Simon," she said, as she moved over to check on the infant. "He got scared, got cold feet. As soon as he saw you actually arrive at the church." She laid out a sleeper and fresh diaper, then moved to the kitchen, pulling the can of powdered formula toward her. "I'm guessing he's the one who slashed your tires that night," she continued, as though talking about a friend she'd seen at the grocery store.

Ben sat forward. "You think Simon was behind the wheel of the white truck?" he asked. She'd said she couldn't remember anything about the guy. Gloves. Smell of alcohol. But maybe, going back in her mind…

Jen turned, her face looking like she'd seen a ghost. There'd been no sign of Simon's SUV, but if he'd made it to Yuma, stolen the truck…

"No," Jen said, unequivocally. "He was bigger than Simon."

"You haven't seen Simon in six years. He's a man now, not a teenager."

Glancing toward the computer screen, Jen shook her head. "I've just spent half an hour staring at images of him," she said. And then finished with, "The man in the truck was much thicker, broader. Like you behind the wheel, only I think...heavier. And...he had a tattoo, Ben. On his neck. I can't tell you anything about it. It's just a flash of ink on the back side of his neck as he sped past. I just now had a flash of it in my mind's eye, looking back. Oh, my God. I'm so sorry. I should have tried harder. Remembered sooner."

Ben was on the phone before she'd finished speaking.

To Hudson Warner, who'd alert Michaels.

Cody Daniels was a big man, just as Jen had described. And the recent photos Ben had seen of the man, during hours of searches, had shown him a tattoo of his brother's badge number, rounding the back of his neck like a chain.

They had an eyewitness who could identify the man. At least in theory. Had definite cause to bring him in.

Yeah, there was still a mole in Jasper Gulley. But not in the FBI. Mr. Daniels had bitten off more than he could chew.

Ben just hoped that his comrades in uniform were able to catch the guy before Simon led him up the hill.

Jenny changed Ella, wondered if it would be the last night she got the little one ready for bed, and then shut down the thought. She had the baby girl for the moment.

And life was lived one moment at a time. Ben had assured her, at least half a dozen times, in various ways, that the mind reveals what it can when it can. He told her it was in no way her fault that it took her so long to remember the tattoo. As she'd changed Ella. Fed her. Smiled at her when she didn't immediately fall back to sleep.

Stood and danced with her for a second.

Mostly Ben had been at his computer, typing and clicking, studying and then typing some more. But then he'd look up, she'd look over, meet his gaze, and he'd tell her again. She'd done great remembering the tattoo at all.

And he checked in with Sierra's Web. Pretty much on the hour. He didn't share anything with her, other than a shake of the head after each call.

It was almost midnight—Ella had just gone back to sleep for what she hoped would be a good four-hour span—and Jenny knew she had to get some rest herself. She'd be no good for Ben, Simon and, most particularly, little Ella if she didn't.

She just couldn't bear the thought of wheeling the crib into one of the two bedrooms and lying there in the dark alone.

It wasn't that she wanted Ben in there in bed with her. She did not. Well, mostly she didn't. A small part of her, the teenager who still lurked inside her, wanted him there.

The rest of her knew better.

He came in from a perimeter check, just around the immediate cabin. Had his phone in hand. She heard him say, "Will do."

Fear shot into her. Felt like it blew a hole right through her stomach lining. Had he found something outside? He'd been watching the cameras all night. Hadn't said anything.

"Dammit, Ben, if we're going to do this together, then we're doing it *together*. Every step of the way. Starting now. My need to know is at everything status. No more protecting me from things you think will upset me. I'm a fully capable, strong woman." She stopped short of stomping her foot. And broke off the tirade with horror coursing through her.

She'd just berated him. Like the shrew she'd become during the last year or so of their marriage. "I apologize," she said then, while he put his phone in his pocket. He hadn't looked her way. She had no idea if he'd zoned out on her as he had in the past when her feelings poured out of her mouth with no filter. "I'm scared. And feeling...powerless."

There. He could do with that what he'd like.

She saw his chest move over a deep breath. Then he turned to face her. The gaze that met hers was stoic. Mostly professional. "I admit to being guilty of sheltering you from upsetting news in the past," he told her. "That ended earlier tonight." He nodded toward the table, the corner where she'd been sitting when he'd reached out his hand to her.

She nodded. Knew more was coming. And braced herself. "Michaels and his team are in Yuma. They met with the doctor, who, under the circumstances, admitted that there were three women she'd been seeing off the books who'd been seeing her regularly, were past delivery dates and had stopped coming to see her."

Her heart sank. They knew of two recent sales. "Three?"

Ben nodded. "Out of the dozens she apparently sees outside of regular office hours." His gaze, though, it told her there was more.

Jen tensed. Realized she was wringing her hands. Stopped. Mentally glued them to her thighs. She looked over at her ex-husband. And couldn't quite make out the expression in those deep brown eyes.

"They found one of them, Jen. A seventeen-year-old named Macy. She admitted that she'd agreed to give her baby up for adoption to a guy she'd heard about that was arranging such things. She had to see a particular midwife for the birth and turn the child over right away. She was blindfolded before she got to the home, and until after she left. She said there were two people there, one up by her face, helping her breathe, comforting her, and the one who delivered the baby. In exchange, she got five hundred dollars. She was a runaway. Her parents didn't know she was pregnant, and she wanted to use the money to get home."

Her throat tight, she asked, "When?"

"She had the baby two days ago. And the exchange matches exactly with a posting Michaels found on the dark web. The one that signifies that the second deal closed successfully."

Not Ella.

And...that baby... The young woman... So much pain. So much wrong.

He seemed to hear her silent words, almost to share them, as he shrugged and softly said, "She had a bus ticket for Tennessee leaving tonight. Instead, her parents are flying in to be with her until this all gets sorted out." Tears sprang to her eyes. Thankful ones. For the young woman who was taking charge of her life. Reuniting with family. And to the parents who hopefully would wrap loving arms around her and hold her tight.

Because even though people made mistakes, sometimes horrible ones, with consequences that had to be paid, there was still hope. And a chance for happiness.

"And the other two women?"

"They haven't found them yet. One in particular was due to deliver a week and a half ago. She was white."

Like Ella.

So, if they didn't have the mother... "What about this guy? The buyer?"

Ben's gaze seemed to reach out to her, to wrap her in

a warmth to chase the chills away as he said, "He's in the wind. But fits Cody Daniels's description. Macy didn't get a great look at him. He'd insisted on doing business at night, in an alley, and he wore a hoodie. But the facial hair was the same as in the picture they showed her. And the build. He also mentioned during their first meeting that he was from Northern Arizona."

She absorbed. Nodded. "We're sure it wasn't Simon?"

His second nod weakened her a bit, as relief made its way through the stone walls she was building around her. "They showed her a picture of him, too. Cody is taller than Simon. By a lot. And much broader built."

She heard herself earlier, describing the guy in the white truck to Ben.

Wondered about the tattoo. But knew not to waste time asking. The guy had been wearing a hoodie. And was in the wind.

"You were right," she said then, the weight of her words, the magnitude of what they meant, sinking down on her. Him picking up on Molly had started it. Leading to her doctor, who'd known of the doctor in Yuma. Molly had had nothing to do with their situation, and yet his attentiveness, his lead, had led to a major break in the case. "We really are dealing with the kidnapping ring."

"That's the going theory." Ben didn't blink. Didn't look away. Just kept watching her as though she mattered more than their conversation. He wasn't gloating. There was no "I told you so's." Just a roomful of compassion. Wrapped in professionalism.

Because while their enemy had a name, they still didn't have him.

Which meant that, for them, in their current moment, nothing had changed.

Chapter 18

They had to get some rest. Setting his phone to vibrate every half hour, so he could check cameras, Ben glanced at Jen. She was sitting on the couch, next to the crib, her head back, as though she intended to sleep right there.

The night before, she'd seemed eager to get away from him. Had stayed in her room half the morning, until he'd come to get her.

He sat at the table and watched her eyes close, stay closed for a few minutes. As she slowly opened them and turned toward the crib, Ben made an executive decision.

Heading to the room that had, once upon a time, been Simon's, he grabbed the mattress off the twin bed, sheets and spread and all, and carried it out to the living area.

"What…?" Jen sat upright, watched him set the mattress by the crib, slid down to the floor to tuck in the covers beneath it and then looked up at him. "Where are you going to sleep?"

He pointed to the couch. And then went out for one last check—an excuse to give her time to herself to prepare for and get into bed. The lights were low when he reentered five minutes later. Taking care of his own ablutions, he changed into a pair of cotton pants and a T-shirt and carried his gun with him to the living area. He grabbed a cover off his bed to take with him.

Only to find the couch fully made as a bed with sheets, pillow and everything.

Jen's back was to him as he arranged his boots so he could immediately slip them on. He checked his gun one last time to make certain the safety was on, tucking it under the couch cushion at his head, and slid quietly beneath the covers.

"Thank you."

Jen's soft words reached out to him in the dim glow coming from the bathroom light he'd left on.

She was thanking him? She'd made his bed.

When he'd spent so much of their lives together blind to the home, the life she'd been trying to make. "You had every right to be upset earlier, Jen. And your bursts of feelings as you called them...you rarely raised your voice. And never made it about anything other than what was on the table in that moment."

"It was all I had to fight about."

He got that. Loud and clear. Felt the brunt of the words in places only she'd ever found. "I only ever wanted to protect you."

"I know."

She was being more gracious than he deserved. "It was disrespectful, at the very least, to act as though I knew better how to keep you safe. It's like I was diminishing your own capabilities." The admission came through a tight throat.

After years of lying in that cabin alone, playing all that had gone wrong over and over in his mind. Trying to figure it all out. See where they'd first left the course that would have led them to happily ever after. Needing to solve the case.

Those last few years, the aloneness, the beer-induced

talks with Drake. It had taken a baby being left illegally outside Jen's work door to bring him the answers. To bring him the truth.

"I was so filled with my own rightness where Simon was concerned," the words came softly toward him. "I was the child life specialist. We were in my wheelhouse."

He smiled at her use of a word he used to throw at her. Safety, protecting others was in his wheelhouse.

"I didn't realize I'd stopped trying to understand you, Ben," she continued while he was still off reminiscing. He heard the rustle of covers and glanced at the other end of the couch, where he'd placed her mattress, and saw her facing him. Her head on her pillow.

Her expression was all shadows, but he could see glints in her eyes. "You *are* a protector. It's not something you do, it's who you are. I've always known that. And after Simon came to us… I got so caught up in the huge responsibility we'd been given, took the child-rearing part to be mostly mine…and I stopped tuning into you. I failed to understand why you were constantly trying to hold us back."

Her honesty hit him hard. "Because I got so overbearing, I forced you into fight-or-flight mode." He told her what he'd figured out, in pieces, over the past few days. The past couple of years. "The more we became a family, the more I had to protect…and the more I tried to strip you of your autonomy." He heard the last words, wiped a hand over his face as the truth landed there. And said, "God, Jen, I'm sorry."

"Me, too."

They'd put the past to rest. Time to sleep. But he didn't feel over it. "They say opposites attract," he uttered, half to himself, as he lay there gazing into the darkness, his eyes adjusting enough to let him study the flatness of the new drywall he'd put on the ceiling the year before. "It didn't work that way for us."

His words were met with silence. He was disappointed, but thankful that she'd been able to fall asleep. They had no idea what challenges would be calling upon her strength over the next day or two.

"We were newlyweds with grief and a four-year-old thrust on us all at once." Minutes had passed before her words dropped on him. "I remember my parents talking to us about it, before they left town to travel the world. We were so certain we had it all covered. We didn't know what we didn't know."

Yeah. They hadn't known what they hadn't known. His tension relaxed some. She made it sound as though none of it had been either of their faults.

Or, at least, that they were deserving of understanding. Forgiveness.

Which was Jen's way.

And why he'd been so drawn to her from the first day he'd seen her in his eighth-grade class. Her smile…as though she recognized something inside him.

It had all been so pubescent, childish. He'd been a lonely kid who'd seen more than was there, was all.

"You think if we'd known what we didn't know it would have turned out differently?" he asked, curiosity getting the better of him.

"Probably not." Her answer, while harsh in a way, seemed to bring a peace he'd been searching for.

Their lives had been so completely different during their formative years. Creating individuals who were too opposite to become one.

"Maybe we were meant to be friends, not husband and

wife," he said then, relaxing more into the cushions. He was exhausted.

"Maybe. The lovemaking was great, though."

Eyes wide open again, Ben lay still. He'd been hoping they'd had some kind of mutual silent consent not to speak of sex again. Ever.

There was absolutely no future in it.

He had to shut down the thoughts. To prevent the ideas from taking them into a blaze of fire that would ultimately burn their hearts up again.

"Friends with benefits," Jen said, sounding sleepy. But like she was smiling, too.

And wanting her to stay that way, to drift off on a happy thought, Ben kept his tension—his warnings against any hint of conversation or yearnings regarding sex—to himself.

Jenny woke fully conscious. Thinking Ella had woken her, that the baby was ready to eat, she lay there, listening for the small whines she'd already grown accustomed to hearing.

The ones that told her how long it would be before the baby was fully up and hungry. They grew in intensity. She had anywhere from one to ten minutes, depending on how deeply she'd been asleep.

No sounds came.

But something had pulled her out of a decent slumber.

Without moving a bone in her body, she glanced around the dimly lit room. To the couch first. No Ben.

And then farther.

In cotton pants, a T-shirt and boots, he stood at the kitchen table, staring at his computer screen. She couldn't make out words.

But, recognizing the frame around the screen, she slid out from under her covers and joined him. He was watching the cameras around the property.

She saw nothing but darkness and shadowed wilderness resembling the version they'd been looking at since they'd arrived the night before.

"What's up?" she asked. He wouldn't be standing there like that, alert, completely focused, if he was just doing a camera check. Something had prompted him to put the boots on.

Her gaze moved to his gun on the table, less than a quarter inch from where his hand rested.

"I saw movement on the camera." His tone gave her nothing. And the words, not enough. He continued to stare, his gaze only moving between the six live screens lined in two rows on his laptop.

"Human?"

"Seemed that way. Nothing definitive."

"Which one?" Like it mattered. But it would help if she knew what to watch.

"The front trees."

Still forty acres or more from the cabin.

"When?"

"Half an hour ago."

And she was only just then awake and hearing about it? "Why didn't you wake me?"

"There's no action needed, yet."

"I could help watch," she told him, leaving the table to make a quick stop in the bathroom and then collect her own computer. "Get me hooked up, and we can split the duty," she said upon her return. "Three screens on yours and three on mine. That way we can enlarge them."

He nodded. Went to work immediately, popping his eyes

back to the screens constantly. And then, pulling a chair next to him, he put the two computers together and sat down in front of them. Pointing toward the empty chair as he did so.

It wasn't much of a welcome. But it felt like full acceptance.

Jenny sat, letting Ben's choice fill her frightened heart.

He'd seen a figure moving about. He had no proof. Had replayed the frame a dozen times since. Could easily see the ephemeral shadow as brush in a slight breeze. But his gut was telling him differently.

His hope was panning out. His little brother had come to him.

He didn't have all the details figured out yet. Like how on earth had the guy thought he could ditch the merchandise with Jen and not have killers at his back?

Or…hadn't Simon cared at that point? Had he seen no way out? Been desperate enough to figure his last act on earth would be saving the newborn girl?

Simon knew of a place he could hide. The cabin. And if it had been sold and occupied, at least he'd know the area offered a plethora of hiding choices.

Jaw clenching, Ben wanted to promise his half sibling that he could swoop in and save the day.

They both knew he couldn't do that. Not if Simon was in as much trouble as the evidence seemed to indicate. But Ben had a lot of pull. He could get the best attorney, hopefully keep Simon in state, close by. Make certain that he was protected. Maybe, depending on Simon's involvement, they could even swing a plea deal of some kind.

If he could convince Simon to testify against the Las Vegas hitmen.

That particular *if* didn't sit well with him. But he wasn't dwelling on it yet. It just lingered, there, in the back of his mind, as he tried to get another glimpse of the figure.

"It's possible he's asleep," Jen said, breaking a ten-minute silence.

He'd never described the form he'd thought he'd seen. Or mentioned his younger brother. Opened his mouth to tell her that they had no idea who the possible trespasser might be. And then closed it again.

She didn't need his warning. Or his prevarication. Life came with no guarantees. They could have a squatter. Someone who knew that Ben's property was vacant a lot of the time. Who regularly hunted or fished on the land.

His words protected her against nothing. They insulted her.

If he got nothing else right that day, he'd have that one.

"I don't think so," he said slowly. "I only saw a shadow, Jen. He was hunched and looking over his shoulder. I think he saw the camera. It's camouflaged, but after living with me all those years, Simon knows what to look for. He's probably now avoiding them."

"Have you alerted Sierra's Web?"

He heard the tension in her voice. Knew that she feared he'd have the calvary all over his land before Simon had a chance to surrender. To make certain that his brother didn't escape and get himself killed.

Knew, too, that if he felt there was no other choice, that was exactly what he'd do.

"Not yet," he told her. And added, because he'd said he wouldn't hold back, "There's nothing to tell. I saw a shadow that my gut is telling me was made by a human on my property. The footage doesn't delineate enough to confirm that."

"But you're going to alert them. As soon as you know."

Her deadpan tone told its story. With acceptance, disapproval probably, but no rancor.

"I'll know that when I know what I know," he told her the absolute truth. Using their earlier words because she'd understand. Because they fit. He was about to attempt to expound on his thinking, by letting her know that he was keeping her opinions on the table with him regarding letting Simon come in on his own, but that those opinions were a few among many, when she stiffened.

His focus was no longer on words. Or opinions.

"It's definitely a body, Ben!" Jen's voice rose so much the infant let out a cry yards to the side of them. While he kept his gaze glued on the form moving stealthily, slowly, in a direction perpendicular to the cabin—Jen jumped up and went to the crib.

He heard no more sound. Felt her sit back down beside him.

"Look at the size...the length... It could be him."

The hair was longer than in the last photo he'd seen of Simon, from a month prior. But not as long as it had been in earlier photos that year. The shoulders...hard to tell with the backpack he was wearing. The length...fit.

And his gut—he had to believe that his brother was coming to him to do the right thing. To turn himself in.

Trusting Ben to help all he could.

"He's still forty acres out," he told Jen, not bothering to pretend that he really believed the body could be someone besides Simon. "Moving sideways, not toward us."

She leaned in enough that he could tell she didn't have the infant in her arms. "Is he crawling?" she asked.

He shrugged. "It looks like he might be slithering on the ground like a snake."

"Trying to avoid cameras?"

Tense, needing to get dressed and be ready, Ben couldn't take his focus off that screen. "The sun's beginning to rise. It's likely that he doesn't want to be seen by anyone who might be following him."

And there was another key factor to consider. "He's not coming in, Jen. He had about five football fields' worth of ground to cover. Should have taken five minutes max, ten if he was doing it hunched over. Instead, he's moved this way only a fifth of the distance."

"He needs to make certain he's not being followed." Jen's words were filled with tension. He recognized the tone and shored up his defenses. He would not diminish her, but he couldn't give in to her, either. Giving in would leave blood on his hands.

"Or he's not sure he can trust me and he's going to lay out there and get himself killed."

"It's possible he wasn't followed."

He looked over at her. "You willing to risk his life, ours and the infant's on that?"

Jen's lips tightened as she continued to watch the screen. Refusing to turn and meet his gaze, though, he knew, she'd have seen him turning toward her out of her peripheral vision. They were sitting that close.

The sun was rising. Shining on the form, on the fingers that seemed to be almost clawing the ground, the grasses through which it was moving. While feet, one at a time, slowly pushed. As though the man was trying to climb flat ground.

He made out jeans. The images weren't in color, but he could tell the pants were dark. Short sleeves, T-shirt, long, hem down over Simon's butt. Ankle-length boots.

"If you have something to say, then say it, Jen." He couldn't go another round with her. They weren't at home, arguing over what-ifs regarding an activity that hadn't yet taken place.

She shook her head. But the muscles in her jaw were tight and hard.

Compassion…love… They didn't carry guns. "We're dealing with life and death here. I have to get out there." Standing, he reached for the jeans and shirt he'd dropped on a chair the night before. Got into them without a glance in Jen's direction.

She wasn't watching him strip and dress, either. They were both watching their one-time ward move along Ben's land to seemingly nowhere.

"I know." Her voice was somber, disapproving still, but he didn't detect irritation.

The body on the screen moved. Jolting. Senses completely honed, heart pounding, Ben leaned in. The body jolted again.

And then suddenly relaxed, head tilted at an odd angle, face half planted in the eight-inch-long grass.

Chapter 19

Ben's phone landed on the table with a bounce. "Call Sierra's Web and lock down," his urgent words rang out toward the door as, gun in hand, he bounded out of the cabin.

Trembling from the inside out, Jenny bolted the door behind Ben. Threw the dead bolt across. And ran back to the table, keeping her gaze firmly glued to the live images in front of her as she opened Ben's phone app to the only number called.

She pushed to dial…waited. No ring sounded indicating a completing call.

She only had two bars of service.

"Come on," she cried aloud. "At dawn? So many people using…"

A swishing sound from the far wall drew her gaze toward Ella. The baby's body had scrunched up, but then settled back flat.

The baby sensing her tension?

"Tone," she said softly. Her senses settling a mite as she focused on the baby. What Ella needed. More importantly, what the baby didn't need.

She didn't need tension in her nine-day-old life. Wasn't going to begin her journey encased in a world of fear, if Jenny could do anything about that.

Ella had been given to her so she'd provide a loving home.

She had to exude security. Calm. Love.

Ringing sounded in her ear.

Finally.

One ring. She heard a click and "Identify." A commanding male voice.

Reminding her of Ben.

"Jennifer Sanders, wife of Detective Ben Sanders." Her voice trembled with the rest of her. "I…"

"We've got it," the voice said.

No…they didn't… "The screens," she got out. "Security cameras…"

"We've got it, Mrs. Sanders. Have had someone watching all night."

Feeling like she'd been slapped in the face, Jenny shook her head. Confused. Why hadn't Ben told her that he didn't need to call Sierra's Web because they could see what he'd seen?

"He told me to call…"

"Right. My name's Hudson Warner. I want you to stay on the line with us," the voice continued, as, shaking so hard she almost dropped the phone, Jenny sank down to her chair at the table. Watching the images for signs of Ben.

And keeping an eye on Ella, too.

The cabin's walls, made out of treated solid logs with an impenetrable metal over them and then drywall, would keep them safe. There were no windows. Only one door.

It wasn't hers or Ella's lives she feared for at the moment.

"Ben said you're aware of who I am."

"Sierra's Web, yes," she practically bit out. What kind of expert sat on the phone chatting?

Oh, God.

There he was. Flat up against a tree. Gun drawn up to his chest.

"A team of agents is on their way," Warner said then. "We dispersed them as soon as Ben sent coordinates after we saw movement on the screen, just in case. They'd been told to get close but hang back. They're about five minutes out. I'm going to stay here with you now, to give direction if needed."

On top of having already known that Sierra's Web was watching those cameras, that he hadn't had to call them in because they'd already been there, he'd hired her a baby-sitter?

As humiliating as that was, Jenny was a little grateful not to be completely alone as she sat there. Even as she mourned what she'd thought had been a brand-new understanding between her and her ex-husband.

Her heart deadened some at the thought, but she couldn't stay there. She had a bigger bleed going on at the moment. "We just saw our... Ben's brother... You think he's dead?"

"I think it looked as though the body on the video was in distress," Warner said. And continued on almost in the same breath with, "Ben says you're an excellent shot."

She nodded. Rubbed her head with her hand. Looked at Ella, still sleeping. She'd need formula soon. Maybe Jenny should get it ready, just in case they had to leave in a hurry.

"Mrs. Sanders?"

"Yeah." Looking at the formula can on the counter, she realized she hadn't answered the expert's question aloud. "Yes, I'm an excellent shot, and please, call me Jenny."

She had enough tension roiling through her without feeling pangs for what she'd lost long before. She was Ms. Sanders in her current life.

And wasn't all that fond of the change. It spoke of her greatest failure.

Oh, God, Simon!

"Where's the gun Ben gave you?" Warner's tone, kind and calm, came over the line.

"Right over there."

Like the man could see her. She stood. Had to get her wits about her. Retrieved the gun from the drawer she'd put it in by the couch. "I've got it," she said into the phone as she hurried back over to the screens.

For any sights of Ben they might give her. Had her pleadings to let Simon come to them on his own contributed to the situation they were in? If Ben had followed his own instincts, would he already have been out there, catching Simon, bringing him in before…?

She'd just seen the boy she'd raised get killed. Couldn't comprehend anything but her trembling.

"Those jerks…they were the result of gunshots," she said aloud. And Ben was out there, with no idea where the shooter was. Bullets could fly at him from anywhere.

"Possibly."

The response left room for doubt. "What else would it have been?"

"Illness sometimes causes convulsions, which can cause someone to pass out." Another voice answered, female. "I'm Dr. Dorian Lowell, Jenny," the woman's voice continued. "I—"

"You're the one who was in the mountains with Agent Michaels," she blurted. "You know what…you cared for…"

She was having complete thoughts. Just not getting them out.

"I'm here, waiting to offer medical assistance if I can," the woman said then. Leaving so much more unsaid.

To Jenny's relief.

She knew a lot. Dr. Lowell knew a lot. They'd both experienced some of the same types of trauma from the same bad blood. Caring for a newborn in danger on the run.

Didn't mean she wanted to talk about it.

Knowing the connection was there was enough.

She'd lost sight of Ben. He'd moved off camera. Every second he was gone seemed like an eternity. Her heart pounded, and she could hardly breathe.

Daniels or some Vegas hoodlum had just killed Simon. She'd seen it happen. And Ben was out there alone, hunting the murderer.

Could be more than one of them. Daniels had friends. And there was the Vegas bookie…

Illness was something to hope for. That Simon had convulsed and passed out. He'd never been a substance abuser, but then, he'd left home at sixteen. And had gotten himself into bad trouble. He could have just passed out.

Ben could be out there alone, going to his little brother's rescue. Would be on camera soon, lifting the still lifeless-looking form and carrying it back to her.

And Dr. Lowell.

She tried desperately to hope.

Glanced at the crib. She had to hope, for Ella's sake.

And for the first time in her life, Jenny couldn't find a way to do that.

Ben had no phone. No radio. No way of knowing if help was on the premises. He just knew he had to get to that body.

Every second could be a matter of life or last breath.

And he had to get there alive. No way he was going out without getting the bastard who'd hurt his little brother.

Simon was hurt. He couldn't let his mind go there.

Had to get to the body. Assess. Act. Keep the body alive until help arrived.

Senses tuned, he moved from tree to tree. Brush to brush. What should have taken five minutes took closer to ten.

Six hundred crucial seconds.

But they were necessary to avoid getting hit by a sniper bullet. Based on the convulsions, the shot had to have come from closer to the road. Cameras would catch someone moving in on him.

Jen would be instructed to fire into the air if that happened.

And to be safe, he was keeping nature's blockades between him and the road.

Cody Daniels was military trained.

The hits on the safe house…no sign of the shooter, or bullets…but clearly a sniper-type shot.

Taken by a man who'd had someone on the inside, allowing him to escape without capture. To disappear as though he'd never been there.

Ben would find that person, too. And the tire slasher… someone who'd been moving freely about the parking lot? One of them? He was going to get them all. One hunt at a time.

He was almost upon the body. Ten yards away. Would be fully exposed for the last five of them. Getting down low, but still on his feet. Crawling served no purpose—it hadn't saved Simon.

A good rifle scope would pick him up easily. Might as well have a spotlight on him and a neon flashing target pasted to his shirt.

Darting from tree to tree, he made it the five yards he'd already cased out. Could see the body. Not the face, but the torso, limbs. Back.

He tried to detect any movement at all. An occasional breath, at least?

Was ready to explode as he wasted seconds that could save a life. And made a split-second decision. Darting in a series of zigzags, as he'd done during sports practice a lifetime before, he made his way to the body, scooped it up and darted back to the bank of three trees that would protect him from any bullets coming in from the road.

And, his breath catching, he turned to the body he held. It was lighter than he'd expected. And slimmer.

He felt no movement against him. Raised his gun hand to feel the throat with the back of his knuckles, found no pulse and kneeled, lowering the body so that he could get a look at what he was dealing with.

His gaze searching for the bullet holes that would be seeping life-sustaining blood.

There were no gushes. No breath. And no pulse, either. Frantic, Ben pushed the hair away from Simon's face, diving in to administer mouth-to-mouth resuscitation when he took a momentary pause.

Details were jumbled, facts not right, but he couldn't dwell on that. Instead, he concentrated on his training, did everything he could to revive the man.

And was still trying, refusing to accept his failure, when a couple of agents, accompanied by a medic, came to relieve him of his duty.

He didn't give up easily.

A hand pulling at his arm, lifting him away couldn't stop him.

The words, "He's gone, Detective," did.

Tears streamed down Jenny's face as she watched Ben breathing his life into the unresponsive body. She couldn't see Simon's face from the angle they had, could only really see Ben's back as he kneeled over his brother and huffed and puffed.

Once the four FBI agents Michaels had dispatched arrived on scene, they were all she could see. Three males. One female. All dressed in street clothes with vests and guns.

She waited for Ben to stand, to see his expression, her heart crying for what had to be a loss. All that air... If the CPR had worked, he wouldn't still have been trying...

Hudson Warner and Dorian Lowell were still connected by phone, but they were as silent as Jenny. Had probably ascertained, before she had, that Ben's efforts were hopeless.

Did they know she'd asked Ben to wait for Simon to come to them? Was that why agents hadn't been dispatched the second the shadow had been seen an hour and a half earlier?

A medic arrived, and agents spread out, heading into separate parts of Ben's acreage. One of the agents, a male, was on the phone.

No sound came from Jenny's phone. The cabin was deathly quiet.

Except for the beating of Jenny's heart. She could hear it thundering in her ears.

Simon!

And Ben... He'd loved the boy so much. Had done everything in his power to prevent Simon from going down the wrong path...

"Jenny, you still there?" Dr. Lowell's voice sounded loud in the stillness.

Choking back another surge of the tears falling steadily down her cheeks, Jenny said, "Yeah."

"It wasn't Simon."

She heard the words. Was staring at the screen. Saw the

stretcher arriving. Stood. Moved in closer, her nose almost at the laptop screen as she watched the medic move to the head of the body, while the newcomer went to the feet.

They lifted.

And a face came into view.

Beaten, bloody—and very clearly female.

Infant cries were the first thing Ben heard when, after he gave his three taps, wait, then a fourth tap on the cabin's door, it cracked open a few hours after the sun rose that Friday morning. He had decisions to make. And Jen had to be a part of them.

Not for Michaels, or Captain Olivera, but for Ben. He'd given his word.

Bouncing the wailing infant lightly in her arms, Jen stared up at him. Intently. As though reading every thought and feeling he'd ever had.

Needing a shower, and time all to himself, he stepped inside, securing all three locks behind him. "The grounds have been searched on foot," he said, his voice raised to be heard over the infant turmoil. "Multiple times," he added. "And from the air. We did a scoop, agents moving in from all four sides and meeting in the middle. There's no sign of anyone having been on my land, other than…"

He stopped there. Could feel those still warm lips against his. And his own fight against the body's refusal of his offering.

The wailing stopped. Jen, a bottle in hand, was feeding the newborn. "Who was she?" she asked, balancing the bundle in her arms as she stood there with him.

Heading into the kitchen for a cold bottle of spring water, he put distance between them, and put aside the thought of a shower for the moment, too. He'd promised to keep Jen in the loop. She mattered more than his moment of peace. No matter how badly he needed it.

"No idea," he told her, uncapping the bottle and taking a long sip, in lieu of standing under the cold spray he wished for. "She came in off the road. On foot. We found footprints…trampled grass…lost the trail a time or two but found it again with little difficulty."

Jen's frown mirrored his, times a hundred. "There's nothing in facial recognition to identify her. They'll try to get something from her prints. There were no abandoned vehicles in the area…"

"Which means, what? Someone hurt her and then shoved her out of a vehicle and sped on?"

He nodded. As much as he detested coincidences, refused to allow them to convince him to quit looking into things, he had no other explanation for the woman's appearance. The property was barren, in the middle of thousands of acres of barren land.

"Is it possible a bear got her?"

He wanted to nod. In past years, he might have. Because Jen knowing what he did wouldn't bring the dead woman back. It would only shelter her from…

He shook his head. "She'd been punched. Repeatedly. There were still fist prints…" He stopped. And then said, "I'm pretty sure he kicked her, too. Size eleven boot, based on the mark I saw on the front of her shirt. Maybe the shove that sent her from the vehicle."

"She wasn't staying low to keep out of sight, she was hunched over in pain." Jen put it all together as he had. "I'm guessing there was internal bleeding."

The medic had said as much. Noted signs… Ben didn't need to organize them in his thoughts. They'd all be in the report.

They had more immediate challenges to tackle. "We have to assume the place has been compromised, Jen. At least as far as Simon is concerned. If he was close, saw all the cars, the ambulance…"

"Then he'd know that someone else was taken off the property," she said, frowning anew. "Seems to me, he'd hang around, if he felt safe enough. Secure enough. And hit us up later this afternoon. Or maybe tonight, after dark."

The possibility existed. Already on his list.

"And if he's close by and his enemies followed him, they now know for sure that we're here."

"And that we have protection to parallel anything they'd see in a high-security jailhouse. I can't believe how quickly Sierra's Web had everyone coordinated and on the ground."

"It's what they do. And they've been doing it, with remarkable success for more than twelve years."

She'd talked to Warner.

Ben wanted to know what she'd thought. If, maybe, she'd gained some new understanding into his own way of thinking. Into his world.

Which reminded him how badly he needed that shower.

"Warner and his partners are waiting to hear if we want to stay put here or be moved to another location. This morning's incident aside, we're closing in on Daniels, and Simon's on borrowed time. We're going to find one of the other two girls. And the mole in the police department—either ours or Daniels's—will be exposed. Sooner rather than later, I expect." He looked her straight in the eye, avoiding sight of the infant as much as he could humanly do. "Desperation, anger, fear…they're going to be running on high, Jen. I'd like for you and the infant to go into protective custody."

Her chin tightened. Jutted. "Like the safe house that was

compromised? And how would we get there? Traveling over public roads in vehicles that could be run off the road or shot at?"

"This place might have been compromised, as well."

"There's no proof of that. An injured woman wandered onto the property. After probably having been dumped along the road somewhere. Even then, your plans, Sierra's Web, the FBI, they all worked. And even though you haven't said so, I'm sure now they'll be guarding the area. I just hope to God they know not to interfere if Simon shows up."

She was right about all of it. And though he wanted her as far from danger as she could get, he heard himself say, "I think, with the protocol already in place, and our nearly impenetrable fortress here, along with the fact that if Simon is looking for us, this is our best bet for him to find us—"

"We're staying here," she interrupted. Met his gaze. And gave him a smile. Somehow, even with the edges tinged with sadness, that smile eased some of the morning's despair.

That was when Ben bowed out of the conversation and got his butt under cold spray.

Chapter 20

Jenny breathed a sigh of relief when Ben shut himself in the bathroom and turned on the water. They were staying at the cabin.

The only place on earth she felt halfway safe. Her somewhat paranoid, over-protective ex-husband had created the perfect safe house. Complete with steel-sided walls that wouldn't burn even if a firebomb hit the roof. And all the extras—a Jeep camouflaged in landscaping and brush, the propane tank ready to start a fire to set a perimeter around the place if needed. And a nationally renowned firm of experts watching over them twenty-four seven...

Over the past couple of years, he'd created exactly what they'd needed. Giving him and others the time to find Simon. And Daniels and whoever else might be out for blood.

Or another baby to sell.

Jenny was no longer kidding herself that Simon was going to just waltz up to the front door of the cabin and knock to be let inside.

While Ben had been out with the agents, scouring his land that morning, she'd read every report Ben had kept on his little brother since Simon had first left them. Finding out that he'd known where Simon was from the beginning had stung.

A lot.

The nights he'd held her while she'd cried herself to sleep, worrying about their boy on the streets…and he'd never said a word.

Because she'd have castigated him for refusing to do the one thing Simon had asked, to give him his space. As a legal adult, Simon had been within his rights to make the demand.

But Simon…he'd made one bad choice after another. Her heart ached for him. And yearned for a second chance, too. Maybe he wasn't yet in too deep… If he'd learned a hard enough lesson he could turn his life around… She just didn't know.

And Ella?

Over the course of those hours Jenny lived Simon's life vicariously with him, and then moved on to what Ben had on his computer regarding Cody Daniels. With the little Dorian Lowell had told her, just before they'd rung off, about the kidnapping ring…she had to accept that Ben was right.

Ella hadn't been left for her to love and raise by a loving mother or concerned family member. Yes, Jenny had been targeted. By her criminal, in over his head, desperate exward who still had some semblance of the conscience Ben and Jenny had tried to instill in him.

And who had some decent memories of Jenny as a good person, a good mother, too, probably. Or, at the very least, he'd remembered her as a sap who'd been consumed by children and the raising of them. Enough to ensure that he'd trusted her to make certain that the baby didn't come to harm.

She'd do that. Of course. There'd never been any doubt on that one.

But she'd given up hoping that Ella would be hers to raise. Somewhere, that child had a biological family. People who would most likely love her, want her, in spite of the trouble her mother had been in. Or maybe, because of it. Just like young Macy, whose parents had been desperate for word of her and had come running, Ella's mother likely had family, too.

Or her father did.

Jenny had been so naive to believe that fate had meant for her to raise Ella. That she'd been purposely chosen to mother the infant.

Life didn't work that way. It was all about cause and effect. People made choices that caused chains of events that led to effects. From environment to how they treated each other. Choosing to be aware, or not.

Something Ben had known all along. And had tried to show her during their marriage. Over and over and over again.

In a few short hours, she'd seen it all.

And knew there was no going back.

Ben felt as though he was walking barefoot on hot coals. A dead, unidentified woman on his property? It was just too coincidental to allow him to accept it as such.

He got the local sheriff figuring it for a domestic violence situation. And fully understood that out-of-towners frequented the area on a regular basis. Most of the scattered properties in the twenty-mile radius were not used as primary residences. And when owners weren't there, many of them rented out their places.

And it wasn't impossible that someone from the Phoenix valley or Flagstaff had been looking to dump a body. Dead bodies showed up in the Arizona desert often enough that people weren't shocked when it happened.

But the woman had been alive when she'd shown up on his property. Not exactly a body dump. And *his property*? Out of all the stretches of remote land in Northern Arizona? A body shows up at his cabin while he's there investigating an attempted kidnapping and attacks on him and his ex-wife, while assisting in a national kidnapping ring investigation?

That he now knew his kid brother had been involved with.

No way that badly beaten woman was left at his place by coincidence.

At the table, with several windows open on his laptop while he did his own traces, following his own hunches, he glanced up when Jen sat down perpendicular to him. "I'd appreciate being clued in to what you're thinking," she said. "I understand that you are who you are, but it'll be better for you and Ella, for myself, for the case, if I know what's going on. I can't be prepared if I don't know exactly what could be coming at us."

Her tone, the look in her eyes—almost deadpan. It was like he was talking to a woman he'd never met before. Impersonating Jen's body. And even that… Her shoulders just sat there. They didn't seem weak, at all. Just…not ready to jump up and go hunting for the good in the situation, something he was suddenly needing.

He was looking for words to tell her so when she said, "You gave me your word, Ben." He heard warning in her delivery.

Shaking his head, he looked her in the eye. Almost daring her to glance away. Hoping she would, and come back to him as the woman he'd known most of his life. "And I've kept my word. From the moment we agreed you'd be clued in, you have been."

Her eyes narrowed, but stayed right with him as she gave a harumph. What the hell?

"You told me you hadn't called in Sierra's Web yet, but the second danger was on the front line and you were heading out, there they were. Already clued in more than I was. It would have eased my mind, knowing you were heading out there, if I'd known agents were close."

His disregard for that comment must have shown on his face as she quickly added, "Yes, I'd have been upset for Simon's sake. I'd asked you to let him come in on his own, but don't you see how disrespectful that is to me, Ben? And how little I can change anything that's happening without all the facts?"

Right. He took a deep breath and let the undying love he felt for the woman shine through as he said, "First, I didn't call Sierra's Web in." She blinked but didn't look away. So he finished, "You did."

"I absolutely did not."

Ben almost smiled at the anger in her tone. Glad to know that Jen was still in there. Behind the unemotional facade. "You did actually," he told her. "You've known since we got here that Sierra's Web is on the case. They were waiting on my say-so to act. The predetermined protocol for me to give my say-so was for you to call them."

Her brow raised. The tension in her face eased some. Not enough. "Don't you think it might have been a good idea to let me know that?" she asked.

The question hit him on the nose. She'd wanted more. There was so much that went into it, things those on the outside never knew…how did he discern…pick out…

He'd never shared any of it with her. The procedures.

The protocols. Aside from what he'd had to tell her to keep her safe, cases he'd shared only to show her the danger, he'd kept most of his daily activity separate from her. Had wanted to keep the darkness of his work away from her.

"I wanted our home to be my good place in the world." The words fell out slowly. Coming from the rawness his life had become. "I wanted to make sure it stayed that way for you—a good, happy place."

Jen sat back, looking surprised. She'd put her hair back in a tight ponytail and it flipped around, landing over the front of her shoulder. Ben had to stop himself from brushing his fingers over its silkiness.

But he remained right where he was, looking her in the eye. "It was all preestablished protocol," he said, holding up a hand when her mouth flew open. "And I know," he continued, "you should have known. I've just… The detail part is second nature to me after all these years," he said. "Like when I say I'm taking a shower, I don't say I'm going to use a bar of soap and washcloth and wipe it over my body…"

The second the words were out, he froze. What in God's name was he doing?

And yet…curious…that sudden softening in Jen's blue eyes.

Picturing his naked body?

Liking the image.

He had to stop. Get on top of his game before it beat him.

"I just didn't think the minutia was important," he said, his voice a little thick. "I took for granted that Sierra's Web would be tapped into my surveillance cameras and that agents would be ready to act if necessary. It's just protocol in a situation like this. And you calling them being the 'go' trigger…just seemed like good sense. If I was compromised, you'd call them…"

"Just think how much more effective I could have been if I'd known that."

He nodded. "I know. You're right. And…for the record, I'm truly sorry, Jen. Now. And then, too. I should have shared more of my work life with you."

"I'd certainly have been better able to understand, to hear your warnings and therefore take them to heart."

She said the words. Her gaze met his head-on. And…he felt nothing from her. No softening. No warmth.

Because he'd screwed up one too many times. At the most crucial time of their life. When they'd been facing danger head-on.

Ben realized, right there, in that second, that his eye-opening moments had been too little too late.

She'd given him his second chance. Had trusted him not to withhold information from her.

He'd failed.

And he'd lost her.

Now that she'd woken up, was finally aware and living in the real world, Jenny completely understood the way the situation had played out earlier that day.

And had new insight and perspective regarding the past, too. Ben hadn't been belittling her. He wasn't disrespecting or dismissing her. To the contrary, he'd been honoring her. Doing everything in his power to keep the details of a job that dealt with ugliness away from her full-steam-ahead approach to joy. If she'd had more of the details, not just grim results from cases resulting in death or despair, she'd have understood his warnings.

Cause and effect.

And all water under the bridge. Knowing the cause too late didn't change the effects. The causes had happened, creating effects that had turned out to be brand-new causes for so many other effects.

Simon getting so lost.

The divorce.

Her lost dream of becoming a mother.

Ben buying their cabin and spending his free time there. All alone in the wilderness. Creating a safe place so that one would exist.

"You're a great man, Ben Sanders," she told him, from the depths of the heart her new perspective had left her. "It's because of you that we're alive and safe right now. Because of the man you were and still are." She'd spent so many years railing at him. Resisting. He deserved to hear her admit the truth. "In your infinite wisdom, you created exactly the place we needed to get through this. The effect of you, who you are, is this place."

His gaze sharpened, and yet his brow furrowed, too. As though something was puzzling him. She waited to hear what it was, wanting to know, to be able to clear the air completely, but was interrupted by the small beep on his phone.

The alarm he had set. For calls in to Sierra's Web.

He glanced at the phone, then, with concern on his face, and quickly told her, "I don't think the woman being left here was random." The words came out in a rush. "I have to call in, and you're going to hear me tell them the same thing. I think she might be one of the two missing birth mothers…"

Her heart jumped. Then settled back down to its new resting place. "You think she was Ella's mother," she said, stating aloud a possibility she'd reached hours before. "We have to find out her identity, Ben. That child likely has biological family that will love her. And who, once they find out their daughter is dead, are going to need her more than ever." She delivered the words without a hitch, noting that she was doing fine living in reality.

Frowning at her, a situation for which she had no explanation, Ben dialed Hudson Warner from the firm of experts. And waited to hear him reporting their suspicions, perhaps with more detail than she knew, as he'd been working furiously for over an hour and hadn't had a chance to fill her in.

He said, "Yeah."

And...fell silent. Completely so. Turning away from her. But not before she'd seen his mouth drop open. As his face creased...as it had when he'd heard about the car accident that had taken his mother's life.

She'd been standing right beside him then. Had taken hold of his hand.

And she knew...

Her heart lurched. She needed a dark place to hide.

"Thank you, I will," Ben said, ending the call without a word about Ella's mother. She watched his shoulders hunch as his phone-holding hand dropped down to his side. Saw him bow his head.

Stood there, bearing the pain, the knowing, as he slowly turned to face her.

"Simon's gone."

For a second there, her spirit jumped...lifted. Gone. Maybe he'd gotten away. Had learned his lessons and made it safely away to a new life.

No. Ben's demeanor. Simon was gone, gone. Dead. "How?" She had to know. That was her only choice. Knowing prompted choices that would cause future effects.

"Car accident," he said, his voice half breaking over the words. "Hikers in Yuma found his vehicle, with him in it, over a steep ditch just outside of town. He'd been rear-ended. ME thinks at least two weeks ago." He just stood there. A rock out of place.

Jenny moved forward out of habit. Took his hand. Because...she was hurting for him.

Aching everywhere. More than she'd ever known possible. Consumed with the dark agony to the point of being aware of nothing else.

When he pulled her against him, she held on.

And cried.

Tears pouring out of her soul for Simon. For Ben, who'd just lost his last living biological family member.

For the past.

For all the choices she could have made differently.

And for a future that would never know the innate joy she'd once believed was real.

Chapter 21

Ben absorbed Jen's pain. Took it upon his shoulders along with his own. Cushioned her sobs against him. And felt the tears start to slide slowly down his cheeks, as well.

They'd started with such high hopes.

Grief held him in its stupor, an entity that had taken over so much of their existence, that it was all there was.

Until a cry rent the air. Softly at first. It barely penetrated him. Jen's stiffening against him was what got his attention.

The sound came again, and he dropped his arms as his ex-wife pulled away from him.

The infant was awake. The child that had drawn Simon to Yuma to make money to pay his bookie. His little brother had chosen to commit a heinous crime, rather than come to Ben for help.

He'd have paid ten bookies to have his brother home again, seeking a better life.

Jen held the baby in the crook of one arm, her rocking motion having quieted the wails while, with both hands, she was tending to the formula. Still sniffling some. Wiping stray tears away with her face against her shoulder.

Ben wanted to help. To prepare the bottle.

His feet wouldn't move. He stood there, yearning, frozen.

Watching Jen live the life he'd always thought they'd be living together.

Until his mother had been killed and Simon had… Simon had…

Been gone for at least two weeks. Killed in Yuma. Before the infant was left.

"If Simon didn't drop the infant at the church, who did?" he said aloud, blood rushing through his veins as he went back to his computer, to his files. What had he missed? Who else was involved?

The distraction was a godsend.

"Someone from Jasper Gulley who was involved." Jen's words were soft, calm, in deference to the infant she held, Ben knew. Because he knew her.

Kind tone or not, she'd hit the mother lode at the same time he had.

While Jen sat at the table and fed the newborn, Ben typed, searched documents for names that appeared in multiple reports. People who'd been on scene…everywhere.

Someone insinuating himself into every situation.

And came up with nothing. He was missing something. They all were.

The woman…she had to be a part of it.

"Simon was in Yuma because of Daniels," he said aloud, looking over at Jen and then straight back at his computer as he opened the file Sierra's Web had just sent over. The one they'd let him know would be coming. The accident report. "We know that for sure…" he continued, heart pounding as his mind processed what he was looking at, "…because Sierra's Web found a bar receipt, and cameras showed the two of them there, sitting at a high top…" His words tumbled with more speed, adrenaline pumping as he viewed the photo that had just come in.

Jen's open-mouthed gasp hit him.

And he quickly turned his computer around. "I just this

second found out," he said. "I'm going through the files Sierra's Web sent. This is the first one I opened."

It showed an unsmiling Simon, a full mug of beer in front of him, facing Cody Daniels, who'd been leaning in, urgently, saying something.

Making the deal.

Ben pulled the computer back to him, as Jen, holding the bottle with her chin, dragged her chair around and sat next to him.

"What if Simon insisted on meeting the mother, first? To make sure she was really on board, wanting to sell her baby?" she asked, while Ben quickly scrolled past accident crime scene photos. "And then couldn't go through with it?"

Ben turned to her, his instincts clicking into high gear. "What if he told her about you?" he asked back.

"About us," Jen said, meeting his gaze, holding it, before jumping back to the computer screen. "He'd have assured her that I'd care for Ella, keep her safe," she continued. "While you figured out what was going on, got Daniels, and then, when it was safe, she could come get Ella. He told her where to find us in case he couldn't bring her to Jasper Gulley himself."

Ben stopped scrolling. Looked at Jen. "Instead, Daniels caught wind of what was going on…"

"For all we know, he had either Simon or the woman bugged, or followed them. He heard…"

Ben jumped in then. "And when he heard that I was involved…hearing Simon sending his paycheck, the newborn, to me…the cop who killed his big brother… Wait." Ben still felt a hole or two… Like how had anyone known about Ben's cabin? And if Daniels had been the one to drop off the new mother that morning, why had he done so?

Not knowing did not sit well. But Ben had to concede

that unraveling perps rarely made logical choices. And that could be his missing piece. He was trying so hard to fit perfectly shaped pieces into a sickly twisted puzzle.

But if the woman they'd found was more than just a random coincidence—and his gut just couldn't let go of the fact that she was—then how had she, or anyone but Simon, found the cabin?

Even Sierra's Web hadn't known his whereabouts until he'd sent the coordinates that morning.

All his communications were being scrambled through servers in and out of the country. Something he'd paid for himself.

He stopped cold as something else occurred to him.

"What if Cody Daniels isn't the mastermind behind this?" he asked. "What if Evart, the lobbyist who started the ring with his mother, is running it from jail?"

"He probably needs money for his legal defense..."

They were on the right track. Maybe off center a bit, still, but there...

And...thoughts were flying at him, almost faster than he could corral them. "We know that Cody and Simon knew each other at school. We know you found pot in Simon's pants' pocket when you picked them off his floor that time to do laundry. And we know that he cut school more than once. What if he brought Cody Daniels up here to smoke dope and party?"

He didn't need her nod to tell him that Jen saw the very real possibility of such a thing happening. But it was... welcome.

Picking up his phone, he called Hudson Warner. Relayed the theory that he and Jen had figured out. Heard the tech expert ask him to hold on while he patched in Scott Michaels and, thrumming from the inside out, watched the infant fall asleep in Jen's arms.

Life ended.

And life began.

Ben's job was to help keep the world safe enough for it to be possible for children to grow up happy.

And maybe, just maybe, find a little of Jen's happiness for himself.

Friday afternoon crept on. One o'clock, then two, came and went. She bathed Ella in the kitchen sink. And when the baby was fed and back to sleep again, she filled the sink with detergent and water and washed out the dirty clothes the three of them had—more for something to do than because they were going to run out of clean ones.

Laundry had been one of her duties when they'd vacationed at the cabin. She'd devised a system of cleaning, then wringing and, finally, hanging clothes all around the metal bathroom shower. She even found the long string full of clips that Ben had designed that allowed her to clip underwear and socks across it to dry.

She'd been glad to find the string for practical purposes, not nostalgic ones. The past was long past.

She had a job to get home to. A three-year-old class that was hopefully back on track, but which she'd be monitoring over the next several months. There were midterm enrollments to consider. Holidays coming up in a few months. And the budget…always the budget.

A deadline was approaching on a major grant request she was supposed to be writing. As soon as laundry was done, she'd get going on it.

Doing was better than sitting around, mentally exploring the new world inside her. Best just to stay busy. Accomplish things. Her brain knew those were good choices, even if she wasn't feeling the joy in them.

As she grabbed her computer, checking Ella, noting the healthy cheeks and easy breathing, she smiled. She'd feel joy, again. She knew that. Life had beautiful moments.

But it would be a joy based in reality.

She knew that, too. And was a better person for it.

She'd find happiness based on what was. Not go out seeking good feelings that she imagined would be there. As though, around every corner, joy just waited for her to find it.

Hard to believe it had taken her forty-one years to figure it all out.

No wonder Ben had treated her like a kid half the time...

He looked up from his screen as she sat down at the other end of the table with her own laptop. He was working online with Sierra's Web and Michaels's team, she knew. His current project, going through surveillance footage all over Jasper Gulley, was an obvious task for him since he knew every inch of the land, and pretty much every face that inhabited it.

If someone in Jasper Gulley was helping Daniels—and it made sense that someone was, based on the van having been compromised—then Ben would be the one who'd likely put it together quickest. He'd recognize the mundane, or a face that showed up where it wouldn't ordinarily have been.

When she opened her laptop, catching a glimpse of him over the top of it, she saw him still looking at her.

"What?" she asked, wondering if he needed anything. Needing to do anything she could to help.

He shook his head. "I'm just... It's good, looking up and seeing you there."

She smiled at him. Liked the words. But didn't make anything out of them. Those days of dreaming big things into small occurrences were over. Instead, she opened her grant file and got to work.

Or started to.

"I'll be damned." Ben stood. Stared at her, eyes wide. "A couple of FBI agents—part of Michaels's team, ones that were here this morning—just knocked on a door half an hour from here, showed Daniels's photo and found out that he'd been in the diner in Globe-Miami last night. They're on their way there."

Miami, Arizona. The town where the old teacher Grace Arnold had taught school. Where she and Ben had been bussed to high school. "So he was up here," she said. And added, "Did he have a woman with him?"

"They didn't know." Ben glanced at his screen again. "Said he got takeout, but it was a big bag. That's why they noticed him. A big bag of food for one person…"

"He already had her," Jenny said, getting the hang of connecting the dots in the real world. "Or was close enough on her trail, and was sure enough of himself, that he bought food for two…" She stopped, thought about what she'd said…

"I get why he had to find her. She could turn him in. He'd have to get rid of her." Like he, or the bookie, had shoved Simon to his death. Her heart lurched, breath catching in her throat, but she pushed through it and finished with, "But why bring her here, Ben?" Maybe she wasn't as good as she thought at seeing what was right in front of her. Maybe it would take a while to get that good.

He shrugged. "That's something I haven't been able to figure out." He shook his head again. And then, seeming to come to a decision, he said, "Daniels's escalating actions indicate that he's beyond rational at this point. Could be he just wanted her to watch while he took us down, to make her pay before he killed her. Or..." His pause, the strange light in Ben's eyes as he looked at her, confused her.

"What?"

"Maybe she got scared and told Daniels that she didn't know anything about Simon's plan. Maybe she agreed to show up here alone and blame everything on Simon, saying he stole the newborn from her, and demand to have her baby back. At which point, she'd give the infant to Daniels, as originally agreed upon. Only she figured that before it actually got to that point, I'd have figured everything out. Maybe she'd been buying time. And when they got up here, she refused to go through with it. And got beaten up for her effort."

Jenny saw one very clear problem with that scenario, beyond the fact that Ben seemed to be trying to create fairy tales there at the end, for her benefit. "Why would he have left her here, letting you know he was in the area?"

"Why drive a vehicle into your garage? Trash my mother's grave? Shoot up the safe house?"

The questions were moot at that point. She got that. And wasn't quite able to let go of his earlier assertion. Trying to give her hope that Ella's mother had regretted her choice to illegally sell her baby. "Is it possible that Simon told the woman about the cabin?" Jen's voice came softly. "If, say, things went wrong...maybe he always wanted to come back here. I think some of his best memories were here. And he'd know the area was bound to offer her some kind of safe refuge..."

"Or maybe he told her that he was going to head up here," Ben added. "Hoping that the place was vacant. Hoping maybe that she'd meet him up here."

For a second, Jenny's old self lit up. But only for a second. "How would he ever have described how to get here?" she asked. "I can totally see him finding it, having traveled the roads often enough, but it's not like there's a road sign or a house number out at the street. You have to have been here before." As Ben had been, as his father had been. Which added more weight to Ben's earlier theory.

Simon had brought Daniels up to the cabin—a couple of squatters—to party.

Ben shook his head and said, "I only, ever since I bought the place, gave the coordinates to Sierra's Web this morning, after the shadow showed up on the property. It has to be Daniels. But why dump the woman? Why let us know he's close?"

And Jenny got another hard lesson in living in the real world.

Even when you faced all the bad possibilities in front of you, put your mind to all scenarios, you still never had all the answers.

Or prevented the pain.

Chapter 22

It was all conjecture. Pieces fit together, but none of them built a picture clear enough to answer all the unknowns hanging over them.

Simon had gotten himself killed. In Yuma. Within a day and a half or so after he'd met up with Daniels there. Daniels was the last known person to see him alive.

Yuma was where the babies were being purchased. They had proof of that through the young woman who'd come forward. And the midwife, who was out on bail and fully cooperating with police. She'd never met Simon. But admitted having seen Daniels before, outside her house one day after a particularly difficult birth.

And there was a believable possibility that Daniels could know about the cabin.

None of which definitively explained a baby left in Jasper Gulley. Attacks on him and Jen. A dead woman on his remote cabin property.

And the possibility that he and Jen were sitting ducks, waiting for a man to show himself. Not Simon, but Cody Daniels.

The hours passed, and he shared the space with his ex-wife and the infant—a baby that was about as angelic as he imagined they could get. Not at all colicky as Simon had been. Ben dreaded the coming night. Evil happened more often under the cover of darkness. And he had two very precious human beings out in the middle of nowhere with him.

He needed the case done.

He needed out of there for another reason, as well. Spending those quiet hours, him and Jen both working at opposite ends of the table...it was like the calm after the storm. Like they were the family he'd once thought they'd be, at the cabin on vacation.

A very dangerous road to take. He already knew where it led. So he retrained his focus back to looking at every nook and cranny of his hometown, and the people in it, as well as following other ideas that occurred to him, and still finding nothing substantial. The reports from Michaels's team were equally frustrating. A few sights of Daniels in the Miami area, but no credit card receipts. He hadn't been back to his hometown. There was no proof he was still in the area. Or that he'd left.

Until, just after three, five minutes after he'd hung up with a check-in call with Sierra's Web, he saw a report flash up on his screen. And immediately picked up the phone.

When Jen glanced up, her brows raised, he motioned her to join him at his end of the table. He put the call on speaker and set the phone on the table.

Jen, in her jeans and T-shirt, was still on her way when Warner's voice came on the line.

"We got him." The expert's tone was as professional as always. With a hint of pleasure, too. Ben was just processing that much as Warner continued with, "They found him holed up at a place owned by a friend of his brother's. He's in custody, on his way to Phoenix now. Michaels wanted to handle his interview personally, I'm sure to fill in every single blank. They found a large amount of cash stashed in his backpack, along with a tablet filled with bogus adoption forms. Blank ones."

Ben glanced up at Jen, who stood there, arms wrapped around her middle, trembling. Without thought, Ben reached for her hand, pulled her down to his lap, wrapping his arms around both of hers.

Needing her warmth. To share the relief.

Weak at the thought that it was over. That she and the baby were safe. He was filled with bone-deep sadness, too. Simon was gone.

And in a matter of hours, Jen would be out of his life again, as well.

"One other thing," Warner continued, his voice loud in the silence of their newfound peace. "Our lab confirmed that the woman found on your property this morning is the mother of the baby in your custody."

He felt Jen lurch. Then stiffen. And held on to her. Their theory, his gut, had been right.

She took a deep breath, and he felt as though her intake of air was a part of him as Warner finished with, "Still no identity on her. Missing persons has turned up nothing. The midwife in Yuma admitted to helping deliver the baby but knew nothing about her. No one in the area recognizes her photo. The name she gave comes up nowhere, as you'd expect. Michaels's team is working on it, and we've got experts doing the same. Until then, I'm told through child services that she's to be left with Jenny Sanders, as long as Ms. Sanders is willing to keep her."

Ben felt a little softening in the body resting against him. Jen's head, just beside his, didn't turn to him, but he felt the movement of her hair against his cheek as she said, "She's willing."

The voice was strong. Sure. Without a hint of joy.

Warner ended with condolences to both of them for the loss of Simon. And Jen pulled away from him. Stood.

As the call ended, she kept her back to him.

And he got the message.

There'd be no celebrating between them. Simon was gone.

And the case. Them working together. Being in each other's lives...

It was over.

Jenny walked into her home just after seven on Friday night feeling as though she'd been gone for months. Years. Not days.

Setting down the new car seat carrier with Ella still in it, she turned to see Ben coming in behind her with the portable crib. He'd offered to take her to the box store for more supplies, but she had enough formula and diapers to last another week. There was no point in planning beyond that.

Not for Ella. But for them? All the way back to Jasper Gulley, he'd been quiet. Withdrawn. Like he was distancing himself from her again.

Surely, after all they'd been through...

It wasn't like she was hoping for some major return to what they'd once been to each other—or the fantasy version of it that she'd conjured up as a kid—but he'd come back into her life. They'd been able to talk about the past, put it to rest.

More than that, they had a new understanding of each other. And with that, and the fact that she still loved him...

"You want to stay for dinner?" she asked him. He'd brought in the leftover food supplies that had been left in the trunk of the car for them when they'd first gone to the cabin.

He didn't look at her. Just shook his head, as he bent to set the last bag of Ella's things on the couch. "I need to get to the station. Write reports. Wait to hear final details from Michaels."

They'd already heard some of them, in the car on the way home. Daniels confirmed that there'd been no one working with him in Jasper Gulley. He'd been given the chance at a sweet plea deal if he turned in his accomplice. Which he did. A man on Evart's payroll in Las Vegas. That man had also been arrested.

And there'd been receipts, gas and fast food, that showed Daniels in Jasper Gulley. Late that afternoon, after Warner's call, but before they had the all clear from Michaels to leave the cabin, Ben had come up with one photo of Daniels in Jasper Gulley. Taken the day after they'd gone into the safe house, out by the freeway. Daniels wouldn't admit to vandalism and lawyered up when pressed as to what he'd been doing in town. Same as he'd done regarding his time in the Miami area.

Prior to requesting an attorney, he'd admitted to seeing Simon in Yuma. And had acknowledged that he'd given Simon information regarding the midwife, and that Simon had needed money fast. He'd refused to implicate himself any further.

The young man was angry. Scared. And not as sharp, or stable, as he'd needed to be to pull off the undertaking he'd signed on to in Vegas.

The whole thing left Jenny feeling sick. Simon, Cody Daniels…two promising young lives wasted. And for what?

And sweet Ella… She wanted to hope for a happy ending there, too. But reality had set in. The baby's mother had likely been a runaway. Meaning she'd felt desperate enough to leave the place where Ella would probably be placed as soon as identifications were made.

"Okay, that's everything from the car." Ben had come

back in the front door, empty-handed. "I've checked the perimeter. All cameras are on. The new garage door is secure."

His words didn't scare her—or even make her defensive—as he looked everywhere around the living room except at her. Instead, his attentiveness spoke of deep caring.

And she needed him to care.

Needed *him*.

Just couldn't figure out how to tell him. In his world. His way. The reality way.

As he looked at the room, was he just checking for safety measures? Or remembering when it had been his living room, too? They'd shared it for a lot of years. Not all bad ones. None that were all bad.

"You sure you don't want to stay?" she asked.

He turned, headed for the door. "I'll drive by later tonight on my way home," he told her. "Just to make sure things are secure. Right now, I've got to get things wrapped up."

With that, he was out the door.

And Jenny spent the next hour reclaiming her home. Her life. Putting things away. Starting a load of laundry that had been left in her hamper. Getting out some pictures of Simon. They might never know what he'd been thinking toward the end, or exactly how Ella had been left with Jenny at the church, but even Ben had admitted that Simon had to have been behind the choice.

She was in the bathroom, had just finished putting towels away, when she heard Ella's cry on the monitor. The baby wasn't due to wake up for at least another hour. Which probably meant her stomach was upset.

Because of all the tension around her...

Heading out to the living room, taking deep, calm breaths, trying to find cheer for the baby, she reached the end of the hall, and...sharp pain. So sharp. Agonizing.

Zinging from the back of her head to the front.

Ella! Screaming!

Not hungry! Rustling.

On the ground, Jenny could hardly see, knew nothing but blurs. Electrifying pain. A big body, the legs, coming closer. A boot, swinging straight at her.

She aimed a kick, just as Ben had taught her before they'd left for college.

Right between the legs of...

No!

Oh, God. Ella!

And...

Darkness.

Ben drove with the pedal to the floor and knew he wasn't going to get there in time. All members of the Jasper Gulley police force had been notified. Were on their way. He was closest.

And there was no way he'd make it.

He'd been sitting at his desk, going over footage from cameras in town that had just arrived. Mostly to occupy his mind and keep worry about Jen at bay. He longed for her, too, as he waited for the rest of Michaels's report, when he'd seen a blast from his past. A face he'd recognized.

And with the shock of a blast to the head, something had fallen into place. His mother's grave. He should have known...

He'd already put out the APB, was in touch with Sierra's Web on his phone, when he took another glance at the screens on his phone, showing him Jen's house. She'd agreed to cameras for the time being. They'd been installed that evening.

Ben's throat closed as he stared in disbelief. And then tore out of the station.

Bruce Connors was already there. In the living room.

Exacting revenge for Simon's death.

And if anyone had cause to hate Ben Sanders, who'd know how to get him where it hurt most, it was his ex-stepfather. The man Ben had testified against, preventing Bruce from even supervised visitation with his young son.

The man was a master manipulator. Got off on working people. He should have put it together sooner.

Screeching around a turn, he didn't yet know how Bruce had found out about Simon's plan to transfer a stolen baby, or the decision to leave the baby with Jen instead.

The man could only have found out after Simon's death. After the baby had already been left in town. By the baby's mother...

Another corner... Why in the hell had he ever thought it a good idea to own a home far enough away from the station to keep his work life as far away from Jen as possible?

His work was the only way to save her.

Sick to his stomach, he squealed onto the street that led to his old cul-de-sac. He saw a replay in his mind of the man's hand coming down on the back of Jen's head. Watched her fall...

It had happened too many minutes before.

He wasn't going to be able to save her.

His jaw trembling, he rounded the last corner, gun already in hand, just as a dark truck came at him. Bruce Connors at the wheel. Ben aimed, shot through glass and, as he swerved, let go of the wheel to reach for the window release, shoving the gun through the opening as soon as it was big enough.

Gunfire sounded. His car was hit.

He aimed at tires. Shot once. Twice. The truck swerved, three times. And just stopped.

With rage coursing through him Ben was out of the running car, gun up, pointing at Bruce's head resting on the steering wheel.

There'd been no impact. No bullet through the windshield.

There was no way Bruce Connors was passed out. The man was manipulating him even then.

Other vehicles arrived. Ben heard them. Didn't break his focus. He drew closer to the driver's door of the truck. Ready for whatever move Connors was going to make. Forcing himself not to pull the trigger.

And was still standing there, clearly aimed at the man's skull, when his captain tapped him on the shoulder. Nodded toward the front passenger seat.

Glancing down, he noticed the blanketed bundle resting there. Saw the officers swarming the truck's passenger side. And his captain pointing a gun toward Connors.

Shaking, Ben dropped his gun arm and, still clutching the weapon, ran for the house.

He had to get to Jen. To tell her he loved her.

Before they took her away.

Chapter 23

With a hand to her head, Jenny scrambled through dulling pain and a sense of drunkenness to get to the crib.

Bruce Connors. She'd kicked him.

Heard him wail, right?

And Ella...

The crib was empty! And...

"Jen!" The sound came from outside the house. Glancing toward the front door, seeing it stand open, she started to think more clearly. "Jen!"

She heard steps pounding up the walk. Ben's steps.

His voice.

"Ben!" she screamed. "He's got Ella!" Her throat hurt with the screeching sound. "He's got Ella!" she screamed again. Racing toward the door.

She hit solid force before she got there. Was lifted off her feet. Carried over to the couch, where Ben sat her gently down and immediately turned his attention to the back of her head.

"There's no blood," she told him urgently, head throbbing, but no longer taking away her ability to think. "I'm fine, Ben! He's got Ella."

As she said the words, she heard a cry. Footsteps outside. And then saw Drake Johnson's head burst into her vision.

Or rather, caught a glimpse of her ex-husband's second-in-command, before her gaze landed on the bundle in his arms.

Ella, red-faced. Screaming. And unharmed.

Turned out that reality was good sometimes.

Ben didn't know about Jen, but he was done being apart from her. He'd tried to pull himself back. To give her space. She'd changed after they'd heard about Simon's death. Maybe even before that. While he'd been out trying to find answers to the dead woman on his property.

She'd changed after they'd had sex.

He just had to know why. So he could honor her, meet her needs and still find a way to be in her life.

Medics arrived, and Ben rode with Jen in the ambulance, though she'd only agreed to go when she'd been told that the infant, though seemingly unharmed in the few minutes Bruce had had her, still had to be checked out. The newborn had been in the hands of a fiend. He could have injected her with something...

They were back at her house before midnight, having talked some. About the night's events and Ben finding Bruce's photo even before he'd seen the man in her house.

Bruce, it turned out, had fallen from Jen's well-planted blow. Had hit his head. He'd run the infant out to his truck as best he could when he recovered enough. But he'd just managed to get in the vehicle, get it started, headed toward Ben, shot his gun and then had passed out, they figured, from the pain. Some they'd pieced together from security cameras.

Jen's instinctive move to protect the baby had stalled Bruce long enough to give Ben and the others time to get to her.

Bruce had been spitting fire when he'd come to with

the help of smelling salts seconds after Ben headed for the
house. He had cleared up some unanswered questions with
some shocking, unpalatable answers.

He hadn't stolen the truck that he ran into Jen's garage.
He'd borrowed a friend's truck, with permission, and had only
later found out it was stolen. He'd driven into her garage to
get access to the attic. Once there, he'd put a device on her
alarm system that allowed him to disable it remotely. He'd
still been expecting her to return with the infant and had been
planning to get in and take her. Because, legally, she was his.

And he'd known better than to trust the court system.
Most particularly with Ben Sanders involved.

He hadn't known, of course, about the newly installed
cameras.

The woman, the infant's mother, was Anna Brookmeyer.
A woman Bruce had picked up in a bar one night, who'd
become his live-in girlfriend. She'd left him months before,
right after Simon came back from Vegas, and he'd wished
her good riddance. Until he'd recently found out, from a
mutual acquaintance, that she was pregnant.

Ben had watched the blood drain from Jen's face as the
captain had sat in her living room and delivered the news
that Bruce Connors was the infant's father.

Had Ben been less focused on her, he'd probably have
puked himself.

And then the captain had told them both that, though
Simon had been in Vegas the entire time his father had been
with Anna, she'd somehow found Simon after Bruce had
found her, demanding that he have equal rights to his child.

Apparently saying that he was going to raise the new
baby from birth, period. No one was going to stop him.
She was a bar broad, and he was a stable, settled business
owner with a nice home.

How Simon had determined that Anna selling her baby was the better option was anyone's guess. Ben wanted to think that his brother had been thinking of the child, not seeing his father's girlfriend's problem as an answer to his own.

But when the FBI came asking questions about Simon, pointing to a kidnapping ring and a midwife in Yuma, Bruce had done his own checking. Had found Cody Daniels, since he knew Simon associated with him. That's when he'd heard that Ben had killed Daniels's older brother. Among other things.

No one knew for sure, or would probably ever know, how Anna came to leave her baby with Jenny, rather than let Bruce get ahold of her, but everything pointed to Simon. He'd been in way over his head, but in the end, he'd done the right thing.

He'd sent his half sibling home to Jen.

They did have verification that Anna had been the one to leave the child. Once Bruce had caught up with her again and had seen her without the child, he'd convinced her to tell him where the baby was. He also, through persuasive physical means, got her to admit that Simon had driven her up to Ben's cabin, showing her how to get there in case anything ever happened and she needed an escape. She'd told Bruce that she'd ask for her baby back and give the child to him. Which was why she'd driven up there with him.

So they'd had that part right.

As well as the part where, when push came to shove, she couldn't do it. Bruce had pushed her out of his truck. Insisting that she was alive and well that last time he'd seen her.

Ben hoped to God that the medical examiner, with the help of forensics, would be able to prove the man killed Anna.

Now that the authorities had an identity for the deceased

mother, they were expecting to find her family. And child services would be in touch with them to arrange for someone to collect the infant.

Ben hadn't looked at Jen when the captain delivered that piece of news. There was nothing he could do to ease the pain of loss she was going to feel when the infant left her care.

Except…maybe…give her something new to live for?

At least a chance of it…

She'd changed and fed the baby after Captain Olivera left. Ben hadn't made any move to vacate the premises himself. He was trying to work out a way to spend the night there with her, without putting too much pressure on them. Or the future.

He couldn't be sure how she'd feel about him stressing that he'd be staying just as friends, after the lovemaking they'd shared—was it only the evening before?—or if he should just take a leap and tell her he wanted to stay and see where it led.

He sat with her and said, "I know now isn't the right time, but… I don't want to go back to a life without you in it, Jen."

She glanced over at him, a smile slowly appearing on her face, though, he noticed with dread, not in her eyes. "I don't want that, either," she told him.

His heart pounding, needing to make certain that nothing happened to ruin things, he sat forward, turned toward her and said, "We know what happened in the past, and why, so we know how to prevent it from happening again."

And stopped. One long sentence too late. She was nodding. But there was no joy emanating from her. Because he'd just been exactly who he'd always been. The guy seeing potential dangers and trying to prevent them before they happened.

"I agree," she told him. Confusing him.

She agreed? Then why wasn't she moving toward him? Holding out her arms? Jen had always been the one who dove into the touchy-feely stuff. And dragged him along with her.

He'd loved it. But…growing up as he had, he just wasn't comfortable with it, or didn't know how to make it happen himself.

"So…what are we saying?" he asked, needing far more than she was giving him. Needing her to open the door so he could give it right back to her. "We're going to… try again?"

Her smile grew. But her joy didn't seem to. "I'd like that."

Good. Great!

Ben grinned at her. And, being the man he was, did what he knew how to do to please her. He took his ex-wife in his arms and kissed her until passion obliterated thoughts and words from both of them.

Giving them moments of pure joy, instead.

After the first time they made love, Ben carried her naked to the bed they'd shared for so many years and then went back for the crib, parking it in the room right next door. Checking the baby monitor, testing that it worked, he crawled into bed, scooping Jenny up into his arms for a second time around the sun and moon and stars.

When they lay together an hour later, both still awake, she felt happy. Maybe not bubbling excitement kind of joy. But nice.

"This is better," she told him, her head on his shoulder, her hand lightly caressing his chest.

"Better than what?" He was half-asleep. Almost slurring his words.

"Always running toward what could be the best in every situation," she told him. "Your way, it's better. You take what comes and make the most of it when it gets there."

Ben shot up. Displacing her.

Shocked, she stared at him in shadows as he reached for his clothes, stepped into his pants.

"Ben Sanders, what in the hell are you doing?" she asked him, hearing a tone of old come out of her mouth. Wincing as she waited for him to snap back at her.

Instead, he finished dressing. And then, with his shoes on, sat down on the edge of the bed. "I'm leaving," he said softly. Reaching out a hand to run it through her hair. Looking at it as though the dark strands were made of long-lost gold.

Hurt beyond measure, she didn't want to see that look. She wanted to know. "Why?" she asked him.

"Because I'm not going to be a part of you settling for second best."

The words made absolutely no sense to her. Not from the Ben of her old understanding, and not from the new, either. Her heart cried out, so loud she almost couldn't think. She had to fight not to throw her arms around the man and communicate with him in the one way she knew she could convince him. With her overabundance of joy.

"Settling for second best?" she asked, frowning. If he was second…did he think she was settling for him because she couldn't keep the child she'd agreed to foster? The idea was ludicrous…

"You said you're taking what's here and making the most of it. Rather than looking for what you think you most want."

She hadn't said that. Well, she had. But not like he was stating.

"I'm not settling for second best, Ben," she said, trying to stay calm. "I'm just… Oh, hell…" Popping up to her knees, with tears in her eyes, she knelt there in her nakedness and threw her arms around his neck, hanging on to him. "I'll get better at it as we go along, but right now, Ben Sanders, I'm so over-the-top exploding with love for you that I can't even figure out where you're coming from. What danger you're seeing. Or how what you're doing is going to prevent it."

He stared into her eyes. And she held on. Letting herself shine in all her glory. She couldn't lose him. That was the biggest danger facing them. And, in the past, all she'd had to do was wrap her arms around his neck and kiss him and…

Pulling him down to her, keeping her gaze locked with his, she kissed him. Deeply. Not heading toward sex, but as she had as a teenager. With a heart full of love and stars in her eyes as she looked toward the future.

He kissed her back. Just as he had in the past. And then he pulled away.

Not far. He sat down next to her, holding her arms around his neck. And looked at her intently as he said, "Where you ever got the idea that it's wrong for you to face every situation with hope in your heart, I have no idea, Jen. But I swear to you…" He swallowed, deeply. Teared up. Swallowed again and said, "Your joy, your ability to find it, everywhere, is what I've always tried hardest to protect. It's why I finally left. I was sucking it out of you."

She shook her head, reaching a finger to his lips, as her heart exploded all over inside her. But he kissed her finger and pulled it away.

"Your joy becomes mine, Jen. It always has. Our lives together, you showed me something I can't remember ever knowing. And these last few years apart… I've tried to find it on my own. And then I realized, this week…it's love, Jen. I've always guarded against the pain that love brings, which in the end, causes pain. But you…"

"It's all about cause and effect," she told him, with tears in her eyes, too. And all kinds of wonderful light bulbs popping in her head. "When the cause is love, the effect has unlimited possibilities…"

"It's also about your ability to be brave enough to walk into each day with hope," he told her then. "That's what I've been missing, my whole life, Jen. What I took from you. And it's my turn to start giving some of it back…"

His words were interrupted by the vibrating of his phone against the nightstand.

He stiffened, his gaze growing steady, serious, as he looked at her.

"Answer it," she said. "The world, Jasper Gulley, needs you, Ben Sanders. It needs your talents, your ability to see the danger and your willingness to go after it and bring it down…" Words poured out of her until she realized her overflowing heart was keeping him from doing exactly what she'd been telling him he needed to do.

She pulled on a robe as he answered the phone. And then came to the side of the bed to sit with him. To share with him.

Rather than leaving him to live the work part of his life alone, as she'd always done. She'd thought she was giving him what he'd wanted. Had been giving him what he'd said he needed—space to do his job. But maybe he'd been wrong. Maybe he'd needed her glued to his side, reminding him to have hope of good outcomes, too. Showering his world with light during the darkness.

She couldn't hear the conversation. Only got his mostly one- and two-word responses. "Yes. What? Uh-huh. Are you sure?"

And finally, "Thanks, man," before hanging up.

No "I'm on my way."

The look he gave her, stunned, filled her heart with fear. "Tell, me, Ben. Who's hurt? What's going on?"

"They found an apartment. In Vegas. Anna Brookmeyer is listed on the lease with another woman. There was no one home. The super let the agents in. They found a folder. It looks like Anna and Simon were married, Jen. And there was a journal. Anna's, they believe. It talked about Simon coming home to Tucson one night, finding her bruised from another one of Bruce's beatings. He didn't even know her, but had taken her to Vegas with him promising they'd have a new life. The first month had been a dream come true. But Simon couldn't stay away from the gambling. And was in trouble again…"

The words fell into the room with the boom of a fire-cracker.

She couldn't make sense out of the explosion.

"There was more. The name of the midwife down in Yuma. Said they went there to have the baby off the grid so that Bruce wouldn't know. And there were some legal documents. A birth certificate. And a certified order listing you as legal guardian in the event anything happens to Anna and Simon, both. And…um…they found a DNA test showing Simon was… Ella's…father."

Eyes wide, Ben stared at her, swallowing hard again.

Ella…

Was hers?

And…

Joy burst through her. Far too strongly for her to fight. She didn't even try.

Clapping her hands together, up to her chin, she couldn't

be still as the truth hit her. "She's your biological niece, Ben! You have a whole bunch of years of family to raise up…"

Her words followed her husband's back as he was rushing out of the room. She started to follow him but stopped.

Sensed where he was going.

Ben didn't run away. He ran toward.

And that moment was Ben's time. Ben's and Ella's.

She'd noticed his lack of any kind of bonding with the baby, of course. Wouldn't have expected anything different with Ben. Doing his job. Staying detached.

But… Ella was hers! Jen stayed where she was but danced in a circle with the force of her joy. Hers and Ben's! Legally hers, biologically Ben's.

Happy tears were falling as Ben returned, carefully carrying the sleeping baby in with him, the bundle tiny against his huge chest. Protected by it. He stood there a minute, looking at the baby, at Jen and back at the baby.

"Cause and effect, Jen," he said then, his voice clogged with emotion. "The cause was us, a couple of kids trying our best, which led to Simon making certain that his own child had the same chance."

Her chin trembling, she walked over to the two people on earth who owned her whole heart. "I'm up for the second chance," she said softly, her gaze for Ben only in that moment. "How about you?"

"My heart has never left this home, Jen," he told her. "You know why?"

She figured she did, but wanted to hear him tell her that their love never died. Needed him to say it. For the circle to be complete. "Why?"

"Because hope lives here," he told her, his expression boring into hers. As though he needed her to fully grasp what he was telling her. "You, Jen. You're always looking for the good, for the joy… Because you never lose hope that it's out there. And that, at least some of the time, you'll find it."

She'd wanted a simple "I love you." What he'd given her…was more than she'd ever hoped to get from him.

She had no words. Just more happy tears. A smile that took possession of her. And a soft kiss to his lips.

They talked about driving to Vegas the next day. To clean out Anna's things, to keep them in case any of her family ever materialized. And to get married.

And on Monday they would file the paperwork to not just be wards to Ella, but to adopt her.

As they lay in bed half an hour later, Ella's crib right beside the bed, at least for the rest of that night, Jen didn't think she could get any happier.

Until Ben announced, "I've discovered that there is only one safe place on earth. You know where it is?"

Smiling, ready to hear about him wanting to head back to the cabin for a goodbye to Simon and his Anna, a wedding celebration and to welcome Ella to the family, she didn't guess what she knew. She played his game. Because she was just so thankful he was there to play it with. "Where?" she asked.

"In someone's heart."

His words shocked Jenny. Stopped her. And put all of her pieces firmly back together forever. Ben's words were a statement of fact. A truth. And also a promise.

One that Jenny knew would protect all three of them for the rest of their lives.

* * * * *